THE FORT

CHRISTY K. LEE

This book is a work of fiction. Any references to historical events, real people, or real places are used fictitiously. Other names, characters, places, and events are products of the author's imagination, and any resemblance to actual events, places, names, or persons, is entirely coincidental.

Text copyright © 2025 by Christy K. Lee

All rights reserved. For information regarding reproduction in total or in part, contact Rising Action Publishing Co. at http://www.risingactionpublishingco.com

Cover Illustration © Nat Mack
Distributed by Simon & Schuster

Line edit by Tina Beier
Copy edit by Marthese Fenech

ISBN: 978-1-998076-41-3
Ebook: 978-1-998076-71-0

FIC090010 FICTION / World Literature / Canada / Colonial & 19th Century
FIC014000 FICTION / Historical / General
FIC044000 FICTION / Women

#TheFort

Follow Rising Action on our socials!
Instagram: @risingactionpublishingco
Tiktok: @risingactionpublishingco

This novel was written and edited on the unceded traditional territory of the Matsqui, Kwantlen, Katzie, Semiahmoo, Anishinaabe, Chonnonton, and Haudenosaunee First Nations.

To Carrie Gabriele,
whose knowledge of her people and their land
dances across every page

THE FORT

Chapter One

SPRING 1806, JUST OUTSIDE OF FORT EDMONTON

For the third time in the last hour, the wagon lurched to a halt, the mud thick and resistant beneath us. This time, the tell-tale snap of the splintering wheel raised curses from the men who rode alongside me in the cramped wagon bed. A few leapt over the sides, quickly assessing the damage.

"Oh dear, not again." Reverend Smith's hand fell to my thigh, squeezing just above my knee. This was the fourth occurrence of his hand on my leg, and I was desperate to leave his side. But there was not even an inch to spare, and the weight of my six-year-old son, Ben, on my lap prevented me from shuffling farther down the seat.

"Miss Williams, you're the only white woman to come to these parts. And unmarried—the men will be beside themselves." The hand inched slowly upwards, and I held my breath in disgust. "Well, I suppose there's also that audacious French woman over at Fort Augustus." He lifted his hand to wave dismissively at the thought of her, and I used the

1

opportunity to escape. I stood abruptly, dumping a surprised Ben off my lap, kicking the foot of my father seated across from me, fast asleep. He blinked, blearily awake, clearly not understanding my urgency.

"Wheel's broke," one of the men reported from below, the mud squelching under his boots as he approached. "Looks like we need to walk the rest of the way. Better leave now if we're to make it before nightfall."

"What about our tools?" I asked, turning back to the reverend, as he was the only one who had spoken to me on this leg of the trip. "We need our tools to work."

The reverend shrugged, beckoning for me to follow my father down onto the sodden path. I looked back over my shoulder at the pile of blacksmithing tools wrapped in a blanket at the front of the wagon bed. There was no way I could manage them all, and the long journey had already been difficult on my father's health. He would have a hard enough time walking to Fort Edmonton without the burden of carrying a heavy load.

I cursed under my breath, dragging Ben by the hand over to the pile. The wagon creaked as I rummaged through the stack, retrieving my favourites, the ones most comfortable for me to use, as most had been fashioned for the large grip of a man. I held partiality to my farrier's knife as the handle fit my fingers to perfection. To leave it behind at the hands of thieves—unthinkable.

"Abigail," my father hissed up at me, casting a worried look at the men who had already made headway, "come now. We'll remake the tools at the fort. We mustn't fall behind the others."

I nudged Ben down into my father's outstretched arms before I followed, an assortment of iron tools slung through the belt of my dress. It

THE FORT

hardly looked ladylike, but then again, I hadn't felt like one in quite some time. I pondered the words of the reverend at being the only woman of my kind at the fort. While I hadn't expected to make friends, I didn't want to stand out either.

We walked in silence, each one of us lost in his or her own reverie as we trudged painstakingly through the sludge. I smiled as Ben ran back and forth amongst the men with the energy gifted to a young boy. We had travelled for over a month from York, the flagship trading post at the mouth of Hudson's Bay. Long days jolting around in a wagon, canoe, or on foot, and even longer nights trying to sleep on the hard ground, had left me weary to the bone. Still, it would all be worth it when we finally arrived in Fort Edmonton, where my father had secured a position as the fort blacksmith with the Hudson's Bay Company. The work would be steady and the pay good, even if the conditions were primitive. I was no stranger to such a life, working as my father's aid since we had arrived from England over six years before.

"Mama!" Ben panted, breathless at my side, tugging at my skirt. "I see Jack. Over there by the forest's edge."

"Ben," I scolded, smoothing down the lick of hair that refused to stay flat on his head. "I told you to forget that rascal pup."

"Please, Mama! Just over there."

I glanced to where he was pointing, and sure enough, a flash of brown darted in and out of the long grass. I heaved a loud sigh, deciding it was more likely just a fox or muskrat. Still, Ben had cried himself to sleep these last two nights since the dog had wandered away from our wagon. My father said I coddled him, but I couldn't help myself. Every time my child smiled, the wound in my own aching heart closed just an inch.

3

"Stay with Papa," I said, ushering him towards where my father walked in the middle of the pack. Then I ran out into the field toward the brown animal.

The iron tools in my belt slapped against my thighs as I jogged through the waving grass. The air blew fresher here, away from the stench of the men. I breathed deeply, my endurance strong, as the past years spent horseshoeing in my father's shop had left my body lean and muscular. I quickly caught up with the mass of brown fur. It *was* the pup.

The pup and I reached the edge of the woods, and I leaned down to scoop the small dog into my arms, barely breaking my run. But, alas, the pup squirmed, not impressed by the loss of his freedom, and escaped my grasp. I watched in dismay as he disappeared into the dark trees of the thick forest.

"Dammit," I muttered, my entire face scrunched up in a scowl. "Benjamin Allen Williams, you're going to pay for this, young man."

I was not but three steps into the dim forest when my body slammed into another, knocking me to the ground. I let out a squeak as I landed on my behind, looking up with alarm to see a man. I scrambled backwards, the unwelcome encounters with the revered fresh on my mind. This man was wild-looking, with an unruly silver and brown beard covering his face. He leaned down toward me, his piercing blue gaze like that of a madman. I got myself up on my feet, ready to flee.

The man's eyes narrowed with disdain, and he grabbed my shoulder in a rough manner. My heart hammered in my chest, unsure if he meant me harm. I scuttled a few more steps backwards. As usual, I had acted without thinking and had foolishly wandered away from my father without letting anyone know where I was headed.

THE FORT

"My son's dog ..." I managed, not entirely sure why I still lingered, "ran into the trees."

He took a quick step away from me as if I were a hot ember, taking in my entire length. His gaze swept from the tip of my brown braid down to the mud on my leather boots before coming to rest on the tools hung from my belt. On instinct, I withdrew the long tongs, holding them as a weapon. If I swung hard enough, I could inflict harm, as my arms were strong and my aim accurate. I stared back defiantly into the ice-blue eyes across from me.

His face suddenly screwed up. "Va-t'en!" he barked in French. "Get out of here! These woods are full of dangerous men. It's no place for an *English* woman." He said the word like he would say 'plague,' and I tightened my grip on the tongs.

His hand flashed out, grabbing my upper arm. "Did you not hear me, girl? Get out." He swiped the tongs from my grasp, and they landed in the nearby grass with a thud. With that, he turned and stalked back into the dark depths of the trees.

I shook my head, adrenaline coursing through me like oak-barreled whiskey. I stood for a moment, letting my heart resume its normal beat, and then remembered my father and Ben walking to the fort. With one final look down the forest path, I ran to rejoin the others.

By the time I arrived back at my father's side, a few men in uniform had joined our group on horseback. One dismounted to walk beside us, and I wiped the sweat from my brow, glancing over at him. He was tall, with a straight back and chiselled chin.

"Hello there." He nodded my way, the tops of his cheeks turning pink. I smiled back, noticing my father look away to give me a semblance of privacy. "The rumours are true then. A beautiful woman will be a breath of civilization in this place." He thrust out his hand at me as we walked. "Henry Davies, ma'am. I'm an officer posted at Fort Edmonton." I felt a pleasant glow at his words but quickly reminded myself of my position: an unwed mother with an ailing father in tow. Not to mention my work with the horses and the steel in my father's shop. It was unlikely such a man would truly think me a beauty.

"Abby Williams," I said, shaking his hand. "My son, Benjamin, and my father, Peter, the blacksmith."

Henry furrowed his brow, looking around the group. "No husband? A widow, then?"

I gave him a half smile, making no attempt to correct his false assumption. I could feel my father's eyes on me, willing my mouth closed. We hadn't fled England to this desolate land of ice and snow for me to reveal my shameful past to a handsome officer.

"Officer Davies," I ventured, making sure to flash the dimple in my cheek in his direction, "we had to leave our blacksmithing tools behind in the wagon. I don't suppose one of your men would be able to retrieve them for us?"

"Miss Williams, it would be my pleasure," he said, quickly giving instructions to another soldier on horseback. The soldier rode off in search of our abandoned wagon, and I sighed in relief. We might have been able to remake our tools at the fort, but it would have been time-consuming, and I was certain there was much work to be done. My hands fell to the tools slung through my belt, my fingers resting on the tongs that I had tried to use as a weapon a mere ten minutes before. That strange man had so easily disarmed me, showing how defenceless I really was. I was a woman in a man's world, and no matter how capable I was, I depended entirely on their support for my safety and well-being. I

THE FORT

searched the forest for the Frenchman with a sweeping gaze but only saw dark shadows cast by the massive growth.

"I'm sure you will find fort life an adjustment, but it's really not so bad. There are other women there, Métis and Indian women, who are married to some of the men. And the accommodations behind the smith's shop are among the best in the whole fort. Quite spacious, really." Henry had moved closer to me, his long legs keeping an easy stride with my short ones. I let him prattle on, sneaking a look up at him every so often. He appeared to be about thirty years of age, not far removed from my own twenty-five. And he had made no mention of a wife, nor did he sport a ring on his finger.

"Abigail, look." My father drew my attention away from the officer as we rounded the top of a hill. Below us, the fort came into view—an impressive collection of buildings hemmed in by its wooden palisade. The river lay gleaming beside it, with flashes of blue and silver on the surface.

I smiled at my father, then down at Ben. At long last, we had arrived.

Chapter Two

T he fort bustled with activity, and I grinned as we passed through the gates. The air was fragrant with the smell of meat roasting on a spit, and Ben happily exclaimed as we passed a few young pups chasing their white and grey tails.

Some of the men looked up, nudging each other as I approached. My cheeks grew hot as I followed Henry to the blacksmith's shop, a whispered hush left in our wake. Everyone was staring at me. Would my presence be welcomed, or would I interfere with their bachelor way of life? For the most part, they seemed rough but self-sufficient. I caught sight of a few men doing tasks normally assigned to women, such as mending trousers and scrubbing laundry.

"Don't worry about them," Henry said over his shoulder as we passed. "No man in the fort will make himself overly familiar with you. I'll see to that personally." He puffed out his chest as if daring anyone to cross him.

I wondered if he knew about the reverend's wandering hand but said nothing. I was used to being seen as out of place—after all, I spent

THE FORT

most of my days working a man's job, earning a decent wage. Truthfully, though, I was looking forward to belonging to this community of seventy or so, as I had felt lonely in York. No one ever stayed long there, either boarding a ship back to England or making their way back to the trading posts farther inland.

"Here we are." Henry led us into a building at the east corner of the fort. The blackened smith's shop was undercover, and someone had already lit the forge in anticipation of our arrival. The large brick fireplace would always stay ablaze, day and night. During the day, it roared with heat for my father to work his metal, and at night, it would be banked in order to be easily stoked for the next morning. We were seldom cold, even in the winter, and the smoke kept away most of the bugs in the summer.

We passed through the shop to our living quarters behind. As Henry had promised, it was spacious with a large sitting room in front and a bedchamber tucked in the back, furnished with a bunk bed, a small table and chairs, and a woven rug on the dirt floor. An extra hearth for cooking and warmth took up residence in the front room, and a deer hide was tacked up over the only window. No doubt the place needed a good scrub, but it looked cozy and comfortable.

Ben ran excitedly around the house, inspecting every corner, his blond head bobbing up and down. Henry chuckled at Ben's enthusiasm, and I took the opportunity to look more closely at him. Henry had light brown hair and eyes to match, a straight nose, and broad shoulders. He turned and caught me looking, his face breaking out in a wide grin. My stomach flipped pleasantly, and I looked away, feeling heat on my face. He really was quite handsome.

"Your father will be busy for the first while," Henry commented as I walked with him back outside the shop. "It's been almost half a year since we've had a smith. And Fort Augustus is without one as well."

"Where is the other fort?" I asked, wondering if we would be expected to work there in addition to Fort Edmonton.

"Across the river. It's part of the North West Company, our competitors." He explained that for more than a century, the Hudson's Bay Company had dominated the fur trade in Rupert's Land. But in recent years, the Scottish and French in Montréal had collaborated to create their own company, travelling farther west to source the best furs. The HBC, which had previously relied on the Indigenous to bring them furs, had been forced to build forts farther inland to compete against the 'Nor'Westers,' who now dominated the trade. Thus, a bitter rivalry had begun.

I trailed Henry through the fort, my father and Ben lagging behind. Henry told us that the fort was a small walled settlement with a mill, a carpenter, a boat builder, a harness shop, and a meeting hall, where meals were taken. Men were busy with furs—fox, muskrat, raccoon, deer, and, of course, beaver—which had been treated by the Indigenous peoples, tying them into tight bundles to be transported back across the country to York, and then to England. There, they would be turned into felt for top hats or fur for jackets of the highest fashion.

We ended up at the meal hall, where the last of the traders and trappers were finishing their midday meal. We had plates thrust into our hands, and my father, Ben, and I gratefully ate, tired and hungry after the long journey. "Let's go back and meet the other women," Henry said after I had finished, urging me into the kitchen. "You'll need to report for meal duty to help."

THE FORT

"Oh." I shifted from one foot to another, twirling a strand of hair that had come loose from my thick braid. "Actually, I'm the farrier for my father. So, I'll be busy in the blacksmith shop most days."

A frown flashed across his face, and bitter disappointment crept up my throat. I shouldn't have been surprised. Eligible men like Henry wanted a woman who didn't prefer spending her day with the horses, getting her hands dirty, but was instead capable of keeping house and bearing children.

"Still, I think you should help when you can," he said, continuing to usher me towards the kitchen. "It's best for appearances."

I bit back a sigh and pasted on my sweetest smile as we approached the group of women. They were Indigenous and Métis, their skin a chestnut brown and their hair sleek and black. A few were gathered in the back of the kitchen, whispering as we came closer. My cheeks flushed again at their obvious stares. I was an outsider, and I was aware that my privilege as a white woman would set me far apart from their close circle. Hiding out with the horses was so much easier than meeting new people.

"Ladies, this is Abigail Williams. She's just arrived with her father, the new blacksmith."

"Abby, please," I insisted, clearing my throat nervously as none of the women greeted me, no smiles gracing their faces. "I prefer just Abby."

Henry smiled down at me kindly, putting my fluttering pulse at ease. "Yes. Abby helps her father with the horseshoeing, but she'll also work here when she can."

"Are you married?" one of the women asked rather abruptly. She was young and very pretty, with a baby on her hip. I was taken aback by her question and wondered at the meaning of it. Had she seen Ben and wondered, or was she merely taking stock?

"A widow," Henry answered, saving me from the lie. I breathed an inward sigh of relief—with him spreading the word about my status, I wouldn't be forced to speak of it often. Only one other person this side of the ocean knew my secret. My father would take it with him to his deathbed, I was certain. Still, the shame of it lurked deep within me, and it was heavy to carry. My son had been born out of wedlock, and I had never, in fact, been married.

"How did he die?" the same woman asked, looking me up and down. Another woman, a bit older than the first, gave her a stern look.

"No, it's all right," I answered, casting a look at Henry, who was listening intently. I might as well flesh out the falsehood now to avoid creating suspicion. "It was a hunting accident. Back in England," I added, reciting my carefully rehearsed story. "His name was George." That part was true, at least. What I didn't add was that he was an earl. That I had been under his employ, and he was married to another, albeit unhappily. That I had foolishly fallen in love. That after our affair came to light, I had been forced to flee, my womb heavy with his child. I only had one memento of George that I still treasured—a pocket watch that lay buried deep in my rucksack, folded into a pair of winter stockings.

The women nodded at me sympathetically. Hunting accidents were a common cause of death in these parts. Still, I swallowed back my nerves, wiping my palms on the front of my dress.

"Come, Abby, let's clear the tables together." The woman who had scolded the pretty one came and linked her arm through mine. She wore a dark blue dress with a high collar, an apron and a pair of moccasins. "I'm Mabel. Don't mind Elizabeth. Her husband has a wandering eye, so she'll be hateful towards you until she's sure you won't succumb to his charm."

THE FORT

My cheeks coloured again at her words, and I swallowed hard. If these women knew of my illicit affair, they would never trust me. No one liked a woman who had allowed herself to become a mistress to a married man.

"You'll do well to find yourself another husband soon," Mabel whispered at me as we cleared dishes and wiped the tables. "There are plenty of available men here. Henry seems to have taken a liking to you already. He's a good man."

I glanced to where Henry still lingered, chatting with other men at a table. The light flittered in through the open door, basking him in a halo. He must have felt my eyes on him and lifted his own to meet mine with a smile. I crossed my fingers briefly before following Mabel back to the kitchen.

The next morning, I woke at dawn and prepared a simple breakfast of porridge for the three of us. The officers had dropped off our tools the evening before, and now, there was work to be done. A pile of traps and items needing repair had already been accumulated in the shop. My father would be kept busy for long months ahead while I needed to sort through the horseshoes, deciding what could be used and which ones needed to be heated and re-formed.

We were just finishing breakfast when a tap sounded at the door. Outside stood a white boy of about twelve wearing a leather apron, standard wear for working in a smith's shop.

"Good morning, ma'am. Father sent me over. I worked with the last smithy as his striker. See?" The boy rolled up his sleeve and flexed the lean muscle in his arm, giving me a cheeky grin. "I'll no' complain, no matter how hard the work."

My father came up behind me and spoke over my shoulder. He had been slow-moving this morning, and I'd feared we would have no one to do the heavy metal work. "What's your name, boy?"

"Edmund, sir. My father is a local farmer, just yonder." He waved past the walls of the fort.

I exchanged a look with my father, and he nodded. We couldn't exactly afford to compensate him, but we needed the help, and a boy who already had experience hammering iron would be invaluable.

"We'll take you on for the week as a trial," my father said, donning his own apron. He was an excellent teacher, and this young boy would learn well from him. He seemed eager and friendly, which would be a nice change from working alone with my father, who preferred the company of his own thoughts. When we lived in York, I had often hung back in the shadows of the workshop, shoeing the horses alone. Many of the patrons were shocked to realize that their favourite farrier was, in fact, a woman. My father explained that blacksmithing was a family trade, and it was not unheard of for wives and daughters to help.

I set Ben to the task of collecting the horseshoes that lay abandoned around the shop while I gave the floor a quick sweep. The previous blacksmith had left behind a lot of clutter and scrap metal, which would need to be sorted eventually. Nothing ever went to waste, though, as we fashioned anything and everything that was used in the fort, from nails to stirrups to barrel hoops. I found a chest in the back of the shop and hauled it to the open area, where I would tend to the horses. I had

THE FORT

traded for a collection of horses' blankets, brushes, and a spare saddle that would fit perfectly in the chest. Although it was not my job to groom the animals, it brought them comfort and calmed them before the shoeing.

By midmorning, I had started shoeing my first horse, brought over by an officer. It had been some time since the shoes had been replaced, and the growth on the creature's sole also needed attention. I gathered the animal's leg between my knees, gently pried off the old shoe with a pincer, and slipped the used nails into the pocket of my work trousers. Then I took my farrier knife and hoof pick and began to scrape away the bottom of the hoof, the consistency much like a human fingernail.

As I worked, I felt a presence close by, like someone was watching me. I lifted my head, looked around, and found the piercing blue gaze of the man from the forest. He stood, leaning against the shop with thick arms crossed over his wide chest, inspecting my work.

"Can I help you?" The adrenaline from yesterday returned, and my body grew hot. I wasn't afraid, as my father and Edmund were not far away, but this man's demeanour irked me. Both his hair and beard were in dire need of a trim, and it seemed like a smile hadn't graced his face in quite some time.

"I was expecting your father," he said in a thick accent, taking a step closer. He muttered something under his breath in French, irritating me further, as I couldn't understand. Who was he to make a judgement about me and my work? I was a steady hand with the horses and more than capable at the forge as well. He gave me an arrogant smirk, and my temper flared.

"My father's in the shop. This is *my* job." I suddenly remembered the feeling of his hand gripping my shoulder, and I gave an involuntary shudder. This man was rough and boorish. "I didn't have the chance to

15

introduce myself yesterday as the farrier when you accosted me in the forest."

He gave a snort, rolling his eyes and placing his hands on his hips. He was only a few inches taller than me but built like a tree, solid and muscular. "I hardly accosted you. As I recall, you were the one wielding a weapon. Would you have preferred I let you wander into the forest to be raped by another man or step into an animal trap? You should be thanking me, girl."

"Gabriel!" Henry approached from across the clearing and threw a friendly arm across the Frenchman's shoulders. He smiled down at me, crinkling his eyes in the afternoon sun. "I see you've met Abby. Abby, this is my friend, Gabriel Bouchard."

"Friend?" I raised my eyebrows at Henry, not bothering to conceal my surprise, as anger and annoyance still coursed through me. Henry was decent and refined, even in these crude surroundings. He hardly seemed the type to be friends with this rough-mannered man. "I wasn't aware that proper English officers were in the habit of keeping company with unkempt French woodsmen."

Gabriel let out something that sounded like a laugh and took a step closer to me. I had already dropped the horse's hoof but could not move any farther from him, as the animal was still at my back. The horse shifted and let out a whinny, also feeling the tension in the air.

"It's obvious you work with horses, *Abby*." He sniffed at me, malice in his unnerving gaze. "You even smell like them. A French woman would never degrade herself like this. They keep themselves beautiful and sweet, ready to warm their husbands' beds."

My fists clenched at his insult and the mention of marital intimacy. An eruption of rage built within me at this horrible man. I couldn't even

THE FORT

bear to look at Henry. "But French men can forget to groom, and that's all right?" I gestured to his wild hair with a sneer, but tears percolated in my eyes, and I frowned to cover it.

We stared at each other face to face for a long moment, his eyes softening when he took in my expression. Still, we stared. It wasn't until Henry audibly cleared his throat that I let go of Gabriel's gaze. Just then, Ben ran out of the shop, and I leaned down to snatch him in my trembling arms. Gabriel stepped back from us, crossing his arms once again over his chest.

"I came to tell you," he spat, "that I found your dog in the forest yesterday. He's tied up over there." He nodded his head in the direction of the gates. Then he stomped off, leaving me open-mouthed in shock. Ben wriggled free from my arms, eager to reunite with his pup.

Henry looked at me, a frown creasing his handsome features. Shame washed over me as I recalled how I had insulted his friend. I was not normally so sharp with my tongue, but something had come over me in the company of Gabriel. The way we had locked gazes had left me rattled.

"I'm sorry, Henry, I—"

A bell rang out over the yard, announcing the midday meal. "Our food is ready to be served, Abigail." His tone was stern, and I winced. "The women are waiting for your help." Then he, too, stalked off into the yard.

I blinked back tears, burying my face in the neck of the horse behind me. I took a deep breath and lodged the hoof once again between my knees. I would be missing lunch today, it seemed.

Chapter Three

I took out my frustration the rest of the afternoon at the forge, pounding out new horseshoes. It was methodical and sedating—heating the iron to a buttery yellow and reshaping it into something new. I first cut long bars of iron into four pieces, using the sharp edge of the anvil and hammer. I then heated and shaped them on the cone end of the anvil, making sure to shape the lip on the heel and the cat's ear at the toe. Finally, I punched holes using the pritchel hole on the anvil. These shoes would still need to be fitted to each individual hoof, but having them made ahead of time saved me from dealing with impatient horses during the actual shoeing.

On each shoe I made, I imprinted my touchmark. Every smith had one to mark their work. My father had made me one a few years ago for my birthday, a rose with my initials etched into one of the petals: AW. It had become my trademark, a soft and feminine flower that still bore thorns on the stem. The rose had been my mother's favourite flower, and every time I used it, I thought of her.

THE FORT

My mind turned over and over as I worked, upset at how much Gabriel's words had affected me. I knew I smelled like work—all farriers did, as the stench from the hot shoe pressed against the hoof was acrid and foul. It shouldn't have bothered me. I was my father's best worker, and if something happened to him, I would likely be able to provide a life for my son to ensure he never went hungry. Yet, Gabriel's words stung. It was not that I wanted to be a woman who was only there to warm her husband's bed, but I wanted to be desired. It seemed that with one stupid mistake, one season in the wrong man's bed, I had marred my entire future.

My father trudged back into the shop from supper, Ben and Edmund by his side. We would continue working into the evening for the first month or so until we were caught up with the backlog. I never minded being busy, as it meant that I fell into bed exhausted at the end of the day, with no energy to feed the thoughts that ripped my heart open in the lonely nighttime hours.

"Is there a reason you're not eating? You missed lunch as well." My father grabbed the tongs from their place on the wall, pumping the bellows a few times to stoke the fire even higher. The workshop was in a better state than it had been that morning, as I had made short work of organizing the shop after Edmund had fashioned a few hooks and mounted them to the wall. Working in clutter drove me mad. Once we were caught up on our work, I would ask my father to make a rack to hold my extra horseshoes.

My stomach growled in response to his words, and Ben brought me over a supper plate laden with meat, potatoes, carrots, and bread. My anger at the day's events dissipated at my father's concern, and I thanked him for the food. Our breakfast of oats barely sustained the physical labour of horseshoeing from dawn until dusk.

"That officer was asking after you," he continued, giving me a knowing look. "Did something happen between the two of you?"

I sighed. My father would wheedle the truth out of me, as he always did. I had never been any good at hiding what I was feeling. "I'm afraid it's his friend that I'm avoiding. I had a run-in with him in the forest the other day, looking for Ben's pup. Then today, we had words, and Henry was not pleased."

"Hmmm." He used the tongs to place a long iron rod into the roaring fire of the forge. "I'd like you to think about choosing one of the men here to marry, Abigail. I won't be around forever, and they won't give you the blacksmith contract as a woman. You're already five and twenty years and it's time to think about your future."

I swallowed back a sharp retort, continuing my work on the horseshoe in front of me. He was right, I knew. Yet every time I thought of marriage, I felt the hands of another man on my body, a man who had whispered words of my beauty as he stoked a fire of desire deep within my belly. In the aftermath of the affair, I had often wondered if his proclamation of love had been real or if he had merely seduced me with false ministrations, feeding me what I wanted to hear. Even now, seven years later, the embers of that fire refused to die. I missed the feeling of his lips against my neck, my breasts, my thighs. I may have only been an excuse for him to stray from his marriage bed, but my heart would never be the same.

My father came over and placed his hand over mine, squeezing gently. "Forget that man. Leave him in the past," he whispered, casting a glance at Edmund, who was busy sharpening knives on the whetstone. The sounds of the blacksmith shop were comforting after spending so long travelling across the country. "Make amends with the English officer. You never know, with him at your side, you might be able to return to England one day and see your brothers."

I looked away from him, watching the men of the fort finish their labours for the day. My two brothers were more than ten years older than me and had wanted no association with me after the scandal. It had not helped matters that I had made a fool of myself, crying and weeping outside the earl's estate, begging for him to take me back. We had kept my pregnancy a secret from everyone at first, but once I had started to show, my brothers had shamed me, calling me horrid names. Our mother had raised me better than that, they said, better than making myself available to a married man. Only my father had taken pity on me, making the decision to leave behind his entire life just so I could start over. I thought of the gold pocket watch that had belonged to George, which I had re-hidden in the chest of horse blankets. It was time to stop lugging around that burden, to let go of my pain.

"Abigail, you must marry. You are still able to bear children and will make a fine companion for any man. Put aside these foolhardy notions of love. For me. For Ben."

I blew out a breath, nodding, even as I blinked back tears. Perhaps that was why Gabriel's words had stung so much. I knew well that my son needed a father, a man to teach him the things I could not as a woman. And although my father had not had an issue with his health since we'd arrived, there had been a few instances during our travels. I needed to secure my future with marriage.

"Yes, all right. I will try to capture the affection of Henry. Even if he has poor taste in friends." I shifted uncomfortably at the thought of Gabriel with his intense stare.

"Bring him one of these in the morning." My father placed a tiny horseshoe in my palm, making me smile. I had made a collection of these good luck charms, selling them along our journey from York. They had done quite well, as many single men had been eager to trade for a token made by a young woman. I had even started placing a kiss on the horseshoes in front of my customers, evoking whistles and cheers. Yes, perhaps Henry would like one as well.

I looked over at Ben, sitting near the fire, his eyes drooping with exhaustion. "Come, small bear. Time for bed." I scooped him up in my arms, though my back complained at his weight. He was getting big and old enough to understand the finer complexities of life. My father was right. It was time.

I slipped into the mess hall the next morning just as the earliest risers were sitting down to eat. Mabel pounced on me as I entered the kitchen, a mischievous grin on her face. "It's good to see you back today. I heard that you had words with Gabriel."

"You did?" I asked, widening my eyes at her. The altercation hadn't been *that* extreme. If everyone knew, perhaps Henry was angrier than I thought.

Mabel chuckled as she tied back her long black hair. She had a shawl over her shoulders to keep out the morning chill. "Abby, the fort is small. Everyone knows everything about everyone." She shrugged, though her eyes fell to the men in the dining room. "I'm sure you will hear stories about me in the days to come, too."

She led me over to the stove, where we dished up the breakfast fare onto plates. "Don't worry about Gabriel. He's just crotchety and prefers his own company over everyone else. The trappers spend a lot of time alone. And he's un homme libre, which means he isn't tied to either fur company by contract. You won't see him all that often."

"Well, good. Is he really friends with Henry? They seem so different."

She nodded. "Gabriel helped Henry through his first winter here, showed him how to use snowshoes, a dogsled, and hunt for game in the deep snow. Like most white men in their first season, Henry was not prepared for the long months in the freezing cold. He's learned since then, though."

I remembered my first winter after we arrived from England. We had also been unprepared for the harsh conditions that seemed never-ending from mid-fall to late spring. It was only through the help of others who had already lived through a previous winter that we were able to survive. "Yes, I remember—"

"Abby."

I spun around to see Henry leaning up against the door frame of the kitchen. Though his arms were crossed across his chest, his face was calm and welcoming. "Might I have a word?"

"Of course."

Mabel nodded at me encouragingly as I wiped my hands on my apron and followed Henry through to the dining room. Had he heard the entire conversation? The horseshoe charm sat heavy in my skirt pocket, and now I wasn't sure if I should give it to him. He might find it childish. Although I had my own child, I really had no idea how to behave in a romantic way towards men. Most women my age were already married and had been shown the ways of womanhood by their mothers. In moments like these, I missed my own intensely.

Henry sat me down at an empty table, and I glanced around the room. I immediately saw Gabriel, who sat smoking a pipe, his eyes trained on us. I turned away, my stomach clenching. Why was he always around? Mabel had made it sound like he wouldn't be, and his presence unnerved me greatly. I looked forward to getting to know Henry without his friend at his side.

"About yesterday, Abby—"

"Yes, I am sorry, Henry, really I am. I know better than to let my tongue run wild."

He frowned. "Yes, I have to say, it was not your better side. Still, it is not your fault that you have been working like a man. It is my hope that in the future you might take up tasks more becoming of a woman." He leaned in closer to me, almost whispering, "More like a mother ... or a wife."

I smiled wanly, not trusting my words. If I were truly to make amends, I needed to appear agreeable. I *liked* my job as a farrier, but I doubted Henry would understand that. Still, he seemed to be respected around the fort and had even mentioned the word *wife*.

"I'd like for you to apologize." He laced his fingers together and nodded over to where Gabriel sat across the room. "I know the French and English have not always seen eye to eye, but it is different here in the New World. We depend on each other."

I stared at Henry, not believing my ears. Apologize to Gabriel? That seemed impossible. A movement caught my eye, and I saw Mabel serving a nearby table of men. She nodded, jerking her head over in Gabriel's

THE FORT

direction. She, too, thought I should smooth things over. I bristled and let out an annoyed huff but stood, straightening my apron and skirt, and marched over to Gabriel, my head held high. I would apologize, but I would not mean the words I spoke, that was certain.

"I apologize for yesterday," I blurted out as soon as I reached his table. "It was rude of me to insult you, as being French is certainly not something you can help." I bit my lip, frowning. That had not come out as I had anticipated.

Gabriel grinned, the smoke from his pipe sweet in the air between us. "I, too, apologize. It was unfair to compare you with a French woman. It is an unequal standard."

I shot him a quick glare for his backward apology. He knew well that was not what had upset me, but rather being told that I smelled like a horse. I whirled on my heel, ready to join Mabel back in the kitchen. Speaking with Henry could wait.

"Abby, sit with me." Henry appeared from behind me, pulling out a bench at the next table, far too close to Gabriel for my liking. "There is something else to discuss."

I reluctantly lowered myself onto the bench. What else could he possibly have to say? I was beginning to make plans to prepare my meals at home. Eating here every day was certain to get me into more trouble.

Mabel came over, dropping off two plates of eggs, back bacon, fried tomatoes, and toast. The smell wafted into my nose, making me feel lightheaded. I was famished.

"Eat." Henry pushed a plate towards me. "You must be hungry. I missed you at dinner last night."

"Yes, well, I was busy." I snuck a look over at Gabriel, who was watching me yet again. Did the man not have better things to look at? The fort seemed too small for the two of us, the wooden palisade confining. I was certainly glad he would be kept busy with his work as a trapper between forts.

Henry cleared his throat, looking between Gabriel and me. Something unspoken passed between the two men, and Gabriel looked away, tapping out his pipe and starting to eat. I breathed a sigh of relief and reached into my pocket for the charm.

"I made this for you," I said, placing it near his plate. "It's for good luck."

Henry picked up the small horseshoe, a smile stretching from ear to ear. His thumb ran over the marking of the rose. "Why, thank you, Abby. That's lovely. I shall cherish it immensely."

There was a *thud* at the other table as Gabriel stood abruptly, lifting his plate. He swung his leg over the bench, raising an eyebrow at me before walking over to another table full of men. My cheeks flushed, but I said nothing, not wanting to upset Henry. But really, Gabriel's manners were quite atrocious.

Henry, seemingly unbothered by Gabriel's departure, shovelled a mouthful of eggs in his mouth. I followed suit, closing my eyes briefly while I enjoyed the first bite. Food on the road had been plain—oats, beans, or pemmican—a mix of dried meat, tallow, and berries made by the Indigenous peoples. Nothing this delicious.

"I've spoken with the Chief Factor, the commander of the fort," he said, wiping his mouth on a cloth napkin. "Fort Augustus is desperate for someone to work in the smith's shop for a few days. Now, I know I told you they are our competitors, but we owe them a favour from last winter when there was a terrible case of flux here at Fort Edmonton. It will just be for a day or so."

THE FORT

I bit into my bacon, nearly moaning in delight at the salty explosion of flavour. Henry grinned at me, sliding the last slice from his plate over to mine. "You need me to go? Or my father?" I did think it was amusing that Henry found my work unbecoming until someone needed my skill.

"I think sending you should suffice, as your father is plenty busy here," he said, taking a final gulp of tea. "Gabriel will take you over, as he's familiar with both forts. It won't be today, at any rate."

I coughed, nearly choking on the bacon. "Gabriel?" I let my gaze slide over to where he now sat, his back squarely facing me.

"Yes." Henry's hand fell to my shoulder as he stood, squeezing it affectionately. "Try not to maim each other, all right?" He chuckled, pocketing the horseshoe charm. With a wink in farewell, he exited the dining room, off to work in the headquarters for the day.

I forced myself to finish my plate, my appetite gone. Then I hurried into the kitchen, back to the relative safety of the women. I would rather shovel the horse stables for those few days than spend time alone with Gabriel. I peeked back into the dining room, finding him looking at me once again. Turning quickly, I put my hands to my chest, where my heart had begun to beat rapidly.

"There. That wasn't so bad, was it?" Mabel was at my elbow, followed by Elizabeth, the young Métis woman who had questioned me the first day. She grinned, but it was anything but friendly.

"Did Henry call things off with his fiancée, then?" Elizabeth asked, cocking her eyebrow. "I see he accepted your gift at the table."

"He's engaged?" I squeaked. How could I be so stupid to assume he was unattached? He was a charming man with a good position and likely a wealthy family back home.

27

"Yes. There's a woman back in England waiting for him," she said almost gleefully, earning a scowl from Mabel.

"Don't listen to her, Abby. There's been no post from her in over a year. She wasn't keen on him accepting the remote post with the HBC. You already know that, Elizabeth. Henry said she has no plans to join him here."

I groaned, hiding my face in my hands. My father was wrong. I had no need for a husband. Men were untrustworthy creatures, just out to woo unsuspecting women into their beds. I would be better by myself.

Chapter Four

The next few days passed in a blur as I worked alongside my father and Edmund in our shop. I managed to avoid seeing Henry, making sure to go to the cookhouse late for every meal. I didn't know what I wanted to say to him with my newfound knowledge of his fiancée. He hadn't made any direct proclamation of endearment towards me—yet. But even though Mabel assured me there was no woman of affection in Henry's life, I was determined I would not be the *other* woman ever again.

One mid-afternoon, I found myself without any horses to shoe. My back and shoulders ached from the strain of always leaning over, coupled with the physical demands of keeping the animals still behind me. The pale spring sun was out; while not quite warm, it filled my heart with the joy of a new season. On an impulse, I took my shawl from the hook and decided to go for a walk to stretch.

I was out of the fort gates and around the corner of the palisade when I came across a group of men chopping firewood just outside the forest. I pulled my shawl closer and ducked my head, trying to hurry past, but still caught the attention of the closest men. One of them, who I did not recognize from the fort, whistled at me, grabbing himself lewdly. I was no stranger to men behaving in this manner but nevertheless looked away, flustered, and turned a sharp right into the forest.

There was no path, but I made my way through the dense grove, stepping over the thick underbrush. I kept close to the forest edge, planning to exit once I had made it out of the view of the men. Remembering the last time I had been caught unawares in the forest, I kept my head up and my senses perked.

Three Indigenous men still caught me by surprise, camouflaged in the trees by their buckskin clothing. I had seen these particular men before, wandering into the fort trading post, but regardless, my heart hammered. I had once again foolishly left on my own without telling anyone my whereabouts.

One of the men cocked his head at me, then stepped around to my other side, the three of them enclosing me in a circle. I tried to squeeze past him, but he widened his stance. I took a deep breath, trying to stay calm. Perhaps he was just curious, as white women were scarce on the western frontier. My eyes darted around the darkened forest, trying to find anything I could use to defend myself. I longed for the comfort of my blacksmithing tools in my palm.

"Abigail!" a familiar French voice called from behind me, and I nearly sagged to my knees in relief. *Gabriel.* Despite our differences, I knew he would return me safely to the fort. I turned, expecting to see his dark scowl, but instead found concern etched into his features.

"Ma chérie!" He squeezed his way through the men, grabbed me by the waist, and pulled me close to him. I stiffened in surprise, trying to push away, his fingers squeezed tightly into my sides, telling me this was

THE FORT

a ruse. I forced myself to soften in his embrace and put my arms around his neck.

"What are you doing out here alone?" he murmured, sounding a little out of breath. He kept his hand at my waist as he turned to the men, obviously under the pretense of being my man. He then addressed the men. It surprised me that he spoke the language of the Natives, and within a few seconds and a pouch of tobacco withdrawn from Gabriel's shirt pocket, the men had turned and made their way back into the forest.

"Thank you," I said, sighing in relief. I glanced up at him nervously. "I'm sorry. I just needed to go for a walk, as my back aches from the horseshoeing."

I was expecting a sharp response, but none came. Instead, he took my hand and pulled me back out of the forest onto the path. We walked a few steps before he released it, stopping to look me over. "Abigail, you must not wander off. I know you are used to taking care of yourself, but there are deadly tribal wars among the Indians. We are trying to keep the peace with them for the sake of the fur trade and other supplies, but if you were taken or harmed, there would be hell to pay."

I looked down at the path, toeing my boot in the dirt. It sounded like he was only concerned with keeping the peace, not about my safety after all. I took a deep breath, hating that I cared. "I know. And I'm sorry. I didn't mean to put you into a compromising position."

He cleared his throat uncomfortably, rubbing the back of his neck. "Well, I told those men that you're mine, so they won't bother you again. But there are many other men who might, Indian or otherwise. If you need to leave the fort, please just ask someone to go with you, Abigail."

I nodded, lifting my head to meet his gaze. His beard looked a little less scruffy today, like he had trimmed it. This was the most I had ever spoken

31

with him, and for once, he was pleasant and not abrupt. I decided to offer something of myself to thank him. "You can call me Abby, Gabriel. It's what everyone calls me, except my father."

He gave a short laugh and continued walking down the path, motioning for me to walk beside him. His red plaid shirt was stretched tight across his burly chest, and I tried not to stare at the space at the top where the buttons were undone. "Why do you want a name like a little girl? You are a woman with a beautiful name, and you should be proud of it." He turned to face me, giving me a grin. "And my name is Gah-bri-elle, in French. Not Gay-bri-el." He mimicked my English accent, making me smile. Truthfully, the way he said my full name was also charming, emphasizing the *I* sound in the middle with his accent.

We walked along the path in silence for a few minutes, and I realized he was taking me on a walk, not back to the fort. I could see the river in the distance and Fort Augustus on the other bank. I sneaked a peek at him, wondering if he had followed me into the forest.

He broke the silence, gesturing out towards the water. "We will go to Fort Augustus tomorrow, oui? The weather should be fine to cross the river."

"All right," I agreed, eyeing the chunks of ice that still floated on the water. I would have to trust him that it was safe. The river *was* narrowest at this crossing, but the idea of accidentally ending up in the frigid water made me shiver.

He walked me down to the riverbank, and we sat on a log, enjoying the meagre warmth from the sun on our faces, until he spoke again. "In the winter, the whole river will freeze, and the men sometimes go fishing through the ice. I can take your son if you wish."

THE FORT

"Oh." I smiled at him, amazed at this different man. He was actually quite agreeable today. "That would be lovely. I'm sure Ben would enjoy that."

He swallowed hard, looking away, before meeting my gaze again. "I have a son, as well. He's just a little older than yours."

My eyebrows shot up in surprise. I hadn't imagined Gabriel had a family, as with the time he spent around the fort, it certainly didn't seem like he did.

He saw my look. "He lives in France with his mother." He turned away once more, picking at a stray thread on his pants. "His name is Alexandre."

I fell quiet, wondering about the woman and his son. Was she Gabriel's wife? I bristled a little, thinking of his comment about French women smelling sweet, but brushed it aside, not wanting to disrupt the peace. I thought about offering the information that my brothers, too, were still overseas, but decided against it. He might wonder why we had left them behind.

"You must miss him terribly," I said finally.

He grunted, not offering any more information, and we lapsed into another silence, this one markedly more uncomfortable.

"How long have you lived here?" I ventured, not knowing how to navigate a conversation with this strange man. I was beginning to think that aside from the gruff exterior, he was quiet and held some turmoil inside, like myself.

He nodded, looking relieved that I had broken the quiet. "This will be my tenth winter." He paused, casting me a sidelong glance. "And you? Will this be your first winter here?"

I shook my head, calculating his time here—he said his son was just a little older than Ben, who was six. Had he made a passage home to his wife at all? "No, we lived in York for a few winters," I said vaguely, not wanting him to realize that I had been pregnant with Ben on the voyage over. I had birthed him during our first winter here, along with a midwife in a vacant trapper's cottage, each birthing pain a reminder of my transgression. I hadn't wanted him—Ben—but the moment I saw his sweet face, I knew my life had forever changed for the better.

He seemed pleased by my answer, his eyes crinkling in a half-smile. "Good. I won't have to worry about you being underprepared for winter. We just need to do something about you accosting strangers in dark forests."

I laughed, watching as he chuckled with me. His words struck a chord that warmed a place deep inside me, but I dismissed it quickly. This was *Gabriel*, who I disliked. Why would he be worried about me? It must have something to do with Henry, but ...

"Gabriel?" I said his name carefully in the French way, earning another soft laugh from him. "Does Henry have a fiancée in England? Some of the other women think he might."

He sighed heavily, rising from the log, motioning that our time by the river was finished. We climbed back up the bank, him offering me his hand through the steepest parts. The pace he set back to the fort was brisk, and I thought he might have forgotten about my question.

We were nearly at the fort gates when he turned to me, crossing his thick arms over his chest. "There was a woman, but as far as I know, he has not heard from her in quite some time." He paused, chewing over his words. "She was not keen on the idea of living this kind of life. Not many women are."

THE FORT

I bit my lip, thinking again of how he didn't see me as a lady and had said I smelled like a horse. What he clearly meant was that no *proper* woman would live this kind of life. I gave him a weak smile, then continued making my way inside the gates. No doubt there was work waiting for me.

He reached out and caught my arm, pulling me back. His blue eyes bore into mine, and for a second, my pulse quickened, but not in fear. "I shouldn't have said that," he mumbled, "about the horses. Learning your father's trade is good for you. This land is cold and unforgiving and has killed many unskilled men."

He released my arm but leaned down closer to speak again, filling my nose with the scent of him, a mix of sweet tobacco and the outdoors. "You should know that Henry is due to be reposted next year. Likely to the far north, where the winter is the only thing on anyone's mind all year long. You may be hardy enough to survive, but it is no life for a young boy."

As if I had beckoned him, Ben ran through the gates of the fort, looking for me. "Mama, come quick! It's Papa. He's speakin' nonsense again."

"Oh no!" I broke out in a run towards the blacksmith shop. Father's episodes of forgetfulness were happening more and more often. I had to attend to him quickly before anyone noticed. It would be just our luck to lose the blacksmith contract due to his confusion so soon after we'd arrived.

I let out a soft curse under my breath, seeing Henry loitering outside the shop. The deep frown that creased his forehead told me he'd likely encountered my father. "Where were you?" he barked as I approached,

Gabriel and Ben just behind me. "Your father's been wandering the fort, looking for a woman named Mary. He's quite distraught."

"We were just discussing tomorrow's plans to visit Fort Augustus," Gabriel piped up. "Down by the river. Abigail was feeling nervous about the crossing."

I hid my surprise at his lie but then realized that he was saving me from Henry's wrath about walking in the forest alone, and I smiled at him gratefully.

"Mary was my mother," I explained, trying not to wring my hands. "She died near-on ten years ago from consumption. My father hasn't been the same since."

"He frightened some of the women and children in the yard, Abby. He was not acting of sound mind." Henry's face had softened, and he reached out to place his hand on my arm in exactly the same spot where Gabriel had just moments before. "He's unwell."

"Please." My voice took on a desperate tone, and an uneasy churning started in my stomach. "Please don't say anything to the Chief Factor. We cannot afford the journey back to York just now. They'll let him go, and we have nowhere to go."

"Abby—"

"Abigail—"

Both men spoke at the same time, and I looked from one to another. Henry, with his upright stance and officer's uniform, and Gabriel, with his unkempt hair and wood axe slung through his belt. A strange hush fell, punctuated by the sharp twang of Edmund hammering in the shop. Finally, muttering something under his breath in French and sending a nod to me, Gabriel took his leave, heading back towards the gates of the fort.

THE FORT

"You won't end up alone, Abby. You have my word," Henry said, brushing a few strands of hair away from my face in a gesture that was quite forward. "I won't speak of this to anyone, but it was more than just me who saw him." He glanced down at Ben, who was close by my side. "Actually, I was coming over to speak with your father. About a courtship with you."

"A courtship?" I could hardly believe my ears. We had been here a mere week, and he was already sure he wanted to court. The woman in England must not be important to him any longer. A man would not approach a woman's father if he had ill intentions.

"Yes. You're beautiful and kind. Everything I've wanted for a wife."

"A wife? Henry, I—"

He laughed, filling my heart with hope. "I won't scare you off. Just a courtship for now, Abby. But I will be restationed next year, and I'm hoping you will join me as my wife."

I remembered Gabriel's warning about the winters in the north. Surely, it couldn't be as bad as he had described. Yet, something niggled in the back of my mind. Why had it seemed like Gabriel was trying to warn me off Henry?

Henry leaned forward, planting a bold kiss on my cheek, throwing my worried thoughts far away. Instead, I was imagining myself as Mrs. Henry Davies, my belly swollen once again, carrying his child. It was a pretty picture, and I thought of it long after I went inside our home to check in on my father.

Chapter Five

*T*he arrival of Mrs. Wilkes, the head housekeeper, interrupted my dusting of the bed chambers. She twisted her hands in her apron. "Abigail, you're wanted in the drawing room. An urgent matter, I'm afraid." I had never been summoned during my employ at the earl's estate, and by the look on Mrs. Wilkes' face, the news was not good.

"All right, thank you," I said as calmly as I could, though a solid lump of dread formed in my stomach. It joined the cramping I had been experiencing since yesterday. Every time I went to relieve myself, I prayed that my monthly courses had arrived, but alas, there was still nothing. I couldn't think of anything else, and with each passing minute, I became more and more convinced that what I feared was true—I was with child. There was also the matter of the earl's gold watch that sat like a hot ember in my pocket. In a moment of romantic whim, I had picked it up off his dressing table, feeling its cool weight in my palm, when the earl had his back turned, dressing after our relations. Before I knew what I was doing, I had slipped it onto my person. I hadn't meant to steal, but here I was, pregnant and a thief.

THE FORT

I had just arrived at the door of the drawing room and was reaching for the brass doorknob when it flew open, and a wrinkled hand grabbed me by the collar. I stumbled into the room, dragged by the earl's mother, the Dowager Countess of Grisham. Her son, my lover, was older than me by some degree, though we had never spoken of our exact ages.

"Well, George?" Her tone was venomous, and I dared to peek at the audience in front of me. George and his wife, Elenore, sat at opposite ends of the room, and another man, perhaps the family lawyer, smoked a pipe near the window.

"Yes, she's the one." George's voice—my George, who had a mere ten hours ago told me he loved me as we rolled together in the sheets—was flat. He refused eye contact with me, instead staring out at the lush green garden through the window.

A punishing slap landed on my cheek, and I fell against the bookshelf, my eyes stinging. "Do you have anything to say for yourself, girl? For defiling my son? Your family shall certainly hear of this. Spreading your legs for a man of position, what were you hoping for? A bastard heir?"

Bile rose hot in my throat as I looked at the earl's wife, sitting primly in her chair. Her eyes were red-rimmed, and she kept her hands clenched tight in her lap. There were rumours that she was barren, and now I might be carrying her husband's child in my womb.

"I'm sorry," I whispered, pleading with George to look my way, to give me one shred of hope that his affection had at least been true. Instead, he stood, excused himself from the room, and walked out, leaving me alone.

I woke from my dream with a start, gasping loud enough to make Ben stir beside me. I blinked awake, shaking off the scene in the drawing room. Those days were over, I told myself sternly, and Ben was far away from England and the grasp of that horrid family. One day, when he was older, I would tell him the truth, but today was not that day.

I hung my head down over the edge of the bunk, checking on my father. He was thankfully sound asleep and would likely stay that way for most of the morning. Each time he had an episode of absentmindedness, it would ravage his strength for the next week. I had started to notice small differences in his day-to-day life, too: forgetting what he was making in the shop mid-task and not remembering events that had happened a week or month before. It was upsetting for Ben and had created a constant worry in me. What would we do if his health started to decline rapidly? Now that I'd had time to think about it, the discussion with Henry about courtship did little to ease my concern. I couldn't marry Henry and leave my father behind in a fragile state. Yet it didn't seem likely he would be able to travel with us or survive the conditions of the far north.

I sat up, suddenly resolving to ask Henry directly about the woman he had been promised to in England. I may have been childish back when Ben was conceived—innocent and gullible to my lover's false promises—but I would not live in that fantasy again. I wanted the words of truth straight from Henry's mouth. I would also talk to him about care for my father. He seemed a decent man and would understand my dilemma.

As I sat there with my thoughts, I became aware of a light tapping at our door. It was early, the sky still dark outside the window. It was likely Edmund, as I had explained to him yesterday that my father would need

THE FORT

to rest today. Thankfully, the boy seemed confident that he would be able to manage the shop alone while I was away at Fort Augustus.

I climbed down the ladder of the bunk, then put on my robe over my nightdress and slipped into a pair of moccasins. When I opened the door, I was surprised to see Mabel who was carrying a pot of stew and bannock, a flatbread staple that had come over with the Scots and adopted by the Indigenous people and Métis.

"For your father," she said, keeping her voice quiet in the early morning darkness. She slipped in through the narrow doorframe. "I figured he might not make it for meals today."

"Thank you," I replied, feeling a surge of gratitude. Outside, Edmund had let himself into the shop and had begun to stoke the fire in the forge, adding more charcoal to bring it to a hot enough temperature. I caught his eye and smiled, thanking him silently for coming so early. He was a good lad, and I would make sure to send him home with anything extra we earned in trade.

Inside, I stoked our own hearth, setting the pot to hang on the trammel to warm for my father when he awoke. Mabel would take Ben for the day while I travelled to Fort Augustus, as he was happy to do his chores and play with the other children. I turned, meaning to get the kettle filled for tea, when I caught sight of Mabel's face, now illuminated by the light of the fire.

"Oh no, Mabel." I reached out to touch the bruising that marked her light brown skin with shades of purple and red. She pulled away, likely embarrassed. I had seen this before, of course. Women hiding their faces in the shadows, pulling their shawls close to conceal where they had been abused. It was on the tip of my tongue to ask what had happened, but it wasn't hard to guess. Her husband was often seen lurching around the

41

camp, drunk in the late evenings. It was common enough for the white men to push their Métis wives around, and nobody said anything, but Mabel was becoming my friend.

"It's nothing," she whispered, but a tear fell onto her cheek, betraying her words. Another followed, and I came over, drawing her into an embrace. "I *hate* him," she gritted out between clenched teeth. "The day he dies, I will celebrate and never allow my children to utter his name again."

"I hate him too," I agreed, pulling away to put on the tea, "and I will celebrate with you."

She laughed through her tears, wiping her face with a handkerchief from her apron. "Thank you, Abby. I know other women have it worse off than me, so I try not to complain."

"That doesn't make it right," I said, though I knew that there was nothing that either of us could do. "Does it happen often?" I asked, giving the stew a stir on the hearth. My stomach growled as the smell of venison, barley, and potatoes greeted my nose. I wasn't sure what time Gabriel wanted to leave to cross the river, but I needed to eat before what was sure to be a long day.

"Often enough." She sighed, coming over next to me.

I helped myself to a bowl and a piece of bannock, digging in greedily. The events of the day before had taken a toll on me, too, and I had yet again missed the evening meal.

"I heard Henry asked to court you," she said, perching on the edge of the hearth and nibbling on a piece of the bannock. "And that you said yes."

"I did." I nodded, taking another spoonful of stew. I wasn't sure I liked how quickly gossip flew through the fort. There was no privacy at all.

THE FORT

"Though I want to speak with him about his fiancée. Just to make sure." I paused, thinking of my afternoon with Gabriel by the river. "Is Gabriel married? He told me he has a son around Ben's age."

Mabel nodded. "I'm not exactly sure, but there are stories. They came over from France together and—"

A sharp rap at the door interrupted us. I gave Mabel a wide-eyed look, and she stifled a giggle. Sure enough, the Frenchman in question stood outside my door, a blue toque pulled over his head to keep out the morning chill.

His cool gaze flickered over me, taking in my untamed hair and robe, and the bowl of half-eaten stew in my hands. "We leave in ten minutes," he said briskly, already turning to leave. "Everything you'll need is at Fort Augustus." He ducked back out of the shop, taking long strides back through to the common yard.

"Well, I see we're back to being unfriendly again," I muttered, not surprised. What I had seen of Gabriel so far indicated that taciturn was his preferred mood.

"She left." Mabel moved to stand at my shoulder, watching him disappear. "His wife left. With another Frenchman and his son. That's the story, anyway. He never speaks of it."

My cheeks flushed unexpectedly at this revelation, and I closed the door quickly, not wanting to look at his retreating form any longer. "That explains a lot," I said, frowning at my reaction. Why was there heat creeping up my skin? I didn't care if he was married or not. Or that his wife had run away with another man, leaving him childless and alone.

Mabel shrugged, putting on her shawl to leave. "I'm not sure if it explains why she left or why he's always angry. Maybe he was a miserable man to live with." She touched her face as if remembering her own miserable plight.

"Yes," I agreed, still musing. Or perhaps that's what he'd meant yesterday about most women not wanting to live in these remote conditions. Truthfully, I hadn't given much thought to being far removed from the comfort of home. It had seemed like the best place to go for both my reputation and Ben's. Part of me *liked* living more simply, away from the bustle of London.

I roused Ben and dressed him quickly, sending him on his way with Mabel. Then, I washed myself in the basin, got dressed, and started to braid my hair in its usual style. I had grown accustomed to wearing it down like a young girl, not pinned up in the style of grown women. I hesitated, thinking of how Gabriel had commented on my nickname sounding like that of a girl. Perhaps he was right—if I were to court Henry, it was time to put those childish ways behind me for good. I dug my hair pins out from the bottom of my chest and spent a few minutes securing my hair up, then pinched my cheeks for good measure.

Despite Gabriel's comment about the fort having everything I needed, I stopped in the shop to gather a small crate of keg horseshoes and a bag for my farrier tools. I worked faster with my own supplies, and if the fort had no shoes, I would spend half the day fashioning them.

I was pleasantly surprised to find Henry waiting for me at the fort gates, Gabriel beside him, smoking his pipe with an impatient look on his face. I huffed in annoyance at his expression. He had failed to mention yesterday that we were leaving at first light, and I had gotten ready as quickly as I could. Well, except for my hair, I supposed.

THE FORT

"Here," I said, shoving the heavy crate at him, relishing as he gave an *oof* at the weight. "Would you mind carrying these? Unless you're sure they have them at the other fort."

"I can carry them, Abby." Henry reached over to take the crate from Gabriel. "I must say, you look lovely this morning. How is your father faring?"

"He's all right," I said, shifting uncomfortably at the thought that the whole fort now knew of his ailment. "Edmund will work alone this morning so my father can rest, but I'm sure he'll be back at work by midday."

Gabriel tapped his pipe against the gate, indicating the end of our conversation, then took the crate back out of Henry's arms. "We must go. I will bring her back in time for the evening meal."

I waved goodbye to Henry and ran to catch up with Gabriel, who was marching down the path to the river at a rapid pace. Yesterday, we had walked leisurely, but today, apparently, we needed to rush.

"Your father should take on Edmund as his formal apprentice while he still has the role of Master Smith," he said over his shoulder as I scrambled to keep up with him. "That way, Edmund can take over the contract and keep you on as the farrier."

"Yes, that might be a good idea," I agreed breathlessly. "Why are we in such a hurry?"

Gabriel slowed his stride marginally, allowing me to finally walk alongside him. "I have much to do today. I will bring supplies to the fort, and then I will check my traps on that side of the river. If they are full, I will deliver them to the Indians to skin and treat. And I must return you on time, or Henry will not allow you to come again."

"I am a grown woman. I hardly need permission from Henry." The words fell from my mouth before I had a chance to think them through, and Gabriel cocked an eyebrow at me.

"You have practically agreed to marry. Henry is not the type of man who will tolerate a woman with a sharp tongue." He gave me a level look. "Of course, a week is hardly enough time for you to know that about him."

We had started our way down the riverbank, my thoughts full of Henry, when I stopped short. There were two birchbark canoes resting in the water. One was full of supplies, with only room left over for Gabriel to row. The other, where I would sit, would be rowed by a young Indigenous boy, and there was already another passenger on board.

"Miss Williams, hello!" the reverend called, patting the bench in front of him. I exhaled sharply at the thought of spending the entire ride across the river that close to Reverend Smith. I was sure he would waste no time continuing where he had left off on the wagon ride into the fort.

Gabriel peered up at me from the riverbank. "What is it, Abigail? We must make haste."

My mouth opened and closed without a sound. I could hardly explain to him with the reverend in earshot. I might have a sharp tongue for a woman, but I was no fool. Men like the reverend were powerful, with the backing of the church and the entire HBC.

"I thought I was going with you," I said finally, imploring him to understand with the pleading in my eyes. "I *prefer* to ride with you," I added in a quieter tone.

He stared at me, the blue of his eyes darkening in understanding. "Merde," he muttered, followed by a steady stream of French, which I was sure was not fit for the ears of a woman. Thrusting the crate of

THE FORT

horseshoes back at me, he stomped down to the shore and grabbed the carefully packed supplies in his own canoe. The reverend's canoe bobbed violently up and down in the water as he threw the supplies unceremoniously into the second boat. Water splashed up over the side, and Gabriel let out an evil-sounding chuckle when the Reverend complained.

"Allez-y!" he shouted to the Indigenous boy once most of the supplies had been moved. The boy nodded but struggled to row with the added weight. Gabriel waded farther into the water, giving the canoe a push. Once he was satisfied they were successfully on their way, he came over to me.

"What happened?" he demanded, hands on his hips. Like most trappers, he wore trousers that came only to his knees. The lower half of his legs were covered in woollen socks and buckskin boots, which would dry quickly, as he was in and out of the water all day checking beaver traps.

"On the wagon ride in, he touched my leg a number of times. It got to the point where it seemed he was meaning to touch ... other places." I felt my cheeks become hot at having to explain and lowered my head so as not to have to meet his eyes.

"Did you tell him to stop?" When I shook my head, he made a growl deep in his throat. "Abigail, you live in a fort full of men. You must exercise more caution. I cannot be around to ensure your safety every day."

I blew out a sigh of frustration, glaring back at him. I felt a bit like Mabel, trying to explain away an injustice I had no control over. "That's hardly fair. Men like the reverend do whatever they please. I'm sure me telling him to stop would do nothing except encourage him."

"So, when you encountered me in the forest, you drew your tongs like a weapon, ready to hit me over the head, but when the reverend made an

47

advance, you hid like a lamb?" He sighed, running his hand over his face, leaving his beard standing on end. "You should be carrying a gun. Men aside, there are dangerous animals everywhere. These are not the streets of England."

"I'm afraid I'm a rather poor shot with a gun, though, Gabriel. Growing up in the city gave me little chance to practice." I stepped around him, eager to change the topic. I bent over to pick up the crate of horseshoes I had abandoned on the grassy shore. "Should we go? You said you had a busy day."

I heard another grunt of disapproval behind me, and then, to my surprise, I was swept up into his arms as he lifted me into the canoe. After I was seated, he pushed the boat farther out into the water, the stones scraping along the bottom. Then, he leapt into the canoe in an agile manner, retrieving the paddle from the bottom of the boat. He deftly rowed us out into the river, droplets of water flying in the air each time he lifted the oar.

"Claudette, the French woman, will stay with you at Fort Augustus," he said once we had been underway for a few minutes, "but please stay away from the men. The Nor'Westers are mostly French and Scots, and we are not known for our good manners."

He gave me a sly grin over his shoulder, and my laughter echoed over the water.

Chapter Six

C laudette was nothing like I expected. Instead of a spindly Parisian matron, a plump, middle-aged woman practically smothered Gabriel in kisses when we arrived at Fort Augustus. He tolerated her endearments with ease, surprising me. I hadn't thought of him as a man who liked physical touch, but perhaps the French were more affectionate in that way than the English.

"Ah, Gabriel, she's beautiful," she said, fawning over me. She crossed herself over her ample chest in the way of the Catholics. "I've been asking our good Father to send me another woman from the Continent, and here she is." I was suddenly enveloped in her bosom, the smell of onions strong on her apron. When she released me, Gabriel had gone across the yard and was hoisting the bundles he was delivering on his shoulder. I watched him for a moment, feeling a strange void at his absence. Oddly enough, I was beginning to enjoy our time spent together. He was prickly, to be sure, but he listened when I spoke and seemed to care about my well-being.

"He's a handsome man, oui?" Claudette asked, following my gaze. "I've been begging him to cut that mangy hair. Perhaps with the attention of a beautiful woman, he might agree." She turned on me, lifting my hand to hers, finding no ring on my finger. "No husband?"

"No, but I am courting Henry, an officer—"

"Ah, non. French men are much better lovers than the English. Et Gabriel est très français." She chuckled loudly, sending me a suggestive wink.

I grew embarrassed at her salacious words, my mind conjuring images of Gabriel engaged in lovemaking with one of the unmarried women. By the way Claudette was describing things, it sounded like maybe he had been with many women. I remembered his comment about French women being sweet and warming their husband's beds, and my cheeks grew even hotter.

"Ah, jolie fille, I didn't mean—"

"Where is the blacksmith shop?" I cut her off, eager to get away. I would focus on the work to be done for the day and send Edmund next time. I had been here no more than ten minutes and already had an uncomfortable knot in my stomach. I did not like the way this woman had dismissed Henry and made suggestions about Gabriel. I may have had a sordid past, but I had no intentions of being seen as available to any man at the fort.

"This way." She gave me a knowing look, which further raised my ire. The French and the English were not friendly for a reason, I decided. I stomped ahead of her, arriving at the forge, which had thankfully already been lit. Piled around the shop was a large collection of items needing repair. Claudette stood silently by as I sorted them: animal traps, cooking utensils, lanterns, hooks, and door hinges. The odd horseshoe had made

THE FORT

it into the pile, and I set them aside to be used later. There were also heavier items, such as parts for wagons and ploughs, that I would not be able to manage on my own.

I decided to start with the traps while Claudette pulled up a seat and a large basket of clothing that needed to be darned. It was obvious that she had been told to mind me for the day like I was a child. I turned my back to her and got to work, glad that working in a blacksmith shop was loud and I wouldn't be forced into small talk.

We remained together for an hour in silence, her with her darning needle and me working over the forge, until a man came by the shop. They conversed in French, sending looks in my direction.

"There's four horses that need shoeing," she said, nodding at the man. "He's wondering if you are able to do it."

"Yes, of course," I answered, holding up one of the horseshoes I had brought with me. "I'm the farrier at the other fort."

Claudette moved with me to the area behind the shop for shoeing, she and the Frenchman intently watching as I put on my leather gloves and shod the first horse. I removed the shoe and filed down the growth, taking special care as one of the hooves had an abscess.

"I've never seen a woman blacksmith before," she commented finally, taking a seat and picking up her darning needle. "You seem to be very good at it." As I held the hot shoe from the forge against the hoof, she made a noise in the back of her throat, wrinkling her nose. The smell was like that of burning hair, and although I was accustomed to it, it was not pleasant for those around me.

I shrugged at her compliment. "I'm not really a smith. I just help out my father."

51

She smiled kindly, and I felt that perhaps I had misjudged her earlier. Like Gabriel, she had a forthright way that grated on me, but perhaps the English danced around the bush too often instead of saying what they meant. Claudette seemed to be a busybody but harmless, and perhaps lonely.

"He's lucky to have such a daughter. I've heard you have a son. Will he learn the trade of the blacksmith, too?"

I moved onto the second horse, a pang in my chest at her question. "My father is ill. I'm afraid my son won't have the chance to learn his trade." This weighed heavily on me, as blacksmithing was a family craft passed down from fathers to sons. One of my brothers had learned, but Ben was too young, and my father's failing memory was becoming worse.

Claudette shifted in her seat, the chair squeaking under her weight. "I imagine that Gabriel would teach your son to trap if you asked. He's the best trapper in these parts. It would be a skill your son could use to secure his future."

I gave her a careful smile, not wanting her to push Gabriel on me again. "Perhaps."

"Dear, I know you think Gabriel a difficult man, and he is. But do not mistake the reasons why. He misses his own son something fierce. Teaching your son his trade might help ease that pain." She finished her with the last of the socks, then dug into the baskets for a pair of knitting needles and yarn. They clacked together as I mulled over her words.

"Is it true then? His wife left him and went back to France?" I did not normally like to engage in gossip, but it had also been some time since I'd had friendships with other women, and I missed the sharing of news. Besides, it seemed the perfect time to find out if there was any truth to the matter.

THE FORT

Claudette leaned closer to me, lowering her voice. "I was not here then, so I do not know for certain. But *Clarisse*, as I've heard, fell into another man's bed while he was away in the north. Gabriel nearly killed him, of course, but in the end, he let them go together. They were in love, you see."

My stomach churned at the story, and I turned my face away from her to blink away tears that threatened my vision. That had been *me*. I had been the woman who had driven a wedge into another marriage without any consideration of how the earl's wife might feel. But beyond the guilt, I also felt something shift in my chest for Gabriel. I couldn't imagine losing Ben across the ocean.

Drowning in my own thoughts and guilt, I finished the last two horses with Claudette's inquisitive stare on me over her knitting basket. She must think I was an emotional fool, having reacted twice to her mention of Gabriel in the space of a few hours.

I stood to stretch my back, then brushed off my work apron and tied the horse to the post nearby. Claudette rose from her seat, giving me a wink. "All right, it's teatime, then."

"Tea?" I asked, my stomach growling at her suggestion. "It's only midmorning."

"Oui, but I am in some need of sustenance just from watching you work so hard. You need fattening up, girl." She came over and linked her arm through mine. "Les hommes français like women with a little flesh on them."

She laughed at my wide-eyed expression, but I followed her anyway. She made me eat two slices of tourtière, a deliciously spiced meat pie served with piping hot black tea. After an hour in the kitchen, she walked me back to the smith's shop and spent the rest of the afternoon filling me in on all the comings and goings of Fort Augustus.

Gabriel and I arrived back at Fort Edmonton just before the supper hour. The reverend had thankfully stayed behind, with a plan to make his way to other local communities to spread the message of his faith. I cringed at the idea of him spending time with young Indigenous women, taking advantage of them with his lecherous caresses. He probably took more liberties with them than he would with a white woman, feeling that his superiority somehow resolved his actions in the eyes of God.

As we walked in through the gates, it was clear that something was amiss as a crowd stood gathered around the meal hall. Shouts, loud and urgent, filled the air, and we ran over to investigate. I searched the throng for Ben, my heart in my throat.

A man lay on a table, an open bear trap beside him. The large, thick teeth of the trap were glistening, wet with the man's blood. His leg was mangled, with bits of flesh and bone visible through the remnants of his trousers. The man writhed in agony, making a ghostly wail that sent chills down my spine. Henry stood at the helm of the table, his normally handsome face ash gray.

"Mon Dieu," Gabriel whispered in my ear, pushed close to me in the crowd. "He went missing the day before last. This is why you must not wander the forest, Abigail."

THE FORT

"Bone's crushed," one of the men near the table declared, holding a sharp kitchen knife and a saw. "We'll have to take it off."

Gabriel disappeared from my side as the crowd, watching the preparations for the surgery, inched closer. There was no doctor anywhere nearby, and medical emergencies such as these were often left to the men with the most mettle. Henry plied the man with whiskey, forcing generous amounts down his throat. Another supplied a leather strap for biting, and a third cut the man's trousers above the knee.

"Where's the smith?" the man with the knife asked. "We'll need this cauterized after we take off the leg."

Henry looked around the room frantically, finally catching my eye. He shook his head, mouthing the word *no*. I nodded, not wanting to volunteer for the gruesome task. Thankfully, Edmund wove his way through the crowd to the front, his face pale. I wondered if my father had gotten out of bed at all today, as I didn't see him anywhere.

"Mama, what's going on?" Ben arrived at my side in Gabriel's arms. His boyish face was tight with worry, and he clung tight to Gabriel's neck.

"He doesn't need to watch this," Gabriel said, a gruff tone to his voice. "Let's go."

Also not wanting to see, I nodded and followed them back out into the yard. Once we were inside the blacksmith shop, Gabriel put Ben down and withdrew a small pouch from his pant pocket. Inside, much to Ben's delight, was a collection of small wooden animals, each intricately carved—a horse, bear, wolf, fox, and raven.

"Gabriel, that was a lovely gift," I exclaimed as Ben ran into our home with his new treasure. "Did you make those?"

55

"No." He shrugged, glancing up into my eyes briefly before looking away. "One of the Indian elders made them. I traded a fur for them today." He turned to leave, but I reached out and caught him by the hand. It was warm and rough, and his fingers tightened around mine.

"Please," I started, very aware of where our fingers touched. "Will you teach Ben about the traps? He has no father to teach him about the wildlife or guns and I ..." I trailed off as a pained expression crossed his face. I remembered Claudette's words about his son and decided to surge forward with my request, my hand still warm in his. "Claudette says you're the best trapper in these parts. Ben won't have the chance to learn blacksmithing from my father, so I thought maybe you could teach him your trade."

Gabriel was staring down at me, and I could see the reflection of myself in his eyes. He reached up his free hand to push back a few strands of my hair that had fallen free from the pins in the busyness of the day. "You look different today, Abigail."

My breath caught in my throat at the look on his face. Something snapped between us, like a crack in a hissing fire. "I don't know," he murmured, his finger falling to gently stroke the side of my face. "I think I prefer your hair in its usual braid."

A cough sounded behind me, and I spun around, dropping Gabriel's hand. My father stood in the doorway of our quarters, leaning heavily on a cane.

Gabriel shoved the hand that had been on my cheek in his pocket and cleared his throat. I turned to find his face stoic and cool. "I can take Ben out two days from now if that suits you, Abigail. And I'll make mention to Henry to provide you with a gun." Not waiting for my response, he strode off, leaving my face flushed from his touch.

THE FORT

"Supper will be delayed, Father. There was an amputation in the cookhouse," I said, hiding my face and wandering over to the hearth to make sure Edmund had banked the fire. It gave me time to regain my composure. My heart was pounding in my chest, and my stomach was swirling. I dared a peek over at my father and grimaced at his frown.

"Abigail, what was that I just saw? I thought the English officer had captured your affection."

"Oh, yes, he has. Henry wants to ask for your permission to court." My voice trembled slightly, and I avoided his gaze, making my way around the workshop, tidying it up. My pulse quickened again at the thought of Henry, thankful he hadn't seen that encounter with Gabriel. Had I initiated it by grabbing his hand? Or asking him to teach Ben? And why hadn't I moved away, but rather, wanted to step closer into his embrace?

My father remained quiet, watching me sweep the metal shavings into a pile in the corner. "That Frenchman—"

"It was nothing," I snapped, finally meeting his eyes. "I was upset about the amputation and asked him to teach Ben to watch for traps in the forest. That's all." I felt embarrassed by what had just happened and resolved that it would not happen again. I would move forward with my intentions to court Henry.

"Just be careful, my daughter."

"I *am* careful, Father. I am not a child. I have learned from my mistakes." There was a wash of remorse and then resentment at his reprimand. "You do not need to worry about your wayward daughter. Henry wants to marry before he is restationed next year, and I will no longer be a burden to you." I pushed past him into the house, hot tears pricking my eyes. I was so tired. Tired of the worry, tired of my shame.

I passed by Ben, who was playing with the wooden animals near the hearth, and my throat grew thick with unshed tears. I scooped him up into my arms, hiding my face in the crook of his neck, trying to quell my feelings. *No.* It wasn't possible. Could Gabriel—the man who had threatened and insulted me—have feelings for me? For us? And worse, what was happening inside my own heart towards this wild man from the woods? I shook my head, furiously brushing away the tears that had started to fall. *No.* Henry was the smart choice, one that would make my father proud.

I gave Ben one final squeeze, then put him down, heading into the bedroom. Not bothering to undress, I climbed up into my bunk and buried myself under the furs and blankets that covered our bed. I squeezed my eyes shut, willing the whole day to disappear under the comfort of sleep. My father was right about one thing. I needed to be more careful.

Chapter Seven

The next morning, I asked Edmund to accompany Gabriel to Fort Augustus, claiming that the work was too heavy and required strength I did not possess as a woman. Gabriel gave me an inquisitive look when I presented Edmund at the gates, but I shook my head and lowered my gaze, not wanting him to see that my eyes were still swollen from crying the night before. It was best that I keep my distance. Gabriel was Henry's friend, and I didn't need the fort gossip to wonder if I were courting two men at the same time.

I wandered down to the kitchen to help with breakfast duty, hoping to find Mabel. I had decided that she was a trustworthy friend, and I could share what had happened with Gabriel. She would help me sort out these mixed-up feelings and set me straight on the path to Henry. That's what friends were for, after all. Perhaps one day I would even divulge the truth about Ben's parentage to Mabel. Perhaps it would help ease the aching burden of it all.

Instead of Mabel, I found Elizabeth, the younger Métis woman, handling the kitchen duties. She wiped the sweat off her forehead as I approached, giving me a slight frown.

"Oh, it's you." She thrust a sack of potatoes at me. "We need these washed, chopped, and fried. And be quick about it. There are hungry men out there, and we're shorthanded." She motioned out to the dining room, where a lone woman was serving at the long tables. "I'll be out there if you need me."

I nodded, taking the potatoes over to the wash bucket and giving them a scrub with a stiff brush. Then I carried them over to the table, where I chopped them into mouth-sized morsels, pushing thoughts of both Henry and Gabriel from my mind. I placed them in the pan to fry, seasoning them with salt. But as I reached for the lard, I noticed the pail was nearly empty.

"Well, that won't do," I mused, looking around me to see if there was another. There wasn't, and I sighed heavily at the inconvenience. I would have to go to the cellar, and the men would have to wait a few minutes longer for the meal.

I found a lantern on a hook near the trapdoor of the cellar, lighting it before reaching for the handle of the door. It stood slightly ajar with a rock wedged in the opening. The hinges creaked in protest as I opened it, and I jumped back as a mouse scurried out of the hole past me.

The cellar was wide and airy, and the shelves held preserves, bags of rice, oats, beans, and other root vegetables. I marvelled that the fort still had so much supply after the long winter, thankful that I wouldn't have to worry about Ben or my father going hungry. I scanned the room for the barrel of lard, finding it near the small window in the corner. As I reached for the paddle to scoop some out, shuffling behind me caught my attention.

"Hello?" I called, turning just to catch a pair of trouser-clad legs darting up the stairs. I followed them, curious that a man would be in the kitchen cellar. I called out again, coming to the base of the stairs. I spotted the man—or, a boy, by his height—just as he reached the top and disappeared around the corner, out of sight.

"That's strange," I muttered to myself, coming back into the room. Just as I reached once more for the lard, something fell from a shelf across the cellar with a whoomph. I found a burlap sack on the floor, dust flying into the air from the floor. I lifted it up, surprised at its weight. After I heaved it into place, I rummaged for the opening.

My hand brushed something prickly. I widened my eyes to see a thick stack of beaver furs concealed in the sack. I quickly went to the next sack on the shelf to find more of the same. There were at least ten sacks, all filled with furs.

My heart thumped in my chest. I had been in the New World long enough to know that to steal furs was akin to treason and murder. Furs were a man's livelihood, a way to feed his family. And they certainly didn't belong in the kitchen cellar.

"Abby!" Elizabeth called down the stairs, and I jumped guiltily as if I had been the one who had stolen the furs. I scrambled back over to the lard barrel, hastily digging in with the paddle. I came to the bottom of the stairs with the lard bucket in hand, trying to calm my heavy breathing.

"Lard," I said, holding up the pail as if producing evidence. I climbed back up into the kitchen, ignoring how she stood with her hands on her hips, ready to chastise me for not having the potatoes ready.

"Were you down there with Jonathan?" she asked, frowning again at me. "I could have sworn I saw him come up from the cellar."

"Jonathan?" I shook my head, hoping that she couldn't hear my pulse racing. Whoever it was, I was not going to share my findings with Elizabeth. I would go to Henry in confidence.

"Yes," she said with a huff. "Mabel's son."

My heart dropped into my boots. *Mabel's son?* It wasn't possible that Mabel's family was stealing furs ... was it?

Elizabeth peered down at me. "Are you quite alright, Abby? Those men are still waitin' on their breakfast."

I nodded, hurrying back over to the pan. I busied myself with my task, trying to hide my shaking hands. Certainly, the boy had been up to no good. Did Mabel know about her son's whereabouts? I had been sure I would report the incident to Henry just a moment before, but now I was not so sure. I remembered the bruises on her face the day before—perhaps Mabel needed the furs to compensate for her husband's drinking. I couldn't find it in my heart to believe that my new friend was a criminal.

I paced outside the door of the officer's quarters, working up the nerve to knock. The last week had passed by without having the opportunity to catch Henry alone, as he was a man of duty and often busy around the fort. I wanted to ask about his fiancée and perhaps the stolen furs, but

THE FORT

somehow our brief encounters in the common meal hall didn't seem like opportune times or places.

The door of the office flew open, catching me by surprise. Henry stood on the step, his features creased in a frown. "Abby, I just saw you through the window. What's the matter?" He paused, coming closer and lowering his voice. "Is it your father?"

I shook my head, pulling my shawl closer. Though the weather was warm during the day, it was still chilly in the mornings. "No. My father's been well. I've been wanting to ask you a question of a personal matter."

Looking curious but smiling politely, he ushered me inside. A common office was in the front room, with a large oak desk and chair and a fire cracking in the hearth. Unlike the rest of the fort, it was laid with wood flooring, and the furnishings looked expensive. I ran my fingers along the edge of the desk, glancing at his ledger.

"I'm sorry to interrupt your work," I said, trying to quell my nervousness. "I just never seem to catch you alone."

"It's me who should apologize," he said, pulling up a spare chair for me, "for not seeking you out. We've had a bit of a conundrum with the furs, unfortunately." He sat down across from me, running a hand through his light brown hair, making it stand up on end. "Missing bundles from the storehouse. It happened last year around this time, too."

I tried to control my facial expression as he pushed the ledger across to me. I couldn't read well, but I knew the general trading value. Prepared beaver skins, or 'soft gold' as they were fondly nicknamed, were the primary currency, and trades were completed for every pelt. A large HBC blanket, with its colourful stripes, was set at five skins. A bolt of calico and a collection of sewing needles were worth two. An axe was also worth two, and a gun fourteen. A pound of the ever-popular tobacco was two beaver pelts.

"Were they stolen?" I asked, trying to decide what to say. I hadn't addressed the issue with Mabel, as I hardly knew what to say. I had also realized it was possible Mabel didn't know. It would be best if I gave Henry a hint that he might need to search the cellar.

"We suspect so. Two of Gabriel's bundles were stolen, and the company will not subsidize the cost, so he's lost quite a significant amount." He sighed heavily, looking out the window to the yard. "The Northwest Company has offered him quite a lucrative contract, and I'm afraid this might be the tipping point for him to join the other French trappers."

"Do you think he'll accept?" I asked, ignoring the way I broke into a sudden sweat at the mention of him. As much as I still felt uneasy in his presence, it would be strange to never see him again.

"I hope not." Henry leaned back in the chair, stretching his neck from side to side. He wore his uniform, though he'd discarded the jacket and laid it over the top of his chair. "We are close to operating at a loss as it is." He waved his hand, though the worried crease did not leave his brow. "Never mind this talk, Abby. It's the business of men." He cleaned his throat, then tugged on his collar as if it were too tight. "Speaking of Gabriel, he's informed me that you need to be taught to shoot properly."

"Yes, I guess that's true," I replied, eyeing the rifle propped up in the corner of the room. "He's been taking Ben out to teach him about traps and animals." Ben had arrived home each time, ruddy-cheeked from excitement and the fresh air. Though he had not said as much, I thought Gabriel also looked forward to their days together as well, as a smile seemed to be more of a regular occurrence for him these days.

THE FORT

"Good. Now, what did you want to speak about?" He reached a hand over to cover mine. It was soft and warm and his nails were trimmed to perfection. I had a vision of holding Gabriel's rough one in the blacksmith shop and how a sudden heat had coursed through my veins, making my heart pound. I shook my head, forcing away the thought. It was better that I focused on the man in front of me—one that could provide stability and security.

Remembering my original mission of the day, I cleared my throat, blurting out the words before I could lose my nerve. "I'm sorry for being so forward, Henry, but I've heard that you were betrothed to a woman in England. I just wanted to make sure that your intentions in courting me are ... moral, and that you no longer have affection for her," I finished, glancing up to meet his eyes, seeing a quick frown cross his face before he changed it to a chivalrous smile.

"Darling, thank you for asking. It shows me that you are quite the virtuous woman." He stood, palms on the desk. "But you are right. This is a good time for me to write a letter to Margaret to let her know that I'm officially dissolving our relationship. I shall do that today. Would you like to read it before I send it with the voyageurs? The brigade should be here any day now."

"Thank you," I said, pleased by his answer, "but I can't read well."

"Really? I'm surprised, with your father being a blacksmith and all. They are usually quite literate in arithmetic. They can often read, too."

"Yes, well, he taught my brothers but didn't have time for me, I guess," I replied, standing to take my leave. I couldn't work up the nerve to mention the stash of furs I had uncovered. I would think about it more or perhaps speak with Mabel first.

"Brothers? I wasn't aware you had siblings."

My heart pounded at the slip, but I forced myself to smile up at him. I did not want Henry poking around in any part of my past. "Yes. They are much older than me and are still back in England." I prayed he did not find it strange that I had accompanied my father to the New World alone. The last thing I needed was my affair to come to light. I had no doubt that Henry would change his tune about my virtue.

He was quiet as he strode over to open the door for me. "Thank you for stopping by, Abby. How does it sound if I take you out to practice shooting tomorrow afternoon? With your father's permission, of course."

I eyed him warily, my pulse returning to its normal pace. Perhaps it was of no consequence to mention my brothers. He seemed to have forgotten it already. "I would love that, Henry. The weather should be fine for a picnic. Shall I pack a meal for us?"

"Splendid idea." He leaned down to kiss my cheek. "Until tomorrow."

As promised, Henry arrived at the workshop the next day around noon, a rifle slung over his shoulder. He greeted my father and Edmund with a handshake and ruffled Ben's hair. Taking the picnic basket from me, he offered me his arm as we walked out of the fort gates.

It was a warm day, and the insects of the midsummer had still not made their dreaded appearance, so we strolled along slowly. I enjoyed the way it felt walking next to him, as he was a good head taller than me, and for a brief moment, I imagined our bodies entwined together in marital

THE FORT

relations. It was not ladylike to think so, but I hoped that we would enjoy it often.

After we had walked for ten minutes or so, he put down the basket and gun and stretched out his hand to me. "Come. Let's inspect the beavers at work." He motioned over to the nearby pond, just visible through a thin growth of birch trees.

We wandered over, hand in hand, to where the large rodents were swimming with collections of twigs, branches, larger logs, and mud. They piled it up in one area, damming the water to create their lodge where they would birth and protect their babies. In the spring and summer months, they were safe from the trapper's nets as the men waited until the winter when their coats were at their thickest.

"For all the fuss over beavers," I said, taking the opportunity to move closer into Henry's presence, "they sure are unattractive creatures." I caught a glimpse of one's teeth, large and yellowed.

Henry chuckled, showing a soft set of lines at the corner of his eyes. "I agree. But the hats are considered a sign of fortune and wealth. My own grandfather has bequeathed his to me in his will."

"Really? I can't quite imagine you in a top hat."

"Well, not in these uncivilized lands, to be sure. But in England, I'm quite dapper, I assure you." His hand moved to my waist, pulling me against him. "Perhaps we can move back there after my posting is complete. You can put your days of blacksmithing behind you and live as a lady. Tell me, Abby, what are your brothers' names? I wish to reach out to them as a sign of respect."

I froze. Having Henry reach out to my family was a *horrid* idea. I could not completely trust my brothers to keep my secret safe. But what could I say? "That's not necessary, Henry. I'm actually not very close with them."

He frowned down at me. "Still, it's the proper thing to do if I am to wed their sister."

I smiled up at him with what I hoped was a demure look. "Those words give me shivers down my spine. I will be lucky to wed a man such as yourself. Handsome, charming, polite ..." I wound my arms around his neck, pulling him closer. "Do you think it improper to kiss? I wish to know what my future husband's lips will feel like against mine."

Henry's gaze moved down to my mouth, and I knew my ruse had worked—for now. His lips met mine, brushing lightly at first before he deepened the kiss. I kept one hand behind his head while the other moved to his chest, earning a sound of approval from him.

"Abigail Williams," he whispered in my ear, "you are quite the woman. I shall have to lay claim to you soon, as there are many men wishing to woo you out of my arms." He chuckled, taking my hand and leading me out of the grove. "Even Gabriel seems to have developed a fondness for you."

I blew out a hot breath, my mouth suddenly going dry. Had he heard of the encounter in the blacksmith shop and kept it to himself until we were alone? There were many prying eyes around the fort, I was beginning to realize. I decided to ignore his comment and busied myself with setting our picnic out, spreading the wool blanket on the ground. Mabel had helped me prepare quite the feast—cold buffalo, bread, cheese, and scones with strawberry preserves. Henry offered me a flask of ice-cold water he had filled up at the spring.

Once we had eaten our fill, I packed up the basket while Henry set up a few targets for practice—leather bags stuffed full of grass and tied off

THE FORT

at the top. Although I was already somewhat familiar with the workings of a gun, he showed me how to load and unload it, as well as clean it. He helped me hold it tight against my shoulder so I wouldn't be injured by the kickback. He instructed me to control my breathing, drawing in the air slowly to focus on the shot. I missed the first few, but after a while, it got easier, and I hit some.

"That's good," he said after we had practiced for twenty minutes or so. He sat me down, showing me how to clean it. "Gabriel was quite insistent on your safety. He even went to the trading post and bought you this rifle." He showed me the butt of the gun, where my initials had been etched into the wood.

"Oh," I stammered, "I'll have to make sure to thank him." This was the second time Henry had brought up Gabriel. Was he jealous of Gabriel's affection towards me? I glanced at Henry, who was busy setting up another target. "Did you ever meet his wife? Claudette, the French woman at Fort Augustus, told me what happened."

He turned quickly, his eyes flashing hot into mine. "No. I don't pry into the personal lives of my fellow man, and you'd best not meddle either, Abby. Women who gossip are not to be trusted. I do hope your time there is not spent in idle talk."

I flinched at his reprimand. "No, I—"

He took the gun from me, hanging it over his shoulder by the leather strap. "Perhaps that's enough practice for today. I have important work to complete at the office."

I trailed back to the fort behind him, wondering what I had said wrong. Did he truly dislike my question, or had I provoked something with my curiosity with Gabriel? I'd best make amends. "I'm sorry, Henry.

I didn't mean to gossip. It's not my affair, after all," I said, trying to rebuild the relaxed mood of earlier.

We stopped just outside the fort gates. "Darling, I'm sorry for snapping at you." He leaned down to brush my lips with his. "I'm just worried about those missing furs. Nothing to concern your pretty little head about." He gave me the gun, eyeing it dubiously as I slung it over my shoulder. "Perhaps we should practice again before you start carrying that about. I don't want you having an accident."

I stifled a sigh of annoyance, trying not to roll my eyes. I may not have enough skill to kill an animal, but I was not a complete novice. Our afternoon had seemed to take a sour turn. I'd have to find a way to make it up to him. "I'll see you at supper, Henry."

Making my way back to the workshop, I found Ben outside with Gabriel, playing with his pup. I was flustered from the slight altercation with Henry, but I tried not to let it show. "Thank you for the rifle, Gabriel. I'll make it up to you somehow."

He stood, brushing off his trousers. A dirk in a beaded sheath was hooked into his belt, along with a longer hunting knife, and his hair was tied back neatly with a leather strap. "That's not necessary, Abigail. Consider it a gift." He lifted a rucksack from the ground, slinging it over his shoulder. "I'm just here to say goodbye. I'm headed north for a while to inquire about some new huskies for my winter dogsled. I'll be gone for a month or so."

"Oh, for so long? Ben will miss your time spent together." And I would, too, I realized when he nodded. I hesitated for a moment, considering how I had put careful distance between us in the last week, then ducked into the workshop. I retrieved one of my horseshoe charms with my initials and the rose and held it out to him. "For safe travels."

THE FORT

He stared at the charm in my hand, swallowing hard. "I don't think—"

"Just take it." I shoved the charm into his hand quickly, not wanting to make contact lest I feel the same warmth when I touched his hand. "For my favourite Frenchman."

He slipped the charm into his bag without giving it another look. "The voyageurs are coming soon. Stay out of their way. They are trouble even when sober."

I laughed at his overprotective concern. "You forget we lived in York. Don't worry; I have much experience avoiding the advances of an uncouth voyageur."

He made a displeased sound in the back of his throat but gave me a smile. "Au revoir, Abigail."

"Au revoir, Gabriel. Bon voyage." I rolled the unfamiliar sounds over my tongue, amazed to see his face break out in a full, ear-to-ear smile. He bent down to whisper something in Ben's ear and then was gone, towards the north.

Chapter Eight

Sixteen voyageurs arrived three days later, carrying their long birch-bark canoes up from the river. They brought much-needed supplies for the trading post, letters, and small comforts from abroad. In turn, they would take the winter collection of furs back to York for shipment on the yearly ship to Europe.

I was tending to the garden with Mabel and some of the other Métis women, but I stopped my task to peek at the voyageurs through the cracks of the palisade. Now that we had caught up on the backlog in the blacksmith shop, I spent half of my day helping around the fort. There was much to be done in preparation for winter—growing and harvesting vegetables for the cellar, drying meat as the trappers brought in fresh game, repairing snowshoes, toboggans, moccasins, and buckskin winter clothing, and, of course, the preparation of pemmican, the dried meat and berry concoction that would sustain the outdoorsmen on the bleak days of winter.

"Don't stare at them." Mabel pulled me away from the thick beams of wood that protected our fort from intruders and wild animals. "If they

THE FORT

catch you looking, they'll take it as an invitation for something else later tonight, once they've been into their rum cups."

It was true. The families of the fort had hidden away their daughters for the three days that the rowdy Frenchmen would visit, as they were notorious for indulging in food, liquor, and women on their stops. It was told that their voyage was gruelling—nearly three thousand miles over rough terrain from the York factory in the north to Fort Vancouver in the American territory. They followed the waterways in their lightweight canoes but were often forced to stop and portage, carrying their loads on their backs and shoulders, secured with a strap around their heads. Paddling for seven weeks, they worked fifteen to eighteen hours a day, at up to forty-five strokes a minute.

"I'm prepared for the worst, don't fret." I patted the heavy tongs I had borrowed from my father's shop and hitched into my belt. "I'm not afraid to defend myself."

Elizabeth, who had still not warmed to me, snorted. "You're more likely to have that used against Henry or anyone else who tries to defend you. Drunk or not, the voyageurs are no strangers to a brawl. After supper, it's best to just lock yourself away in your quarters."

"You're probably right," I admitted, remembering how Gabriel had so easily disarmed me on our first meeting. Still, I felt safer with some protection. Henry had already told me that he might not be able to watch out for me, as he was tasked with controlling the consumption of alcohol at the evening festivities, which would be no easy feat.

"Elizabeth's right, I'm afraid. You should put the tongs away, Abby. There's no need to provoke." Mabel seemed agitated today, and I had surmised that her husband was likely to join in the festivities and bring home his fists in the later hours.

"Why don't you bring the children over to my place tonight?" I offered. "You can all sleep in our sitting room." Mabel and the other women lived in the common dormitory with their families, but I had a spacious room in the front, and it would be safer for them there. Aside from that, I had hoped that it might provide the opportunity to ask her about the furs in the cellar. I had snuck down the day before with the pretense of gathering a few supplies and found that they were still there, the sacks now covered in an HBC blanket. I was surprised that none of the other women had found them, and it determined my resolve to speak with Mabel before I brought the matter up to Henry.

Mabel gave me a thin smile. "I might just do that. Thank you, Abby."

"Abigail!" Claudette called from across the yard, catching me by surprise. She waved and came over, kissing me on both cheeks.

"What are you doing here?" I asked after introducing her to the other women. Claudette wore a hat for the special occasion and what I assumed was her Sunday best. I looked down at my clothes, covered in dirt from the garden.

"My husband has business with the voyageurs, and I thought I would come for a visit." She took my hand, patting it in a motherly manner. "Do you have time for a cup of tea?"

"Of course." I took her back through the yard, narrowly avoiding a voyageur carrying a crate of guns. He gave me a bold wink, showing a mouth of missing teeth.

"My goodness, those men smell something awful." Claudette wrinkled her nose as another passed in front of her. "Must be the skunk oil and bear grease they slather on to keep the pests away. Let's hope they take the opportunity to bathe in the river."

THE FORT

I laughed as I led her through the blacksmith shop in my quarters to prepare the tea. "How are you, Claudette? Gabriel is away, so I haven't had the chance to visit." I swallowed thickly at the thought of him, hoping he was safe.

"Oh, I'm all right," she said, settling down at our small table. I offered her some bannock to go along with the tea, but she declined, waving it away. "My husband is speaking of retiring, so we may be heading back to France in a year or so. Or perhaps we will settle back east. He hasn't decided yet."

"Are you happy about that?"

"Well, I'm not rightly sure how I feel. I will be happy to live in a more civilized manner and not struggle through another one of these godawful winters. But I will be sad to leave the people behind. And I'm ever so curious as to how *your* story is going to end, ma fille."

I raised my eyebrows at her as I poured our tea into tin cups and placed them on the table. "I'm going to marry Henry, and he will be restationed next year. No real story, I'm afraid."

Claudette looked down into her teacup, a smile pulling at the corner of her mouth. "Where is he, this officer of yours? I expect he's busy with the voyageurs' arrival, but you'll have to point him out to me."

I peered out of the small window, where I had pinned up the deer hide to allow air and light in during the day. "He's just over there with that rather rough-looking man." I pointed in Henry's direction. The voyageur beside him was tall and scrawny. I'd heard that their diet in the wilderness mainly consisted of a daily ration of cornmeal mixed with water and a strip of pork fat. It seemed that it would not be enough sustenance to maintain the physical feat, but perhaps that's why they indulged when they stopped at the forts. Henry and the man appeared to be having words, as Henry's arms were crossed over his chest, and his eyes narrowed suspiciously. The man shrugged and left, likely in search of something to eat in the kitchen.

"Oh yes, he's quite handsome. To marry him will improve your status, will it not? An officer's wife? And your son will receive the finest education."

"I suppose." I frowned, not sure what she was implying. "But that's not why I have my sights on him. My son needs a father, and I need a husband. It makes sense to marry again."

"Oh, to be sure. Someone to show your son what it is to be a man."

I glanced back out the window, watching Henry as he took the mail from the HBC clerk and sifted through the stack. There was nothing wrong with him—he was kind and courteous, with a steady income and a good position. Why was Claudette making it sound otherwise? Or perhaps it was my own feelings coming through, as there were moments when I wondered what Henry and I would talk about in the long evenings alone in the north. So far, we had only spoken of trivial matters here in the fort. I knew nothing of his family or interests or even his favourite meals. Still, I told myself firmly, marriages had been built on far less, and there would be plenty of time to get to know one another once the busy life of the fort was behind us.

"Dear, come and sit down and enjoy your tea before it's cold." Claudette pulled me back into the room with her, motioning to the other seat at the table. "Now listen carefully. I'm going to tell you how to make that delicious meat pie you like so you can serve it to your man once you're wed."

THE FORT

The supper hour was nothing short of bedlam. It was roast goose, with hearty servings of turnips, parsnips, and carrots brought up from the cellar. The women were all kept busy in the kitchen, and the children ran around freely, scampering underfoot. The men of the fort sat gathered around the voyageurs, listening with envy to their adventures—perhaps living vicariously through them. They also brought news from the other forts—of skirmishes between the Indigenous, deaths, illnesses, and even a fire that had left one fort smouldering. At one point during the meal, the sixteen visitors broke out in song, harmonizing in a melodious rendition of *À la Claire Fontaine*. I caught Henry's eye across the room, breaking out in a grin, wondering if Gabriel would have joined in with his countrymen, or sat quietly in the corner, smoking his pipe.

I was helping to clear away the last of the plates when I noticed my father's seat was empty. It had been taken over by a boisterous man whose face bore the claw marks of some wild animal, making his mouth sit permanently to one side. Worried, I glanced around the mess hall. My father had indulged in a few cups of rum despite me voicing my concerns to him earlier. He had likely just retired early to our room, but I wanted to make certain. I checked on Ben, then asked Mabel to watch him for a few moments.

"Abby!" Henry was close behind as I left the building. "Where are you going?" He caught up to me, pulling me into a close embrace. I could smell the rum on his breath, realizing that it might not just be the voyageurs' advances I would be dodging that evening.

"I'm going to check on my father," I said, indulging him in a kiss. "I'll be back."

"All right, but don't linger. Some of these ruffians are quite disagreeable. I don't want you to end up on the wrong side of things. I've been charged with making sure they don't get out of control, so I must stay."

I suppressed an annoyed sigh as I thought he might have made time for me and asked one of the other officers to help. But I did not have time to hesitate, so I made my way quickly across the deserted yard, glancing around to make sure I had no unwanted company. I pushed open the door to our room, ignoring the impending feeling of dread that lurked in my gut. He was probably fine, tucked away in bed.

"Father?" He wasn't there.

I took a deep, steadying breath, trying to calm myself. There were plenty of places he could have gone. Perhaps he had just gone to relieve himself away from the mayhem of the fort. Still, I took the rifle from the rack in the workshop, fitting the leather strap across my chest. Grabbing a lantern from the shop, I set out to look for my father. I was filled with guilt, procuring a memory of everything he had given up for me.

"Abigail, are you in here? It's time to leave, my dear."

I was sitting on the floor of the dusky blacksmith shop, my legs tucked up against my chest. I did not want to go, nor did I want the babe that grew in my womb. Despite my ill-wishes, my belly had become rounded and heavy in the last weeks, a visible reminder of everything I had lost.

"There you are." My father heaved a sigh of relief as he spotted me. "I've been looking for you for the past hour." I had chosen the darkest corner in which to conceal myself, ignoring the sounds of a scampering rat. I sniffed back my tears as he pulled up a stool to my hiding spot. All I had done these

last days was cry, and I knew he was becoming impatient with my state of melancholy.

"We must leave for the docks, my dear. Your brother is here with the wagon."

"I don't want to leave," I managed, my voice wavering. "This was the home I was born in. Everything of Mother is here."

"Yes," my father agreed, his voice husky. "But they are just possessions, my dear. We will always have our memories. Those will never fade."

A sob escaped me, ragged and sharp. It was my memories of George that refused to leave me, haunting my every waking hour. "You should let me go alone," I said, relishing the idea of being discarded. At least I would be left to attend to my wounds in peace.

"No, Abigail, I will never leave you. You are my child, and life's burdens are meant to be shared with the ones we love, my dear. We are not meant to carry them alone. Now, we must make haste. I do not wish the earl to learn of your condition, as he might lay claim to the babe. Let us leave."

He reached for my hand, pulling me out of the darkness, across the ocean and at home in the New World.

I frantically searched the entirety of the fort for my father, even ducking into the root cellar in case he had fallen down the stairs. I circled back to our room, hoping he had made his way back. He was nowhere to be found. Finally, I peered back into the window of the mess hall, seeing the party with the voyageurs going strong. Most of the women had taken their leave for the evening, but the men still lingered, their faces turned red from the drink. I eased my way inside the door, hoping to catch Henry's eye without drawing too much attention to myself.

He saw me and came over.

"My father's missing," I said. I tried to keep the emotion from my voice, but it wavered nonetheless. "I've looked everywhere. I think he's left the fort."

He frowned, a mix of concern and annoyance. "He's likely just gone to have a private moment. He'll be back soon, I'm sure."

I rubbed the back of my neck as two of the voyageurs left the table to wander our way. "I don't think so, Henry. I'm worried ..." I lowered my voice to a whisper. "He might be having one of his forgetful moments."

"Is this your woman, Davies? Aren't you a lucky one?" The man I had seen earlier in the day with the missing ear gave me a salacious look. "A feisty girl with a gun."

Henry gave an exasperated sigh, a thunderous expression clouding his normally fair features. "Please go back to your quarters, Abigail. I'll be by in an hour to check on you and help you look if he has not returned by then."

I left, my stomach in a knot, wishing Gabriel were here. He would have helped me look for my father. I understood Henry had a job to attend, but could he have not spared a few minutes of his time for me? It made me question how often he would leave me to my own devices when we moved to the north. Promising my father to choose a husband was turning into a task that left a bitter taste in my mouth.

Deciding to take matters into my own hands, I took a deep breath and passed through the gates of the fort.

I began down the path down to the river, calling out for my father as I went. I eyed the edge of the forest but did not dare step inside, remembering the man whose leg had been crushed in the trap. Thoughts of my father suffering the same fate pushed at the edge of my mind, but I mustered the courage to send them away. Instead, I quickened my

THE FORT

pace—dusk was beginning to fade into night and soon my lantern would be the only light I had.

I walked along the river's edge, forcing myself to check the murky depths for a floating body. My chest became a beacon of hot panic, and I berated myself for encouraging my father to take this remote post with the Hudson's Bay Company, far away from the comforts of a city. At least in York, I could have taken a job as a maid once my father was no longer able to work. Here, I needed the support of a man, as they would never allow a woman to blacksmith alone.

I rounded the top of a hill, my fear becoming frantic sobs. *Where was he?* I would be forced to turn back soon before I lost my way. A wolf howled in the distance, setting my heart to racing. I stopped and tried to take a steadying breath.

By the light of the moon, I spotted a small cabin at the bend in the river and headed toward it. I would rest there for a moment to gather my wits and then make my way back to the fort. There, I would enlist proper help. If Henry refused, then I was sure I could charm another officer into aiding me.

As I approached, I saw a figure slumped over the front steps. Could it be him?

I broke out in a run, not bothering to even consider that the person might be armed or dangerous.

"Father!"

The man sat up, looking around in a bewildered state. It *was* him!

"Father, what are you doing here?" I sat next to him, lifting the lantern to check him over for injuries. Thankfully, he seemed fine. Relief coursed through me, but it was tinged with fear—a fear that his condition was worsening and he might not be so lucky next time.

"Abigail, I've been looking for you everywhere. I thought you were lost, so I came here to find you." His eyes had glazed, and I broke out in a sweat despite the coolness of the night. I had been right in the same room with him, meaning that he was clearly confused.

"Where is here, Father? Who lives here?" I lifted the lantern to the cabin, which looked vacant, as there was no light inside despite the late hour.

"Why, your Frenchman, of course, Abigail. You know that."

"Gabriel? I've never been here before, Father. And besides, he's gone north."

"Abby!" Henry's voice echoed over the hilltop, and I scrambled to my feet.

"Henry! Over here!" I called, cupping my hands around my mouth. I was still smarting from his neglect, but I didn't fancy walking home alone with my father in such a state.

"Abby!" Henry sprinted towards me, three men following. "Thank God you're safe!" He gathered me in his arms, kissing me multiple times on the mouth in front of everyone. "Mabel told me you left, and I realized I'd been an ass, not coming to help you right away. Can you ever forgive me?"

I wiped more tears from my eyes, my anger towards him dissolving. "My father came here to look for me. He thought I was lost. He says this is Gabriel's home."

"It is. But you've never had reason to be here, have you?"

"No." I shook my head, brushing off the accusation that lurked behind his question. "I don't think he has either. But maybe Gabriel brought Ben here, and he told him."

THE FORT

Henry leaned down to help my father to his feet. "It's time to go home now, Peter. There's a nice warm fire set in the hearth."

I smiled at Henry, grateful for his assistance, though I remained fraught with worry. My father could have easily ended up dead or injured. I needed to make a decision about our future before his condition worsened any further. Marrying Henry sooner rather than later would provide myself and Ben with some security, at least. If my father became unable to work, at least we would have somewhere to call home.

"Abby, come along now. Stick near me, please. You've already given me quite a fright tonight." Henry offered me his hand, and I accepted, taking comfort in its warmth for the moment at least.

Chapter Nine

The next morning, the fort was unusually quiet as the men slept off the remnants of their inebriation. I puttered around our room, fussing over my father. He seemed to be in fine spirits and insisted on meeting Edmund in the shop to continue their tasks from the previous day. Edmund had happily agreed to a formal indenture with my father and arrived every morning, bright-eyed and ready to work. Although it would take years for him to become a Master Smith, I was exceedingly grateful to have the young man around, even if just to keep an eye on my father.

Henry caught up with me while I was in the kitchen with Mabel, preparing a late breakfast of porridge, tea, and toast. His mouth was set in a firm line, and I held back an exhausted sigh. It was certain to be a long day.

"I was just called to the Chief Factor's office," he explained in a hushed tone as to not reach the ears of the other women. "He wanted to know what happened last night with your father."

THE FORT

I pursed my lips, trying to keep back the tears that had threatened all morning. So, this was it, then. My father would be let go, and I would be forced to secure a place for us—either through marriage or another form of servitude.

"I tried to downplay the event," he continued, "but I'm afraid he's concerned. He'll be coming around later today to speak with him."

I nodded, not trusting my voice. Henry pulled me close, and I leaned against him for a moment, breathing in his masculine warmth. "There's something else," he said, pulling me back to look at him. "I want to tell you in person so you know there are no falsehoods between us." My stomach fluttered—there were many falsehoods between us, all of them on my part. He pulled out an envelope. "This arrived with the voyageurs. It's a letter from my betrothed, Margaret, asking to reconcile our relationship."

I stared up at Henry, a strange feeling washing over me, not entirely disappointed. "Oh, I—"

"I've already written her back, explaining that I've moved on with you," he said, squeezing my waist. "I just wanted you to know because you asked about her."

"All right, thank you for telling me," I said, my mouth going dry. I should have been happy, and yet, I was apprehensive about this continued courtship. I felt as if I could never tell him the truth about Ben and would live in constant fear that he would find out. Still, I intended to use my voice. "About last night, Henry. When I asked you for help, you brushed me off. As your wife, I will expect a fair amount of attention and affection, especially when I require your aid." I knew my request was bold, but I needed to clear the air to express my disappointment.

It was Henry's turn to stare, and then his brows pulled into a frown. "Certainly, Abby, but as you might recall, I asked you to wait for me in your room. Chasing a senile man about—"

"Senile? My father might be forgetful, but—"

A shout from outdoors interrupted us, indicating a ruckus. Henry released my waist and ran out to the yard, with me following close behind. Mabel's husband, Luc, was in the dirt, a voyageur pinning him down, knee pressed against his neck.

"He's a thief!" the voyageur shouted as another officer pried him off Luc. "He stole the tobacco from my coat while I slept."

"I did no such thing," Mabel's husband roared, spittle flying from his mouth. I cringed as his hands formed into fists, taking a swing at another voyageur who had come to help his friend. Henry left to join the men in pulling apart the fight, and I slipped back into the kitchen, finding Mabel pressed into the wall near the door, listening to the altercation. When I reached for her hand, I found it shaking violently. I pressed it between mine, trying to calm her nerves.

"Luc *is* a thief, Abby," she said in a hushed tone. "He steals to trade for his liquor. Last winter, he barely collected enough skins to meet the quota to stay on at the fort. We shall be cast out, with nowhere to live ..."

"No one will let you starve," I assured her, though it was a false promise. I bit my lip, then told her the entire story of her son in the cellar and finding the stash of furs.

"No." She sobbed when I told her that Elizabeth had seen Jonathan come up from the cellar. "They'll shoot him or send him away to prison if he's caught doing Luc's dirty work."

"I think," I said, pulling her into an embrace and whispering in her ear, "that we should return the furs to the storehouse. Everyone is so busy with the voyageurs' visit, they won't notice. And we should talk with Jonathan and explain the dire consequences."

She nodded, wiping away her tears. "I think that's a good plan, Abby. Do you think we should tell Elizabeth?"

I thought of Elizabeth and her snide demeanour. Was she trustworthy? "Yes," I said after a moment of hesitation. Though Elizabeth continued to be prickly to me, I knew she would protect Mabel. "I think it would be wise to ask for her help."

"There's so many," Elizabeth said as we stood staring at the pile of burlap sacks full of furs. "How did Luc imagine he was going to trade them all?"

"Perhaps we should just leave them here, and Abby can inform Henry," Mabel said, her eyes still red and swollen from crying. She started to sob again, putting her heads in her hands.

"No." I didn't want Mabel to have to implicate her son, and if we accused Luc outright, it would likely cause harm to the entire family. "I think it's best if we let them discover them on their own. They can puzzle it out themselves."

"Yes," Elizabeth agreed, rubbing Mabel's back. "And besides that, if they discover the kitchen was used as a hiding place, they'll never give us a moment's peace." She lowered her voice, looking up the cellar stairs. "The kitchen belongs to the women. It's *our* place."

"Then it's settled," I agreed, smiling at Elizabeth. "Where should we move them to?"

We looked at each other, thinking of all the possible hiding places at the fort. There weren't many nooks and crannies, as we used every corner for living and working.

"It would make sense to return them to the storehouse," I suggested, but that was too far, on the other side of the fort. It would take us multiple trips, and the furs were heavy.

"There's been an officer posted there since Henry discovered them missing," Elizabeth said. "We might be able to create a diversion, but not for that long."

"The graveyard?" Mabel suggested, then dismissed her own idea with a wave of her hand. "No, the men will notice if we are out there digging a new hole."

We mulled it over a few moments longer before Elizabeth snapped her fingers. "I know! The men have emptied out a few casks of rum during the voyageur's visit. We can stuff them in there. The cooper will find them sooner or later."

"No." I shook my head. "They won't be easy to open. We'll need a prybar, at the very least." This I knew for certain, having worked alongside the cooper in York fashioning the hoops for his barrels. I frowned in thought. "Under the boats of the voyageurs? ... No, I don't think there will be enough room. Besides, as uncouth as they are, it seems unfair to implicate them."

"Damn," Elizabeth swore, surprising me. She looked me up and down, a light dawning in her eyes. "Well, what about the smith's shop?"

The cellar was quiet as both Elizabeth and Mabel watched me for a response. I couldn't possibly—

"Yes, that will be perfect, just until we find somewhere else to put them." Elizabeth grabbed Mabel's arm, nodding enthusiastically.

THE FORT

I shook my head, heat rising in my chest. "It might implicate me or my father if they were found. I would rather they stay here until we decide."

"We can't risk Jonathan like that. He's just a child."

"And I have a child of my own to protect," I shot back, feeling a twinge of anger. It was one thing to help a friend but quite another to put myself and my family at risk.

"Abby, it might work. The blacksmith shop is halfway to the storehouse. We could move them there to start, then to the storehouse when we have the chance. They only need to stay there a day or two, a week at most." Mabel implored me with a desperate look.

"And it wouldn't be unheard of for your father to have a stash of furs, paid for his work," Elizabeth added.

"I suppose that's true," I said reluctantly, "but where would I hide them? My father and Edmund, the striker boy, work in the shop every day. I don't want them to know." Not to mention Ben, who, like most children his age, struggled to keep things secret.

"Is there some place that's just for you and the horses?" Mabel asked, her expression hopeful.

I sighed, bemoaning what I would do for my friend.

It was in this way that I found myself that afternoon emptying out the chest in which I usually stored blankets for the horses, using the sunny weather as a ruse to hang them for some air. I borrowed a rug beater from Mabel, taking my annoyance out on the blankets, earning a few raised brows from men who happened to pass by.

Later that evening, when the men were well in their cups for the second night in a row, we got to work. Elizabeth decided that it was better that we transport the furs under the guise of regular work. The voyageurs had brought with them a supply of dry goods, and we told our families that we were going to organize the cellar now that mealtimes were over for the day. We hefted the burlap sacks, one by one, across the fort in the dusky twilight.

"In here," I said, keeping my voice low so I didn't disturb my father and Ben. I led Mabel and Elizabeth to the back of the shop, wincing at the creaking hinges as I opened the chest. We laid the sacks in, almost breathlessly, before going back for more.

It took us an hour, sweat soaking our brows and undergarments, faces red with exertion. I slipped George's gold watch back into the chest while Mabel and Elizabeth collected the horse blankets from the line. Then, we took our time folding them into neat squares and placing them on top.

"There," Elizabeth said as we arranged the cellar to fill the space. "Problem solved."

I stood back, brushing the dust off my skirt. It wasn't solved, not really. I wouldn't get a proper night's sleep until the furs were back in the storehouse, where they belonged.

It was midafternoon, and hot. The next day had passed without any further commotion from the voyageurs, and this was the last evening before they would pack their canoes to continue their journey. The occasional loud outburst came from the kitchen, and I knew that some of the men were already into the drink before the dinner hour. This last night was likely to be the most taxing of all, and I planned to avoid it altogether.

THE FORT

I found myself wandering towards the gates, desperate for a quick walk to escape the stench and noise of the fort. With the early summer heat, game that was hung to dry, and the smell of the unbathed voyageurs, I longed for the fresh air by the river. Ignoring the danger of leaving alone, I once again slipped out past the palisade.

My spirits lifted immediately as the river came into view. It would be lovely to swim, but I didn't dare, as the current was strong, and I was likely to be carried downstream. The women and children had their own private bathing area in a smaller stream nearby. We had gone just a few days prior, stripping down to our shifts and undergarments, washing away the many winter months of only having a basin to clean ourselves.

My feet followed the same path I had taken two nights before, heading toward Gabriel's cabin. What had led my father there? He had no recollection of it now, of course, but I found myself curious to see it in the light of day. I reached the cabin, hesitating slightly. It was an invasion of his privacy, and yet I did not turn away. I would just take a quick look around and then head back to the safety of the fort.

As I stood there, I realized what I had not noticed at night. The view from the cabin was spectacular, lying nestled above the river. In both directions, as far as the eye could see, the glistening water stretched out, curled like the body of a snake. The afternoon sun hung midway in the sky, which was coloured a brilliant blue that reminded me of Gabriel's eyes. I imagined he must enjoy many sunsets in the same spot where I stood, when the pinks and reds and purples bled into one another at the end of the day.

I turned, biting my lip as I began along one side of the house. There was a collection of beaver traps, many of them needing repair. I frowned, picking one up to inspect it closer. Why hadn't he brought these to the shop for me to fix? Surely, he needed them done before the season started.

I continued around the house, finding a stump with an axe lodged in it, and a pile of firewood piled beside. There was a well and a bucket on a long rope and, to my surprise, a large garden that looked well cared for, though a few weeds had grown in his absence. I let my fingers trail along the walls of the cabin, built in the French way, with the logs going up and down instead of across. As I made my way to the front once again, my hand paused only for the briefest second, and then I pushed open the door.

I blinked in the darkened room; a hide tucked snugly over the window kept out the light. I propped open the door with a piece of wood near the hearth, allowing a stream of afternoon sun into Gabriel's living space. I walked inside the simple one-room cabin with a bed tucked into the corner. For the most part, it was clean and tidy. There was a small table and two chairs and a tin mug of tea left forgotten. A collection of dishes and pots were on a shelf, and next to the hearth was a neatly stacked pile of firewood.

I walked over and rolled up the hide over the window, bathing the cabin in light. Near his bed was a small chest of drawers—and knowing that I was now indeed absolutely intruding on Gabriels' privacy—I pulled the top drawer open. I had been expecting clothing but instead found it empty, save for a book.

It was a French novel, and when I picked it up, my heart pounding, it fell open to where the spine had been broken. Inside lay a hand-drawn picture of a young boy, around two years of age. *His son.*

My heart bled as I beheld the worn drawing, wondering how often he had sat here, running his calloused fingers over the likeness of the

THE FORT

boy. I shook my head, thankful for the thousandth time that I had never divulged the news of my pregnancy to the earl. He hadn't wanted me, I knew that now, but he may very well have wanted Ben. I couldn't fathom not having my child here with me.

I slid the picture back into the page, meaning to put it away, when the book fell open to another spot. My eyes widened as I found another picture, this one commissioned by a professional artist. I looked down into the face of a much younger Gabriel, a beautiful woman in his arms. Golden curls cascaded down her back, and the artist had shaded her cheeks in the most becoming soft glow. A fiery heat spread across my chest as my gaze slid back to Gabriel. The expression on his face was of the highest adoration, enraptured by the woman in his embrace.

I hastily put the picture away, slamming the book back into the drawer. Why did I feel as if I couldn't breathe? I had no right to feel envy, but there was no other explanation for the nausea roiling in my stomach. I must be going mad. Gabriel was nothing more than a temperamental, unkempt man whose country had been at war with mine for as long as anyone could remember.

I left the cabin, shoving the log aside with my foot and pulling the door closed, not caring if he knew someone had been there. It served him right for leaving his door unlocked. Turmoil bubbled up from inside me, and I only made it halfway down the hill when the emotions caught up with me. I sank to the grass, sobbing into my hands. Truthfully, I wasn't at all sure about my match with Henry, except that my father's illness made the decision imminent. I saw my father's days coming to an end, or at least I was losing the sane, capable man who had been my rock in turbulent times. And Gabriel ... I couldn't make sense of the pull I had toward this conflicted man. And yet, I wanted desperately to know if he felt the same about me.

I sat there for some time, letting the breeze from the river soothe my heart. It was not until the sun had started its descent into the horizon that I stood again, taking a final deep breath. I must put these feelings aside, focus on my work, and continue my plan to wed Henry—the responsible thing to do.

The din of the fort reached my ears before I had even arrived at the palisade. The voyageur's farewell party was in full swing in the central yard, with a fiddler and men dancing the jig. I slipped past the party, staying hidden in the shadows, as I planned to barricade myself in my room and try to have an early night's sleep if that was possible with the revelry that was sure to last late into the night.

"Abby!" Mabel raced over to me, a look of panic on her face. "I've been looking for you everywhere. You must come with me."

"What's the matter, Mabel? What's happened? Is it Ben?" With a surge of anxiety, I thought of the furs hidden in our shop. As a newcomer, my father and I would be considered suspect, as no one could truly vouch for our character. The longer they sat there, the more I realized what a mistake it had been.

She shook her head. "Gabriel and his travelling companions are back. They ran into problems with a group of Indians, so they turned around only a few days into their journey."

"Oh." I bit my lip at the excitement that swelled in my chest. Regardless, I wasn't up to seeing him amid the drunken escapades of the voyageurs. "I'll say hello to him in the morning."

She grabbed my arm, her face still drawn with dread. "Abby. He's badly hurt. There was a cougar attack this morning."

THE FORT

"What?" The blood left my head, and I held onto both of her hands with mine. "Where is he?"

"In the officer's quar—"

I left her behind, picking up my skirts and weaving my way through the crowd of men as fast as I could. *He's badly hurt.* Was he going to live? Cougars could be deadly, and an attack by a wild animal of any sort could be fatal.

I burst into the officer's quarters, slamming the door behind me. A small group of men, Henry included, were gathered around one of the beds.

"Is he alright?" I asked, my voice trembling as I pushed my way through the men. Gabriel lay in a bed, his normally tanned skin pale. They had removed his shirt completely, and one of the men was suturing one of a few gashes that ran across his upper belly. In horror, I saw that his left arm had been clawed almost beyond recognition. The skin lay in shreds, the muscle exposed beneath gleaming red.

"Gabriel!" I choked on my tears, falling to my knees near the top of the bed. Without considering what Henry might think, I stroked his forehead, pushing his hair away. My other hand cupped the side of his face, my thumb running over his beard.

One blue eye opened with effort. "Abigail," he slurred. They had obviously given him quite a lot to drink. "Tu ne devrais pas être ici."

I shook my head, not understanding his meaning. "Will he? His arm ..." I brought my tear-filled eyes up to Henry, whose face was etched with empathetic agony. He came behind me, taking my arm and helping me up from the floor.

95

"Leave him be, Abby. Some of the Métis women are preparing a medicinal paste. It might be our only hope to salvage his arm. But for now, you must let him rest."

I shook my head stubbornly, getting up and dragging a stool over from the corner of the room. "I'm not leaving."

"Abby—"

"No." I snapped, meeting Henry's eyes with a glare. "Stop telling me what to do, Henry. You're not my father." *Or my husband*, I thought bitterly. I reached out and took Gabriel's good hand into mine. "I'm staying right here."

Chapter Ten

The sky had completely darkened by the time Mabel arrived, bringing a paste made from spruce pitch to apply to Gabriel's forearm and tea for fever and pain. Most of the men had gone back outdoors, either to join in the festivities or to keep an eye on the events. Henry stood post by the door, not willing to leave me alone in the room with Gabriel.

"I've tucked Ben into bed," Mabel said, taking my spot next to the bed. She began to apply the paste, using a flat wooden spoon to gently smooth it over the claw marks. He stirred, moaning in pain as she continued.

"Thank you," I said, coming to his other side to try and rouse him for some tea once Mabel was finished. "I will stay here for the night in case he needs help."

Henry cleared his throat loudly from the door. "You cannot stay, Abby. The officers will need to sleep here later."

"Then he should be moved," I insisted, sending Henry an even look. "I'm not leaving him alone with a bunch of drunken men."

"I agree with Abby," Mabel said, cutting Henry off from his protest. "The fort is overrun with voyageurs, and they are already half-shot with drink."

"What about in my sitting room?" I offered. "Perhaps Gabriel could stay there instead."

"Abigail!" Henry stared at me with his mouth ajar in shock. "That would be completely improper."

I stood, my blood simmering in annoyance. But I knew from when he had asked of my brothers that the best way to convince Henry was not with petty fighting. Instead, I walked over to him and placed my hand gently on his chest. "This is *our friend*, Henry. He would insist on only the best for you."

He let out a defeated sigh, looking over my shoulder. "What do *you* want, Gabriel?"

I turned to see Gabriel awake, a dazed expression on his face. Then he frowned and grunted loudly, his face turning white. Mabel brought the empty bowl to him just in time, as he vomited, filling the air with the stench of sour whiskey and bile.

"Laissez-moi tranquille," he gasped, as Mabel wiped his face with a cloth. "Let me die in peace."

I widened my eyes at his words and whirled around to Henry, putting my hands on my hips. "Move him, Henry. I'll bring the tea and meet you there."

With that, I grabbed the medicinal tea, spun on my heel, and made my way into the ruckus of the yard.

THE FORT

Four men carried Gabriel over to my quarters, and he reluctantly allowed me to administer the tea, sip by sip. When I asked if he wanted something to eat, he shook his head, lying back on the makeshift bed I had prepared in my sitting room. I flitted about, starting a small fire in the hearth but leaving the window uncovered to allow air to circulate through.

"Stop fussing over me." He swatted my hand away with his good arm as I brought over a cool cloth for his forehead. "I'm not your child."

"But you have a fever," I insisted, placing the cloth, even as he scowled at me. It warmed my heart to hear his thick French accent again, even if he was in pain. "And I'll fuss all I want."

He grunted in response. "You are such a stubborn woman. God help Henry in your marriage."

I barked out a laugh, sitting on the hearth, my back against the warmed stones. "Me? *You* are the most difficult man I have ever encountered."

He pretended to ignore me, closing his eyes, but I saw a smile pull at the corner of his mouth. The tea seemed to be working to settle the pain at least. They had bandaged his arm and chest, though he remained shirtless. I had tried to pull a blanket up over him, but he had demanded I take it off, preferring to lay uncovered. I had to admit, it was a little improper to have a half-undressed man in my living room, but with my father and Ben close by and the door left propped open, I had convinced Henry to leave and attend to his duties at the party outside.

"Can I ask you something?" I ventured, unable to get the pictures I had seen earlier from his cabin out of my mind. When a narrow slit of his eyes opened to look over at me, I continued, keeping my voice low to avoid being overheard by my father nearby. "Why don't you send for your son? Why do you let him live so far away when it's obvious you miss him?"

99

Gabriel stared at me, undoubtedly shocked by my forwardness. "A child belongs with his mother," he said finally, turning slightly to stare at the ceiling. "He's eight now, and I have not seen him for almost five years. I'm not fit to be his father."

I frowned, knowing I should leave the topic alone, but barreled forward. "That's not true at all. You're wonderful with Ben. Kind, caring—"

"You said it yourself, I am a difficult man, Abigail. I'm sure he would hate me in the end. Everyone does. I have a bad temper and say unforgivable things."

I thought of our first encounters and reluctantly agreed that his words had been piercing. But yet, when he was with Ben, he was always compassionate. "It's different with a child. Just because your wife left you doesn't mean that your son will not love you. Claudette told me everything, and I—"

"Do not speak to me about that. You know nothing of what you say." His voice rose loudly in the small room, and I immediately fell silent. He was injured and should be resting, and I had gone too far meddling in his affairs. But he was wrong. His son *would* love him, even after all this time.

A lull fell between us, save for the noise from the voyageurs outdoors. Finally, I leaned over, removed the cloth from his forehead, and rinsed it in a bowl of cool water before applying it once more. I decided to offer something of myself to him.

"I *do* know," I said, keeping my tone calm, though I was taking a risk in revealing part of my past to him. "I know exactly what it is to be tossed aside like rubbish. I know what it is to be left by someone I loved, to

THE FORT

feel like I cannot go on. You are not the only one who has experienced heartbreak, Gabriel."

He turned his head to me in surprise, his gaze inquisitive. "Tell me."

"No." I shook my head but met his eyes. "I cannot speak of it more than that."

He nodded to his injured arm but kept his gaze trained on me. "I'm dying anyway. Grant a dying man his wish."

I snorted at him, standing from the hearth. "You're not dying. If you were, you would be asking for a priest and confessing your sins, as Catholics do."

I was rewarded with a soft laugh. "And here I was, thinking my last breath would be with a beautiful Englishwoman."

Heat coursed through me at his words, and I turned sharply away so he couldn't see my face. "You're not dying, Gabriel. You're far too cantankerous to die."

I expected him to chuckle at that, but when silence greeted me, I turned back to face him and found him staring at me thoughtfully. "Was it Ben's father?" he asked, swallowing hard. "The one that treated you badly?"

I came over with a bowl of broth that Mabel had left. "Have some of this. It will give you strength."

"Answer me, and I will."

I sighed, coming back to sit on my perch of the hearth, bowl in hand. "Yes. But Ben doesn't know."

He muttered something in French and took the spoonful of broth I offered.

"What happened with the cougar?" I asked, hoping to lead the topic into a less intimate one. Despite myself, I let my gaze fall to his bare chest, brawny and covered with a light dusting of hair, brown and silver. Bandages covered where the cat had left its marks, and spots of blood were starting to seep through. "Did it get away?"

"No, it's dead. You can expect it in your dinner stew tomorrow, I'm sure." He lay back, looking suddenly exhausted. "I wrestled with it. It was going to get the better of me, but then I remembered ..." He trailed off, looking oddly bashful. I waited for him to continue speaking, using the silence to feed him a few more mouthfuls of broth.

"I'm tired now, Abigail," he said, closing his eyes. "Please go and sleep in your own bed. I'll call if I need anything."

I started to protest, but he opened his eyes, shaking his head. "Henry will never forgive either of us if I let you attend to me all night. And you know he'll check back in before he retires for the evening."

"All right," I agreed, making to stand up, but he reached out and caught me by the hand.

"It was your damn lucky horseshoe in my pocket. I remembered it and hit the cat square between the eyes. It only stunned the animal, but one of the other men was able to shoot it."

I stared at him, my breath catching in my throat. My horseshoe had saved his life. He had been carrying it in his pocket, close to his person. A warmth bloomed from my core, and I ducked my head, trying to hide a smile.

Gabriel closed his eyes again, exhaustion pulling him under. I let go of his good hand, then stood and placed the bowl on the table. I banked the fire, watching the rise and fall of his chest as his breathing slowed into slumber. When I finished, I made my way to the bedchamber door, pausing when I heard him stir. I glanced over to see him looking up at me, a forlorn hurt in his deep blue eyes.

THE FORT

"I think that by now, Abigail, my son has already forgotten me."

I blinked back tears at the raw tone of his voice. Not knowing what to say, I sighed and gave him a weak smile. "Good night, Gabriel."

I woke to the sound of raised voices in my sitting room. Although I couldn't understand what they were saying, Gabriel's angry voice punctuated the air. I nearly fell out of my bunk in my haste to see what was going on. I threw on my robe and moccasins, noticing that both Ben and my father had already risen. I must have slept late and soundly.

Both Gabriel and Claudette were standing near the door, though Gabriel was sagging heavily against the wall. They barely noticed as I emerged from my bedchamber, their French words flying over and on top of each other. Gabriel's face, creased in a scowl, was pale with a sheen of sweat glistening on his cheeks and forehead. He had put on a shirt sometime during the night, and it was creased with pink where his wounds had bled through.

"What's going on?" I demanded, pulling my robe closer around me.

"I caught this homme obstiné trying to leave. He says he's well enough to take care of himself at home." Claudette pointed an accusatory finger at Gabriel, who gave me a weak smile. I kept my face stern, though I fought with the idea of taking him in my arms and leading him back to bed.

"Gabriel," I admonished, "you have a fever. Please stay here."

"I don't want to be coddled," he said in a gruff manner. Then he added in a gentler tone, "Thank you for taking care of me last night, but I no longer require assistance, Abigail."

"Non, tu ne te sens pas bien!" Claudette exclaimed, gesturing to the blood seeping through the bandage on his arm. "I am not letting you walk off so you can die alone in your cabin."

"I'm not dying," Gabriel said, though his tone grew weary, and I could tell his resolve to win the argument had waned. He caught my eye, giving me a sheepish grin at his words, as he had insisted the night before that he was going to perish. Claudette looked between the two of us, her eyebrows raised.

She gestured to the table, where a plate of food sat waiting. "I brought this all the way from Fort Augustus for you. Your favourites. The least you can do is eat."

He gave a low growl in his throat but slowly made his way across the room and sat at the table. I poured him a cup of water, and he nodded his thanks, taking a forkful with this good hand. He gave me another affectionate smile. "Henry came by earlier to see why you had missed breakfast. I told him to let you sleep."

"Thank you," I said, filling a pot with water to boil on the hearth for some porridge. The bucket was nearly empty, a sign that Ben had not done his morning chores in all the excitement. "It's been a trying couple of days. My father went missing during the first night of the voyageur's visit." Not to mention the stress of the hidden furs.

His smile turned to a frown of concern, but then he became distracted by Claudette, who was busy arranging items on a shelf near his makeshift bed. "Ah, non, Claudette! Take those away from here."

THE FORT

Claudette straightened, thrusting her chest out in defiance. "Just because you're angry with our Father in Heaven doesn't mean that He no longer cares for you." She gestured to the items she had set out: a couple of figurines and a string of rosary beads. "The saints will take care of you in your time of need."

Gabriel glowered over at her, and I hid my smile, thinking that he had found his match in Claudette. The two of them stared at each other like the feral cats that prowled the alleyways in London, their hackles raised.

"Abigail," Claudette said, not taking her eyes off the stubborn Frenchman at my table, "I will go and get some fresh bandages, as well as something for his fever. Make sure he doesn't leave, d'accord?" She left the room, letting the door bang on her way out.

"Remind me never to get on the wrong side of Claudette," I said, trying to diffuse the mood. I stirred my pot of porridge, testing the thickness of the oats.

"Effectivement," he agreed in French, moving aside his half-eaten plate. He pushed himself up with effort and made his way to the bed, where he sat, leaned up against the wall. He gazed at the figurines on the table, a pensive look in his eye.

"Why don't you believe?" I asked, bringing my bowl of porridge over to sit near him on the hearth. It was a personal question, but we seemed to have crossed into that territory the night before, and I felt no qualms about asking.

He glanced up at me, his face etched with weariness, and I wondered if he had slept at all. "I used to go to Mass when I was a child. But after my mother died, I saw no point."

"How did she die?"

105

"Pox. I was eleven. My father was so distraught that he threw himself into the Seine and drowned. After that, I figured the Father had no use for me."

My heart wrenched for the boy who had raised himself. "You lost both parents when you were only eleven? How did you manage?"

He shrugged. "It was just me and my brother, Michel. We survived. Worked, begged, stole. It was hard to get ahead in France, so I made plans to come to the New World and secure my future here."

"And your brother?" I asked, enthralled at his story. I wondered how many people knew of it—not many, I thought, as Gabriel liked to keep to himself. "Is he still alive?"

"Oui." He nodded. "But he has not spoken to me in years."

"Why—"

"Non, Abigail. I cannot tell you. I fear that you will hate me if you know the truth."

He became quiet and tried to turn away, but I reached out a hand to cover his. "I could never hate you," I said boldly, watching as his face flickered at my words. "Besides..." I took a steadying breath, "there are things about me, mistakes I've made, that are unforgivable. If Henry knew—"

The door of the room burst open as Claudette arrived back with the bandages, Henry close behind her. I jerked my hand away from Gabriel like I had been burned by a hot coal, sending my bowl of porridge flying across the room with a *clatter*. I surveyed the mess on the floor with dismay, meeting Claudette's inquisitive gaze that asked a hundred silent questions.

"Oh my! I am so clumsy." I jumped up, not able to hide the flush I felt coursing through my body. It looked horrible—me, still clad in my

THE FORT

nightrobe, holding his hand. I kept my eyes trained on the floor as I went to retrieve the wooden broom from the corner. Feeling as guilty as the day I had been dragged into the library at the earl's estate, I busied myself with the cleanup, still not able to meet anyone's eye.

"Ah, Gabriel, I see you've made yourself at home. Good to see my Abby is taking such good care of you. I almost look forward to falling ill so she can nurse *me* back to health." The tone of Henry's voice was not to be mistaken for anything other than jealous contempt, and I flinched.

Gabriel cleared his throat, his face a mask, not revealing that anything had passed between us. "Henry, I'm glad you've come by. I was trying to explain to Claudette that I would like to return home." He darted a look at me, still crouched down over the dustpan. "I do not wish to impose on Abigail's kind hospitality any further. Please arrange my transport."

I glanced up, but he had looked away, back to the religious figures beside the bed. To my surprise, he crossed himself on either shoulder, from head to heart. What had he asked of God?

Claudette tugged on the sleeve of my blouse, dragging my attention away from Gabriel. She jerked her head towards Henry, who was still watching the two of us with a wary expression.

I forced my face into a sweet smile, walking over to the man who wished to make me his betrothed. "Henry, darling," I said, ignoring the way that my voice wavered. "Shall I get dressed, and then we can go for a walk? It's been a rather long night for all of us. I am feeling like I need to get out for some air."

When his eyes met mine, I winced again. He looked hurt and confused, and although he nodded, I knew it was not without doubt in my character. I shook my head, inwardly berating myself. I had allowed my words to belong to one man, yet my heart—another.

Chapter Eleven

Once the voyageurs had cleared camp and were on their way, Henry called a meeting for the entire fort to be held after the supper hour in the cookhouse.

"It's about them stolen furs," one of the women whispered to me as we were finishing the morning dishes. I broke out in a sweat, hastily drying the last of the plates. I found Mabel and Elizabeth in the bunkhouse, stripping the beds for washing day.

"I need your help," I hissed, helping them pile the sheets into big baskets to be taken to the river. "We need to move the furs today."

Elizabeth shook her head, but a worried line was etched in her brow. "They've posted two men at the storehouse, one on either side." She paused, lowering her voice. "We might just have to tell the truth."

My stomach turned in knots at the thought of talking with Henry. Conversation had been strained at best since Gabriel's return. To confess to having the furs hidden in my possession would ensure that I would fall out of his favour altogether.

THE FORT

"I can't," I said, my voice raising slightly. "We are newcomers to the fort. No one will have reason to believe my father and I are innocent." I cursed myself for agreeing to hide them in the first place. Now, I was stuck in a dilemma that seemed impossible to escape.

Mabel wrung her hands, blinking away tears. "There's just no—"

A ruckus in the yard interrupted her. Elizabeth peeked out the door of the bunkhouse and then motioned me over discreetly with her hand, trying to avoid the attention of the other women in the room.

"It's Henry and the other officers," she whispered, pointing to a group of men exiting the cooper's shop. The cooper had his hands up, agitated by the intrusion into his quarters. "It looks like they're conducting a search."

A flood of panic coursed through me, making my hands shake. I thought of my father in his shop, unaware that he was about to be exposed as a thief. "No," I said, my voice trembling. I took a deep breath, blew it out, and stepped into the courtyard.

I walked briskly, afraid I would lose my nerve. Mabel and Elizabeth caught up to me in an urgent half-run, though they did not try to stop me. We arrived in front of the group of men as a threefold, and I was emboldened by their comradery. It would have been easy for them to hide away in the shadow of the bunkhouse, yet here they were, by my side.

"Henry," I said, a sudden chill coming over me. "I need a moment of your time."

"Not now, Abby," he said, frowning as he squinted at me in the morning sun. "I'm in the middle of something important."

109

"Henry," Elizabeth said, though she looked at me for confirmation. I nodded, feeling relief at the unburdening of this secret. "It's about the missing furs."

A hush fell over the men, and the whole fort, it seemed. A bird chirped cheerily from a nearby ledge, proclaiming false promises of things to come. From the corner of my eye, I saw Gabriel making his way towards the group in a slow limp. I closed my eyes in despair, the fort walls feeling too tight, the relief of the moment before vanished. I felt shame wash over me like the morning I had stood in the earl's library, about to be judged for my wrongdoings.

"Well?" one of the officers demanded, narrowing his eyes at us. "What is it?"

Beside me, I felt Mabel shift. I glanced at her, seeing her face harden in resolve. She was going to tell the truth, to expose her family.

"I have them," I blurted out before she could risk the life of her son. Jonathan may only be an adolescent, but he would be judged as a man. I, on the other hand, could play into the feminine guise of ignorance. "They're in the blacksmith shop. We didn't steal them," I added hastily as the group broke out in a low hum of chatter.

Henry stood with his mouth open, his cheeks becoming flushed. I had humiliated him in front of the other officers, I realized too late. I should have insisted on a private audience. Now, everyone knew that he had chosen an untrustworthy woman. Elizabeth reached for my hand, squeezing it. She would stand by me, as women so often did for each other when faced with resistance from men.

"We were trying to return them to the storehouse," she said, taking over the conversation. She beckoned with her head to the blacksmith quarters. "I can show you where they are."

THE FORT

The men followed us over to where my father and Edmund were working, unaware. I caught Gabriel's gaze as we passed, his expression one of confusion and concern.

Elizabeth led the men to the chest, and two of the officers pushed past, tossing aside the pile of horse blankets to the ground. There was a collective gasp as they hauled the burlap sacks out of chest one after another. Henry watched me, his brow creased and his mouth set in a firm grimace. I could tell he wanted to chastise me, to shake the truth from me, but was holding back in front of his men. My father stood at the edge of the crowd, his head bowed. We had stood in this position once before, when he resigned himself to the truth of my affair.

"Officer Davies, sir," one of the men came forward, holding out his hand. My stomach lurched when I saw the chain, glinting as it was transferred to Henry's open palm. The earl's gold watch.

Everyone stared at the watch, and Elizabeth shifted uncomfortably beside me. Henry turned it over, rubbing his thumb over George's initials, etched elegantly on the back. He plucked the chain, dangling the watch in full view.

"Is this yours?" he asked my father, knowing well that it was not. Such a piece of jewelry was not found among the working class, and if it were an heirloom, it would be treasured and valued, not hidden away with the horse blankets. My father lowered his head further, refusing to comment.

"What's the meaning of this?" It was the Chief Factor, looming at the back of the crowd. My face burned, and tears leaked down my face. I was to be labelled a thief—if not by the furs, then for certain by the watch.

"We've discovered the missing furs, sir," Henry said, not taking his eyes off me. His gaze held no compassion, no sympathy. He looked at me as if I were a stranger. "Abigail and her father will come to the office to explain."

"No," I said, hearing how desperate I sounded. "Not my father. He had no part in this."

"It was me." A voice came from the edge of the throng, timid at first but then louder. "I took the furs and hid them in the cellar." Jonathan broke through the line of men. Mabel ran to his side, clutching his arm protectively. I let out a defeated sigh, bringing Henry's attention to me once again.

"Alright, let's clear out," he commanded, telling two of the men to bring the furs to the office. He took my upper arm, pinching it slightly in his grip. He beckoned to Mabel, Elizabeth, and Jonathan, and we trudged to the office together.

They took Jonathan in first, making us wait nervously in the front room. We did not talk but instead held hands, each silently praying to any God that would answer. I thought of Claudette and her unwavering faith, wondering at the right words to choose when Jonathan had all but admitted to the crime. I cursed Luc and his wretched life, hoping, begging that they would lay the blame on Jonathan's father instead. It might leave Mabel without a husband, but she would survive. Some way, somehow.

Jonathan returned after an hour, his eyes and lips swollen from crying. My heart lurched, knowing the consequences would be severe. The Chief Factor had to keep order in the fort, and thievery of any kind was not permissible. My stomach clenched at the thought of the watch still in Henry's possession.

THE FORT

"What is it? What did he say?" Mabel cried, jumping to her feet and grasping her son's shoulders. He was taller and broader than her, but she all but shook him in her urgency. "Will they let you live?"

He nodded, but the tears ran freely down his face. "We must leave the fort by tomorrow, first light." He took a shaky breath. "I'm so sorry, Mama."

Mabel pulled him into her embrace, a cry leaving her lips. "It will be alright," she murmured, stroking his hair as if he were young, "At least it's not yet winter."

My heart fell from its place inside my chest. I desperately did not want to lose Mabel so soon after we'd met. This country was vast, with weeks of travel from one place to the next. Once she left, it would be unlikely that our paths would ever cross again.

"Abigail, please come with me." It was Henry, standing in the doorway of his office, leaning on the frame. His brows drew together in a frown, and I couldn't help a bristle of annoyance that went through me. Although I had some explaining to do, I had not, in fact, done anything wrong.

"Good luck," Elizabeth whispered as I slowly got up from my chair. I nodded at the two women, wishing, for a moment, that I did not have to answer to this man. I wanted to return to my father and son at the blacksmith shop to explain that I had only been protecting Mabel and her child. But I forced myself to smile at Henry, taking a seat at the desk. The gold pocket watch lay on the table, and I stared at it, not daring to touch it.

He closed the door tightly behind us. Before he had even come around to sit behind his desk, I started to talk. "I'm not a thief," I said, pressing

113

my hands to my legs to keep them from shaking. "The watch belonged to Ben's father."

"I see," he said, his expression softening but then turning to a frown. "But why keep it hidden away?"

I swallowed with effort, tired of this lie. I longed for the day when I no longer had to think or speak about George. "Well, I suppose it was a family heirloom. I should have returned it to his mother, but I did not. I couldn't bear to," I added, trying my best to look like a mourning widow.

Henry ran his tongue over his teeth, and I held my breath, waiting to see if he would accept the story. Although it was not unreasonable to believe that I would have married above my position, as I had a fair beauty and was still young in my years, the watch was costly and had, in truth, belonged to an earl. Henry would know the value of such things.

"I will admit, Abby, that it does not please me to think of your heart belonging still to another man," he said finally, and I let out a tiny breath of relief.

"It doesn't," I said quickly, giving him a quick smile. "Truthfully, I kept it for Ben. We were able to carry so little from England, and—"

"I understand," he said, cutting me off. He stood, scooping the watch from its resting place and carrying it to the corner, where he had a small iron box that he locked for safekeeping. He withdrew a key from his pocket and placed the watch inside. As he turned from the corner, his expression remained grim. No, I had not yet escaped his suspicion.

"When we are married, you will answer to me. I expect your loyalty and transparency and respect. None of this," he said as he waved his hand to indicate the events of the morning, "will happen ever again. Do I make myself clear?"

THE FORT

A flurry of replies came to my tongue, and I passed by each one. A sour ache grew in my stomach at the thought of such a life, no more than a doting wife, too afraid to make friends for fear of making a mistake. When I did not answer, Henry leaned down, coming face to face with me.

"Abigail," he said, his tone level, though I knew anger simmered behind it, "the company is in trouble. I have investors coming at the end of the month from England and we must make a good impression. I cannot worry about my betrothed hiding furs to save her friend."

My throat grew thick at his reprimand, but I nodded.

He blew out a hot breath, straightened up, and walked over to the door. I scrambled to my feet, eager to leave. He caught my hand just as I reached the door.

"Abby, I only say these things because I love you. I must ensure that we have a secure future." He squeezed my hand, and I tried not to pull away. I knew the difference between love and possession. It had become clear to me that I wanted to break off my engagement to Henry, but I needed to let him down gently, lest my life become unbearable at the fort. Instead, I gave him a peck on the cheek and let myself out of the office.

My father and Gabriel were waiting outside the blacksmith shop. My father sat on a stool, a blanket over his shoulders, despite the warm weather. Gabriel stood smoking his pipe, a crease lining his brow.

"Abigail," he called as I came over. "What has happened? I wanted to go inside, but your father made me wait." He glanced down at the older man, who peered up at me with hurt in his eyes. I had humiliated my father as well on this day, and I deeply regretted my actions.

"Mabel and her family must leave the fort," I said, looking between them both. "First thing tomorrow morning."

Gabriel swore in French, then muttered, "It is not just that women and children must pay for the crimes of a man."

"It could have been us, Abigail," my father said, holding out a hand so I could help him up. "I don't know what came over you to make such a rash decision."

"I know, and I'm sorry, Father." I brought my eyes to Gabriel's. "And to you too, Gabriel. I know some of the furs were stolen from you as well."

"I do not care about that," he said, holding his injured arm close to him. "I only care that ..." he trailed off, realizing my father was listening to his every word. "And what of the watch?"

I winced, knowing that I could not lie, not after what had passed between us when he lay wounded in our sitting room. "It belonged to Ben's father, George. I ... I took it."

My father let out a sharp exhale, shaking his head. "Abigail, to steal—"

"And did he not steal from me?" My emotions ran high, and I swiped tears from my eyes. "He stole my life, my country, and my dignity." I shook my head with the frustration that I still grieved after all these years. I did not care that Gabriel heard, that he saw all my hurt. I turned to my father, grasping his hands, which still bore incredible strength. "I cannot marry Henry," I announced, surprising myself with my boldness. "I cannot lose more of myself."

Father closed his eyes but smiled, and when he opened them, he looked not at me but at the man over my shoulder. "I know, my dear. I know."

THE FORT

I woke before dawn, rummaging through my belongings for anything that I could spare to give Mabel for her journey east. She had family in the flatland of the prairies that would take them in, and although she would travel with Luc, I fervently wished that some cruel fate would fall on him. Neither of us could write, but she promised to send word when they were settled in their new home.

I managed to find a spare pair of stockings, as well as a box of matches and a candle, and bundled them in a scarf that Claudette had knitted for Ben. Then, I let myself out into the early morning light. A group of women already waited in the yard, waiting to bid Mabel farewell. We walked down to the river together, clutching our small gifts and parcels.

Jonathan and his brothers loaded two boats laden with supplies for their journey. We each hugged Mabel in turn, and when my arms were around her, she let out a small sob into my hair.

"Don't cry," I told her, even as I blinked back my own tears. "You are brave and strong, and we shall meet again one day."

She smiled and kissed me on the forehead. "Au revoir, my friend."

"Attendez!" It was Gabriel, coming as fast as he could manage down the hill from his cabin. He reached my side, holding something in his good hand. It was a horseshoe—*my* good luck charm, that I had given him before his trip north. "For safe travels," he said, putting it into Mabel's hand. "Tried and tested."

We stood together as Mabel and her family finished packing and began to climb into their boats. Gabriel placed his hand on the small of my back as we waved, the canoe slipping into the water. Mabel held her youngest child in her lap and did not look back at the shore.

"It seems to me," Gabriel murmured once they were out of sight, "that in this country, there is always a tragic goodbye."

It must remind him of the day he lost his son, I told myself as we headed back up the riverbank. For all my pain, that was one thing the earl had not stolen from me—Ben.

Chapter Twelve

T he sun shone brightly on this fine Sunday afternoon, and after a late lunch of rabbit stew and biscuits, the men from both Fort Augustus and Fort Edmonton gathered with the local Natives for a round of The Creator's Game. In lacrosse, as the French had nicknamed it, the players held sticks with nets attached to the other end, which they used to capture a wooden or deerskin-stuffed ball. I had seen men play when we lived in York, and they had explained to me that it was often used by the Natives to solve disputes over hunting grounds or prepare men to be warriors. It was a rough and tumble game that left the players sweaty, bruised, and exhausted.

The women sat on the edge of the field where the men played, catching up on mending and the gossip of both forts. I sat with them for a short while, then moved my blanket next to my father, who had brought a chair to sit on while he watched the game. Ben played nearby with the other children, creating a squirrel trap of sticks, rocks, and dirt. I darned a hole in Ben's trousers, casting an occasional glance at the men. Henry took a particularly hard thump, and I flinched, not understanding why men enjoyed such brutal sport.

"Bonjour, Abigail. May I sit with you?" I was pleasantly surprised to see Gabriel making his way towards me. When I nodded, he eased himself down next to me in the grass and sat cross-legged. It had been a few weeks since his run-in with the cougar, and although he was now moving around with more ease, he still favoured his arm and often wore it in a sling. Henry had insisted that we be charitable and go over to Gabriel's cabin to help him with the household duties he couldn't manage one-handed. Just this morning. Ben had asked when we would visit him next, as he had grown fond of helping me weed Gabriel's garden.

"Not joining the game today?" I asked kindly, though I knew he was still on the mend.

"I don't dare incur the wrath of Claudette," he said, winking at me. I glanced over to where she sat, and sure enough, she was watching the both of us with her eagle eye. I also shot a wary look up at my father, who was close enough to hear our conversation. Fortunately, he was still focused on watching the men play.

"I've been thinking about what you said." Gabriel began in a hushed tone, staring out at the field. "About Alexandre, my son."

"Oh, yes?" I nodded, put down my sewing and inched a bit closer to him on the blanket. I could smell the remnants of his pipe on his clothing, a scent I had come to associate with him.

"Oui. Thinking on my life in general." He lifted his injured arm, trying to extend it, but only made it halfway. "I'm not sure I have much of a future left in the fur trade."

I frowned. "I'm sure it will take time to heal. But you're the best trapper around. Surely that counts for something."

120

THE FORT

He shrugged, eyes still focused on the men. "Perhaps. But we are having to go farther north to find the best furs now, and I'm not as young as I used to be. I've saved enough to buy a small farm, and I'm thinking of returning east to Montréal. And perhaps I will make the trip to France and bring Alexandre home with me."

At his words, hot envy swirled in my gut, making its way up my throat. He was speaking of leaving, of starting a new life—a life that I would never be a part of. Yes, I knew that I had neither officially dissolved my engagement to Henry nor spoken of my growing feelings for Gabriel, but I somehow never imagined that he might leave before I had the chance. First Mabel, and now him. I feared my heart would break in two pieces.

He was quiet, waiting for my response. "That sounds ... lovely," I said, my voice cracking and giving me away. "I wish I could go with you."

He jerked his head towards me, and I quickly turned away, embarrassed. I was behaving like a fool, blurting out my feelings in public with my father in earshot. Here I was, still betrothed to one of the officers, making outlandish comments to another man. True, Gabriel had become a close companion, and I held an affection for him, but to say such a thing ...

His hand fell from his knee to the blanket, next to mine. It stayed there for a moment, hidden by the volume of my skirts. Then, his smallest finger reached out and rubbed the side of my pinky. It was my turn to look up sharply while he looked away, our fingers still side by side. A strained tension fell between us, and the flames of a desire I had long forgotten shot hot through my belly, leaving me breathless.

"I can see you there with me," he said finally, wetting his lips and darting a quick glance in my direction. I could barely hear him over the shouts of the men. Our fingers grazed once more before he moved his hand to cover mine completely, tucking his fingers around it. "Ben and Alexandre are playing by the stream while you are in the kitchen, preparing their lunch. I am out in the field tending to our plentiful crops, thinking about how we might have enough left over to sell."

"Will we have livestock?" My heart skipped over the word *we*, he squeezed my hand in response.

"Mais oui. Cows, chickens, and maybe a few—" He broke off suddenly, distracted by something in the field. "Where's he going?"

I followed his gaze and saw my father wandering into the playing field. I jumped to my feet, then I broke into a run, shouting out my father's name. What in heaven's name was he doing? He was at risk of being hit by one of the men.

I had almost caught up with him, aiming to reach out and pull him off to the sidelines, when the wooden ball came flying towards me. I shrieked, trying to dodge to the right, but a *thwack* sounded as a searing pain tore through my shoulder. I fell to the ground, flat on my back.

"Abigail!" Gabriel was above me, helping me up and into his good arm as I struggled to draw in a full breath from the hit. "Ma chérie, are you all right?" His brows were knit together, breathing heavily from the run. As a group of men gathered around us, Henry marched over, taking me out of Gabriel's embrace with a slight scowl.

My attention was pulled to the commotion on the field. I watched with horror as my father snagged a lacrosse stick out of a player's hand and began to strike the ground. He smashed the beautifully carved wooden handle to smithereens, as he was strong and able from his work as a blacksmith. Then, he managed to take another from a man who stood aghast at what was happening. Tears streamed down my face as my father made a spectacle of himself in front of both fur companies.

THE FORT

He picked up the splintered pieces of wood, muttering to himself, the mania within searing out of his eyes. These were not the actions of a sane man, of the father who had raised me with a kind and loving hand, who had carried me when I was heartbroken. A sickness had taken over his mind and drove the mayhem I saw now. He started throwing the pieces of wood at the group of men.

"No one understands!" he shouted, sending some of the closest men scattering. "We must destroy the poison!"

"Enough!" The Chief Factor, who had sat with the spectators, shouted over the murmur that had started among the crowd. "This has gone on long enough. Bring him into my office. The daughter, too." He left, gesturing to the commanding officer to restrain my father.

A hush fell as everyone turned to look at me. I stared back at them as I processed the Chief Factor's words. It was over. We were going to be dismissed from our employment with the Hudson's Bay Company.

Ben ran over to me, his face creased with alarm. "Mama, what's happened with Papa?" he asked as I scooped him into my arms, my shoulder aching where the game ball had hit me. I shook my head, unable to speak, struggling against the outpouring of grief in my chest. I was watching my father, Ben's grandfather, disappear before my very eyes while he was still very much alive.

"Abby, we must do what the Chief Factor says," Henry said softly in my ear. His hand was warm on my back, but I felt no comfort from it. Instead, I looked longingly at Gabriel, who had gone to collect my father. He wrapped an arm around my father's shoulders, leading him back to the fort. Back to our certain doom in the Chief Factor's office.

I put Ben down, took a steadying breath, and straightened my shoulders. We would survive, like Mabel and her family, cast out from the fort.

123

Some way, somehow. I wiped my tears, and not meeting the eyes of any of my friends, I followed Gabriel and my father back into the fort.

"I'm sorry, my dear. It is not my desire for the Hudson's Bay Company to abandon you, but I simply cannot have a senile blacksmith. Your father deserves to live out his days in rest. And with these outbursts, he is a danger to himself and everyone else. What if he had hit the women or children? Or worse, what if he had been holding his smith tools? Or started a fire? He simply cannot be trusted anymore."

I nodded, staring down at my hands folded in my lap. The Chief Factor spoke the truth, and I truly did not blame him for the decision. We would be let go from my father's position and be asked to leave the fort. I blinked back tears but did not let them fall, as I had resolved to stay strong.

"Is there no way we can hire Abby and the boy Edmund while we wait for a replacement smith?" Henry asked, holding my hand tight in his. I glanced to the doorway, where Gabriel leaned against the frame, his injured arm held snugly against his chest. His eyes met mine, and we shared an unspoken moment. He was worried about my fate as well.

"Hire a woman? I think not. It would make me the laughingstock of the HBC. Surely you understand, Davies. We are the face of Europe's most profitable fur company." He turned to my father, whose head hung so low I could not see his eyes. Although he could remember nothing of the actual incident, he was deeply ashamed of his actions and the turmoil

THE FORT

they had caused. I wanted to reach out and console him but feared it would embarrass him further. "I can give you until the end of the month, but after that, I will need you to vacate your premises. Luckily, I had some foresight and sent word with the voyageurs that we need a replacement."

Gabriel cursed and left, slamming the door behind him. I let my head fall into my hands, panic burning my throat. The month's end was only a week away.

My father's hand came to my elbow, urging me up. "Come, Abigail. We have much to discuss." We left the office together, leaving Henry behind with the Chief Factor. The eyes of the fort were on us, and I could only imagine what was being said: *The stolen furs. The gold watch. A crazy father. What a scandal.* I held my head high, remembering how my father had walked me home seven years ago on a stormy English night. The reminder of what he had done for me in my darkest days steadied my resolve to help him through his.

We made our way into the privacy of our shop, and I breathed a sigh of relief that it was Sunday and Edmund was at home with his family. Ben, on the other hand, was waiting for us, his eyes red from crying. I pulled him onto my lap, my insides weeping the tears that I could not show. No, now I must be brave, even though a void cracked open in my chest at the thought of leaving everyone behind.

"Ben, we must leave the fort soon. Papa is unwell."

My son, who had never known a life of stability, had never had a real home, swallowed and nodded, his eyes full of trust. "Where will we go?"

My father shook his head firmly. "*We* are going nowhere. I will head back east alone and board a ship back to England." He reached out and patted my knee. "You should stay and build a life here."

"I will not leave you alone, Father. Besides ..." I trailed off, not sure how to explain to my father how uncertain I was. Just an hour before, I had visions of settling down on a farm, but now everything seemed precarious. I abhorred the thought of my father leaving alone, but the thought of leaving Gabriel lurked like a dark predator in my gut.

"I fear my condition will only get worse. Perhaps we should write your brothers to be my escort."

I sighed. No doubt my brothers would find some reason to find fault with me over the whole ordeal. And to return to England ... it had been many years, to be sure, but if I were to accompany my father, I would need to stay far away from the earl's estate, lest he hear news of Ben.

There was a movement outside the shop, and I looked out to see Gabriel running a hand anxiously through his beard. My body flooded with relief at the sight of him, and it was only the weight of Ben in my lap that kept me from running to him and throwing myself in his arms.

He came into the shop and leaned against the hearth of the forge. "I've spoken with Chief Factor Rowand at Fort Augustus. They're willing to take you on as blacksmith."

"What?" I stared at him from my seat. "I don't understand. Many of the Nor'westers were at the game as well. Surely, he must realize Father's condition."

"Yes." He cleared his throat uncomfortably, darting a quick glance over at me. "I struck a bargain with him. I've agreed to work exclusively for the North West Company as long as you remain there."

My father rubbed the back of his neck. "That's kind of you, Gabriel, but perhaps we should just make plans to leave. I'm afraid I will be a burden—"

THE FORT

"No." Gabriel cut my father off, his blue eyes blazing. "The deal's been done. I shall help move your belongings tomorrow."

I pushed Ben off my lap then, coming to stand in front of Gabriel. Not caring that my father and Ben were audience to my affection, I threw myself against him, wrapping my arms around his neck. When he gave a grunt of discomfort, I remembered his injured arm and pulled away quickly, embarrassed by my forwardness.

His other strong arm reined me back into his chest, pressing me back against him. I looked up at the beard and long hair I had once found so alarming. Now, it took everything in my power not to bring that face, his lips, down to mine.

"Thank you," I whispered instead, my vision blurring with tears. "Thank you, Gabriel."

He let me go abruptly, turning to leave the shop. Watching him leave, I remembered our conversation on the lacrosse field, his plans to retire. In a swift instant, he had given it all up. I closed my eyes at the realization—I was in love with a Frenchman, and if I was not mistaken, he was in love with me.

Chapter Thirteen

The sky was still dark outside the window when a persistent knock sounded at our door. Groggily opening one eye, I groaned. *Henry.* He had likely heard the news by now that we were leaving for Fort Augustus this very morning. I had avoided him for the remainder of the day before, feigning a headache at dinner. Truthfully, I was horribly confused about my feelings for Gabriel and needed the evening alone. The vision of us together at our imaginary farm had possessed my thoughts, and I had scolded myself a few times for thinking of the touch of his hands on my most intimate parts, tucked warm in our bed.

"Is it true?" Henry asked as soon as I opened the door. "You're leaving today?"

I sighed, fighting the exhaustion that threatened to pull me under its tide. "There's no other choice, Henry. So, yes, we're going to the other fort."

"The Chief Factor is livid," he said, coming inside and sitting at the table, despite the early hour and the fact that I was not yet dressed. "He says you've swindled him out of his best trapper."

THE FORT

I raised an eyebrow but said nothing, turning to fill the kettle for some tea. It was better to let him air his frustrations before I had my say. I rubbed my temples, an ache starting to throb. I hadn't slept well, as my thoughts had bounced from my father to Ben, to Gabriel, to Henry. Where I fit in, where my future lay, I wasn't sure.

"We should be wed at once. The reverend is away, but we can get married in the country style, as the men do with the Indians. Once he returns, we can have the church ceremony. We'll move into the family accommodations together. Then there will be no need to move to Fort Augustus."

"And what of my father?" I asked, knowing the fort wouldn't allow him to stay with us. "I cannot abandon him." Besides, I had already made up my mind that I wouldn't be marrying Henry. Not with another man filling my thoughts at every waking moment.

"Another canoe brigade should be passing by in a month or two, coming up from Fort Vancouver. I was thinking we could send him east and arrange passage to England."

"Alone?" I shook my head, giving him a scowl. "Never."

He sighed heavily, running a hand through his hair. "Abby, what do you imagine will happen when I am reposted next year? I can hardly have your ailing father in tow."

"About that." I paused, trying to choose my words carefully. "I was thinking that I might take my father that way myself in the spring. Gabriel is thinking of relocating there, and I thought—"

Henry's expression turned dark. "What is going on between the two of you? You seem awfully close these days. For him to give up his freedom and work for the North West Company just for you? And the way you stood vigil over him, tending to his injury? You spend more time with him than me."

I felt my pulse quicken, remembering how I had dreamt of Gabriel touching me as a man would his wife. I needed to let Henry down gently. "Don't be absurd. I'm just concerned for the well-being of my father."

He gave me a long look with narrowed eyes, accepting a cup of tea. "It's settled then. We shall be wed tomorrow."

"No!" I said loudly, a fiery panic spreading across my chest. "I've already decided to move to the other fort."

Henry put his mug down with a thud. "Now, listen to me, Abigail—"

"I cannot leave my father. You don't understand, Henry. He gave up everything to come here with me, and I will not send him off in the wilderness alone with a canoe brigade."

"I think you're being unreasonable. I'm sure one of your brothers would come to escort him on the journey home."

A rage had started to grow like a living thing inside me, and I turned on Henry, seething. "Have you no heart? He's my *father*!" I shouted, not caring that I was likely overheard by other early risers at the fort. "Next, you'll be telling me that Ben is not welcome, either."

Henry flushed and looked down at his feet. "Well, there are some fine boys' schools I've looked into for Ben. He needs a proper education, and he won't get that clinging to your skirts."

I slammed down my mug of tea on the table, the hot liquid spilling over onto my hands. I would never allow Henry—or anyone else—to separate me from my son. I stomped over to the door and flung it open. "Get out."

He spluttered into his tea. "What? Darling, I'm just being practical about our future."

THE FORT

"I'm starting to think you are nothing more than an unfeeling beast," I snarled at him. "And it's time for you to leave."

His face grew pale, and he pushed himself up slowly from the table. "Abby, I think you've misunderstood me. I just want to take care of you."

"I am perfectly able to take care of myself. Goodbye, Henry." I ushered him out and closed the door behind him, my entire body shaking. I slid down to the floor, sobs wracking my frame for the second time in as many days. The door of the bedchamber creaked open, and my father came out, a sombre expression painted on his elderly face. He took the chair that Henry had just vacated, sighing heavily as he watched me try and wipe my tears.

"My dear, I hate that I've become a burden for you," he whispered. His words set me into tears once more, as I was so fearful of the months to come. How would I manage his illness while taking care of Ben and running the blacksmith shop? What if he harmed himself or someone else? Worse, what if he died and left me alone? He was not just my father but my friend and confidant.

"Father, that argument was not about you," I sniffed, trying to calm myself. "It was about me not wanting to marry Henry."

My father gave me a wry smile. "I know, Abigail. You've never been able to put aside matters of the heart. Your mother was the same way."

I took in a shaky breath, deciding to divulge the truth, as he likely saw it anyhow. "Yesterday, Gabriel told me that he plans to retire and move back east and farm. It ... it frightened me, Father. The thought that I might never see him again. But I'm afraid my love may be one-sided. He's a rather ... stoic man."

"No." My father shook his head. "He cares for you that much is clear. But whether he can give you his heart the way you desire, I'm not certain. Love is always a risk, my dear."

A risk that might end in heartbreak. I mustered a weak smile as Ben came into the room, his little face still heavy with sleep. He snuggled into me, and I stroked his hair. But then again, what would my life be without risk? Safe, yes, but perhaps unfulfilled.

"Come, Ben," I said, rising from the floor. "We must pack. We're leaving for Fort Augustus."

The boat ride across the river was quiet and subdued. As Gabriel was still unable to paddle, he sat with my father in one canoe while I sat with Ben and Edmund, who had graciously decided to accompany us in another. Some of the older boys from the fort rowed us over, and our blacksmithing tools and meagre belongings were rowed over in a third. I stared back at the HBC flag, red with the Union Jack in the upper left corner, rippling in the wind. Many of the friends we had made in the last months came to wave goodbye at the riverbank. Henry's absence was noticeable, and I avoided Gabriel's curious gaze as we rode silently through the water.

Half an hour later, our arrival through the gates of Fort Augustus was met with far less fanfare. A few men greeted Gabriel as we came into the yard, and although I knew some folk from the times I had visited with Gabriel, I still swallowed back the nausea I always felt at having to meet

THE FORT

new people. We would move into the shared accommodation—a long barracks-style building that had men sleeping on one side and women and children on the other. I worried about my father staying alone, but he waved me off, settling into one of the bottom bunks and putting away his clothes in the shared chest of drawers. I found beds for myself and Ben on the women's side and then wandered outside while Ben ran off to play with the other children.

"I'm sorry the bunkhouse isn't as nice as your lodging over at the HBC," Gabriel said, stepping in line with me as I made my way over to the blacksmith shop.

"Please don't apologize," I said, laying a hand on his arm. "I can't thank you enough."

He chewed on the side of his lip. "Do you think we could go for a walk before you start working? I'd like to speak with you alone."

My heart thudded as I followed him out of the gates. A part of me wanted him to proclaim his love, but by his stern expression, I didn't think that was what he had planned. We walked the path in anxious silence until I could see his cabin across the river.

He crossed his arms across his chest, his injured one still stiff. "I wanted to speak with you about yesterday. When we talked of the farm and sharing a life together. I ... I just wanted to be clear about my intentions. I will go there alone, Abigail."

My legs grew weak, and found a nearby log to sit on. He did not think of me as anything more than a companion. I tried to stay calm, but my voice betrayed me with a waver. "I shouldn't have said anything to you, Gabriel. It just sounded like a lovely dream."

133

"Yes." He came and sat on the ground next to me, leaning against the log. "Truthfully, I would enjoy your company very much. It's just ... c'est compliqué."

"It's all right," I said, trying not to let the disappointment that surged through me show on my face. My father was right. I was a fool when it came to matters of the heart. I should learn my lesson, once and for all, and choose someone safe and predictable. I rose from my seat to leave.

He turned suddenly, catching my hand to stop me from walking away. "Do you love Henry?"

My cheeks burned at his question, catching me by surprise. "I ... No," I said, looking away to avoid his intent gaze. "No, I don't love him."

He let out a loud exhale like he had been holding his breath. "I see."

I kept my gaze focused on the river in case I started to cry. I swallowed thickly, my throat aching with unshed tears. "Why do you ask?"

He pulled me back down to the log and leaned into me, resting lightly against my leg. "The woman I married, Clarisse, was first betrothed to my brother, Michel. I stole her away from him, wooing her with a promise of a new life in the New World." He gave a wry chuckle, staring out at the water. "It was nothing short of ironic that she left me just three years later. I hated myself for betraying Michel and hated myself for loving her. When she left, something deep inside me broke open, and I promised myself never to love again."

My own chest cracked at his revelation, but I managed one word. "Never?"

He shook his head. "I'm sorry, Abigail."

We sat together, not wanting to acknowledge what had passed between us. I tried to understand the complexity of what he had told me: he had taken his brother's woman and ended up brokenhearted and

THE FORT

was unwilling to love again. Finally, I shook my head—no, that wasn't everything. He was trying to tell me that he had feelings for me, but he would not allow himself the chance. He wanted to know if I loved Henry, but he was still pushing me away.

"It's not true," I said, standing from the log. My chest hurt with the emotion I was trying to keep inside. "You say this now, but when you move to Montréal, you'll find a nice French woman to settle down with."

"No, you're wrong." He looked up with a pained expression, catching my hand again. "Je rêve seulement de toi. I only dream of you."

My heart felt ready and vulnerable behind its thinly repaired walls. I, too, was unwilling to love and be hurt again. I pulled my hand away, trying to keep myself intact. "I know I am nothing more than a child to you. An annoying Englishwoman who smells of horse. You needn't worry about me any longer, Gabriel." I turned and walked briskly along the path back to the fort, hot tears pricking my eyes. I had enough to worry about without fretting over a burly Frenchman.

I heard him behind me, shouting at me in French. "Attends!"

I quickened my pace, willing my tears away. I had been a sobbing, weeping mess the last two days, and I needed to regain my composure. I needed to focus on my father and Ben and forget these two men.

"Abigail, stop. Please, listen to me." We reached the edge of the palisade, and he grabbed me by the arm, jerking me around to face him. My back dug into the wood of the fort walls as he pressed close to me. "You are a woman, not a child. One that I ..." He stopped, taking a step back. "You belong to Henry."

"I don't belong to *anyone*." I grabbed at his shirt, not letting him escape. He moved back closer to me so that our bodies grazed one another. "Henry and I fought this morning. He doesn't want anything to do with

135

my father, and he wants to send Ben away. I told him to leave. And ..." I paused, staring up into his deep blue eyes. We had said so much already, and I needed to lay my soul bare for my own sake. "And I'm falling in love with you."

I heard a sharp gasp from him, and then his lips were against mine, crushing me against the palisade. My hands flew up to behind his head, pulling him even closer. We kissed frantically, desperately, like two lovers finally reunited after a long journey apart. His teeth nipped my lower lip, the pain quickly dissipating as he ran his tongue over the same spot. I groaned into his mouth, wanting more of him. My hips moved to press against his, and he made a noise deep in his throat, releasing me suddenly from his kiss.

"Merde," he groaned against my neck, his breath ragged and hot. "I think of you every moment of every day, and you are a vixen who calls to me in the night. But I cannot, Abigail. I will only hurt you."

I put my palms on his cheeks. "I am not a porcelain doll, Gabriel. I am the guardian of my own heart, and I do not think of you as a bad man." I leaned forward and brushed my lips against his once again. "Do not cast me aside. I want this life that you speak of."

He kissed me again, slowly, until I became lightheaded, breathing heavily with the desire that swirled hot inside me. His hands spread across my backside, hoisting me up against him.

"We must stop. Someone might see," I said breathlessly as his lips moved down my neck, finding the top of my bodice.

I felt the vibration of his soft chuckle against my ear. "Tu es si belle. Je veux te faire l'amour chaque matin et chaque soir."

THE FORT

I rested my head against his chest, my breathing ragged. "That's not fair. I can't understand when you speak French." I looked up at him, euphoric from what had passed between us.

"I know." He nuzzled my neck one last time, releasing me back on my feet. "You must ask Claudette to teach you some French, ma chérie."

I frowned as reality came crashing back down on me. "Gabriel—"

He put a finger to my lips, silencing my concern. "We will speak again later. You must decide what you want with Henry. I cannot take another man's woman again."

I nodded, understanding what he meant more than he knew. I winced, knowing that he did not know the truth of my past. He had revealed his to me. Would he still think of me as beautiful once he learned mine?

Chapter Fourteen

A
s the next few weeks went by, I found myself loving our life at Fort Augustus. My father was able to rest, as no one seemed concerned when Edmund and I ran the blacksmith shop by ourselves. Ben adjusted easily, often playing with the other children into the dusk hour, his hands and face covered in dirt when he came in to wash before bed. I scolded him gently for always needing a thorough scrubbing at the end of the day, but truthfully, I was glad to see him enjoying the outdoors with the other young boys and girls.

Gabriel and I spent every evening together, first dining with my father and Ben, then leaving the fort for some time alone. Gabriel left first, then me, to avoid suspicion, leaving Ben under the care of Claudette or some of the older children. We sat with our backs against the palisade, eating apples, berries, and other fruit that grew plentiful in the summer. Sometimes, we spoke about the things of our past, but more often, we played cards, laughing and teasing each other in an easy banter. When the sun started to set, we would pack the cards away, and I would curl up in his embrace, tilting my face up to his to receive his kisses while he caressed

THE FORT

my face and hair. It was nothing frantic like our first kiss had been, but I would lie awake in my bunk after he had gone home, reliving the evening and thinking that, for the first time in a long time, I was happy.

"So, what's happened with the officer?" Claudette asked late one morning as we drank tea at a small table set up outside the cookhouse. The sun had not yet reached its full heat of the day, and I basked in its warmth, stretching my sore back and arms.

I shrugged at her question, though I had felt a small pang at how easily Henry had dismissed me. He had made no attempt to reconcile after our argument, and his prolonged absence made me realize that to marry him would have indeed been a mistake.

"We argued over my father," I said, smiling at the Chief Factor of Fort Augustus, who tipped his hat to me as he passed through the yard. "We haven't spoken since."

"Mmmhmm." She nodded like it didn't surprise her at all. "I told you in the beginning you are more suited to a Frenchman. You are too vivacious for a prim and proper man of England. I am not fooled by your accent, mon amie. You have the soul of a French woman."

I picked at the crumbs of the biscuit on my plate, avoiding her gaze. I had no doubts that Claudette had noticed that something had blossomed between Gabriel and me, but I wasn't ready to speak of it openly. "Perhaps you are right," I said. "Henry wanted me to be someone other than who I am. Someone more ... good."

"You *are* good," she said firmly, filling my teacup. "And don't let any man tell you otherwise. Even the French ones." Claudette gave me a wink from her side of the table.

I gave her a shy smile, a warmth growing in my belly, then took a sip from my cup. I wasn't worried about rushing back to work at the black-

139

smith shop. The Nor'westers had a different pace than the employees of the HBC. Men came and went from the fort, running their own fur brigades to Fort William, near Lake Superior in the east. Despite the easygoing atmosphere, the North West Company had outperformed the HBC in recent years, in both the quality and quantity of the furs.

"Claudette, do you think I should tell my son that his grandfather is dying?" My voice faltered on the last word, having a hard time coming to terms with it myself. Even though he had been able to rest more since we had switched forts, I had seen some of the life seep out of him since the incident on the lacrosse field. Now, he pushed food around his plate at mealtimes and his shoulders had become stooped and hollowed, his complexion grey and sunken. It seemed as if his body had caught up with the frailty of his mind.

"Well, it might soften the blow when the time comes," she said, reaching over to squeeze my hand. "I hate to say it, but he might not last the winter."

I nodded, swallowing my tea to avoid responding. I knew what she said was true. Winters in this remote, harsh climate were difficult for even the healthiest people. When the food became scarce, and the wind cut bitter cold through the thickest fur robes, weakened men like my father would fight to survive.

"What will you do? When the time comes?"

"I don't know," I said, pushing away the now vivid dream of sharing a farm with Gabriel. "I planned to marry Henry, but now ..."

Claudette leaned back in her chair, crossing her arms over her ample bosom. "What do *you* want to do, Abigail? What would make you happy?"

THE FORT

I considered her question, running my fingers down the braid that hung over my shoulder. "I like working with the horses, I suppose. But I've always dreamed of having a lot of children. A family to take care of."

She pushed herself up from the table, collecting the plates and cups to take back inside. "Then that is how your story will end, jolie fille," she said simply. She patted me on the shoulder as she passed, leaving me alone with my thoughts in the morning sun.

That night at dinner, the Chief Factor came and sat with us at our dinner table. He was a friendly man, nothing like the one over at Fort Edmonton. Mr. Rowand rarely sat alone in his office but instead socialized with the members of the fort, getting to know them. He frequently came by the blacksmith shop, complimenting me on the good work. Like a flower in the pleasant spring sun, I bloomed under his attention and found myself eager to please him.

"Hello, Mr. Rowand," I said as he sat down at our table, bringing over his plate of fish and garden vegetables. "You've come just in time for my nightly French lesson."

He chuckled, taking a piece of bread from the basket on the table. "Very well. What are we learning?"

Gabriel grinned at me. I marvelled at the difference in him as of late. Gone was the brooding, reserved man, and in his place was a man whose eyes danced when we were together, whose fingers grazed mine whenever they could. I found myself sinking deep into the haze of infatuation

CHRISTY K. LEE

whenever I was around him, always exhilarated and giddy. I could scarcely think about anything else during the day except him.

"Yesterday, today, and tomorrow," he said. "Hier, aujourd'hui, et demain."

I practiced the words out loud, and Ben echoed them after me. He had raced ahead of me in learning French, speaking it with the children in the yard. Once or twice, he had evoked a wide-eyed look from Gabriel, making me think that he was also learning the profane.

"That's charming," the Chief Factor said politely, smiling at each of us in turn. Although we were trying to keep our affection for each other quiet, I was starting to suspect that it was evident to all. I took a quick glance around, but everyone else in the meal hall was busy with their own affairs.

Mr. Rowand cleared his throat. "I was hoping to ask you for a favour, Abigail. A good friend of mine lives in a settlement a few days' ride from here. They are in desperate need of having their horses shod. I have a group of men headed there the day after tomorrow. Would you be willing to go along and do the work?"

"I think that should be fine," I said, sending Gabriel a quick glance. "I'll ask my father. And one of the women can watch Ben."

Gabriel cleared his throat beside me. "I'll be coming along, Mr. Rowand, if she decides to go."

The Chief Factor nodded. "I suspected you would say as much." He turned to me. "I will be indebted to you, my dear. And I will be sure to keep an eye on your father while you're gone."

We finished our meal together, Ben picking over the vegetables on his plate. When he asked to be excused, the Chief Factor left as well, leaving

THE FORT

us alone. Our hands discreetly found each other under the table, his thumb roaming over the top of mine.

"You don't have to go if you don't want to, Abigail. He won't be angry if you say no."

"I know, but it might be pleasant to get away for a few days. And it will be nice to spend the time with you."

He nodded, then frowned. "Have you spoken to Henry? If we are to go away together, we should speak with him."

"No, I haven't. I guess we should, but must we do it today? Perhaps when we return."

He squeezed my hand, sending shivers down my spine. "Today's French lesson was actually something different. J'aime tes lèvres." He leaned down to whisper the translation in my ear. "I love your lips."

"Mmmm. How about I love your eyes?" I said, gazing up into his.

"J'aime tes yeux."

My hand moved to stroke the scars that still marred his arm. "I love your strength."

"J'admire ta force." He glanced around the room before stroking the side of my face with the back of one finger. "And I love your courage. I've never met a woman like you."

My heart felt ready to burst. I wanted him to say that he loved *me*, all of me. Even the parts I felt ashamed of. I vowed that during our time away, I would tell him the truth about everything—about the affair, Ben's father, fleeing my life in England. For now, I moved my chair a bit closer to his. "I love France," I murmured with a twinkle in my eye.

He threw his head back in a laugh that made more than a few people look our way. "I shall take you there one day," he said, giving me an

143

affectionate peck on the cheek. "We will make love under the stars, my Abigail."

My heart thumped at his words, at the promise of a future together. I wanted to say yes to it all—making love, building a life together, having babies. *One day.*

Two days later, we left at dawn. It had been some time since I had ridden a horse for any great distance, and the saddle that had been chosen for me was too large. The man leading the trek kept up a demanding pace, and my legs burned in agony despite wearing my trousers for comfort. When we stopped at midday, I hobbled down to the stream to drink and wash. Gabriel helped me back up from the bank, laughing as I groaned dramatically and leaned heavily into his side.

By the time we reached the site where we would camp for the night, I was almost asleep on my mount. A few men cooked fish they had caught earlier over a fire, and I ate my share before I took my bedroll from the back of my saddle and made myself a place to sleep a fair distance away. The night was warm, so I didn't mind being away from the fire.

Gabriel watched me from the corner of his eye, the smoke from his pipe swirling thick around him. I pulled a blanket over me and smiled at him, my eyes already half closed. Tomorrow would be an equally long day, and if I were to manage at all, I needed to rest. A few minutes later, there was a rustling beside me as he put down his own bedroll behind mine. I rolled over sleepily, the sweet smell of tobacco tickling my nose.

THE FORT

"Is this all right?" he asked, pulling another blanket over himself. "I just don't want you to sleep alone with all these men around."

"Of course," I replied, rolling back over. The men might talk, but we were fully clothed and still far enough apart to be decent. His hand came to my waist and under the weight of it, I fell fast asleep and started to dream.

The rain was unrelenting, streaming down my face. I had been standing vigil outside the gate of the earl's estate for hours. I hardly noticed that I was soaked to the bone, as the wound in my heart was so deep I could scarcely breathe.

"George, please," I whimpered, my hands curled around the wrought iron of the gate. "Please just speak with me one last time. I love you."

It had been a month since I had been dismissed from my employment, and my fears had been confirmed by the absence of my monthly courses. I was with child, a cursed reminder of him. If I could just speak with George, to tell him that his offspring grew in my womb, he might find some sympathy in his heart.

"Get out of here!" someone yelled through the pitch of night, sending my pulse to a frantic pace. "I've sent for the authorities. You'd best leave before they come."

"Please!" I begged, though the voice belonged to a woman, not George. "I just want to speak with him. Please allow me one minute of his time."

A slamming of a door was the reply, and I sank down, the pebbles from the ground digging into my knees.

"Abigail?" Another voice pierced the dark, one that I knew well. A lantern bobbed as my father came into my vision, riding the fat donkey that belonged to my brother. He was drenched, and seeing him in the wet, cold night sent my body into an uncontrollable shiver.

CHRISTY K. LEE

"Oh, my sweet girl." He bent down to help me up off the ground. "Let us go home."

"Father." I wept into his arms, my limbs shaking. I had not yet told anyone of my condition, but I needed to share my shameful secret before it tore me in two. "I'm with child."

He said nothing, helping me up onto the animal. It would not bear the weight of both of us, and my father would walk alongside me for the hour-long ride home.

"We'll both catch our death of cold out here, Abigail," he said gruffly as we started on our way. "And you must take better care of yourself for the sake of the babe."

I started to sob again, hunched over, my arms wrapped around the neck of the donkey.

My father jerked the animal to a halt and grabbed my chin firmly in his grasp. "Stop this now, my daughter. You will not grieve the loss of a man who has disrespected you in this way. You will raise this child as a blessing, not a burden, you hear me?"

I nodded, but then the rain suddenly stopped, and I was instead in the shadowy darkness of the blacksmith shop. I was alone, heating a long iron rod in the forge to cut and bend into a horseshoe.

I heard a sound behind me as someone entered the shop, and I smiled, expecting a Frenchman with a thick beard. Instead, standing before me, clean-shaven and dressed in fine clothing, was George.

"George?" I asked, my stomach filling with a cold dread. "What are you doing here?"

"Where is my son?" he demanded, the gold of his wedding ring glinting in the light of the fire.

"You cannot have him."

THE FORT

He grabbed my arm, his fingers digging into my flesh. I dropped the tongs and the iron rod, which landed at my feet with a clatter. George hissed as the hot tongs grazed his foot, the smell of burnt leather filling the air.

"You worthless whore," he growled, jerking me over to the door. "Go and get my son."

As if summoned, Ben ran into the shop. I cried out, my whole being ablaze with fear. I could taste it, like metal in my mouth. "No, Ben! Leave! You must not go with him!"

"It's all right, Mama," my child said, his grin revealing his first missing tooth. "I'll be back home soon."

"No!" I yelled, thrashing out of George's vice grip. "Ben, you must not go with him!"

Then the shop was gone, and I was back outside the earl's gates, yanking on them furiously. I had no babe in my womb now, only a sense of overwhelming loss. "Give me my son!" I screamed. My voice was hoarse, and I once again sank to my knees. Only this time, my father did not come. For he, too, was gone.

Chapter Fifteen

"**A**bigail!"

I woke, my face wet with tears, my heart pounding so hard the thump echoed in my ears. It was dark, and I was outside. A pair of hands held me tight, reminding me of George's tight grasp. *Ben.* Where was my son?

"Ma chérie, c'est moi. It's me, Gabriel."

I threw my arms around him, burying my face deep in his chest. He stroked my hair, whispering to me in French until my body stopped shaking and my sobs subsided. It had been a dream, I reassured myself over and over. No one was coming for Ben.

Finally, I lifted myself from his embrace, rolling back to my sleeping space. I pulled the blanket up to my chin, shivering despite the warm night. "I'm sorry," I whispered. I wasn't sure if I had woken the other men with my dream, but it seemed that they had fallen back asleep. "I had a bad dream."

THE FORT

Gabriel rolled onto his side, propping his head with his arm. "Is this the George who is Ben's father? And why are you worried about Ben's safety?"

I took a deep breath, blowing it out slowly to calm myself. "Yes, George is Ben's father. I dreamt that he took Ben away from me."

I heard him swallow thickly, then he lay back down and pulled me into his chest. I knew he wanted to know more, and although part of me wanted to confess the whole story, the taste of fear still lingered in my mouth.

"Ben's father is still alive? You're not a widow? I suspected that might be the case, but you should tell me the truth, Abigail." There was a wariness in his tone, and I flinched, George's rejection fresh in my memory.

"No, I'm not." I breathed the words out, barely even a whisper, but I knew he heard as his body stiffened under me. He said nothing, and with each passing second, I imagined the horrible things he was conjuring in his mind's eye.

"George is a married man. An earl. I was a maid at his estate."

Gabriel let out sigh and I scrunched up my face in the darkness, trying not to let out the scream that lurked in my throat. "It wasn't rape," I blurted out, hating myself. "I loved him. I thought ... I thought he loved me."

He lifted my chin to face him, even though we couldn't see each other clearly in the night. "This man employed you, seduced you, then left you pregnant and alone?"

"He didn't know of the pregnancy," I said, my voice trembling. "I would have told him, but I didn't have a chance. His wife is barren, so I think that was for the best."

"I see," he said simply, gathering me back into his chest. I waited to feel him tense, to feel the repulsion course through his body, but it did not come.

"Are you not upset with me?" I asked quietly.

"Of course not. This man, earl or not, should not have taken advantage of a young girl." His arms tightened around me. "But the fact that you loved him makes me jealous. For I find that I am very much in love with you."

"Really?" I lifted my head to peer at him. "You love me?"

He chuckled, the sound vibrating through my body, and a part of the shame that I had held onto for so long melted away. "Oui, ma chérie. From the moment you tried to take my head off with your tongs in the forest. I thought to myself, Qui est cette femme avec le feu dans son âme? Who is this woman with fire in her soul? You awakened a stirring in me that I had not known for a long time. But then, I hated your affection for Henry."

I shook my head against him. "No. Henry is a man I thought I should marry, nothing more. He is a handsome man, but his heart is not kind. Not like yours."

"Handsome, eh? Is it time for me to cut my hair and shave? Is that what my Englishwoman likes?"

I leaned up to find his lips, and he kissed me deeply, his hands keeping my body tight against his. "I love you just as you are, with your hair and beard and eyes so blue. Please never change any part."

He sighed, his hands leaving their spot at my waist to cup my behind. "There are many parts of me I wish I could change. Mistakes I have made."

I laid my hand on his chest, feeling the strength of the muscles beneath. "I bear those scars as well, Gabriel. But I would not be here with you without them." My hands drifted lower to where the cougar had torn his flesh. "They are part of who we are."

He growled, kissing me again. "Come with me to Montréal. Marry me. Let us fill our home with children."

"Yes," I whispered, tears burning hot at the corners of my eyes. "Je t'aime, Gabriel."

"Abby? What is the meaning of this?"

I woke, still snug in Gabriel's embrace. But the voice I heard was Henry's, and he sounded angry.

"Henry?" Gabriel sat up, bringing me upright with him. "Why on earth are you here?"

Henry stood above us, dressed in his officer's uniform, his expression thunderous. "I've come," he gritted out between clenched teeth, "with urgent news. But I did not expect to find my betrothed *sleeping* in the arms of my friend."

"Betrothed?" I leapt to my feet, ready to defend myself. "You did not even say goodbye to me when I left Fort Edmonton. Now it has been *three weeks* without word from you. This is hardly how one treats the one they want to marry."

Henry scoffed in my face, and Gabriel drew me back behind him protectively. "I apologize, Henry. But Abigail and I are in love. We plan to be wed and move to Montréal in the spring. *With* her father," he added, raising an eyebrow in Henry's direction.

Henry crossed his arms over his chest and gave an evil-sounding laugh. "My, my. Well, it seems the universe has other plans for you." He reached into his pocket and thrust an opened letter at Gabriel. "As for my absence, there was a case of the flux at the fort. I didn't want to risk spreading it to you, Abby."

"Oh." I bit my lip and stepped out from behind Gabriel. "I'm sure you could have sent word with someone. But I'm sorry that I did not come to speak with you."

"Mon Dieu!" Gabriel exclaimed, taking a step backwards. He looked at me, his face pale, the letter in his hands. "Clarisse has died from consumption, and Alexandre has been put in a home for orphans."

"Oh, Gabriel!" I put my arms around him, not caring that Henry stood a mere foot away. "You must go to him right away."

"I ... yes, that is what I must do." He looked down at me, his eyes searching mine. "Come with me."

"I cannot. I won't leave my father or Ben alone. And I am sure you can travel more quickly without me." Even as I spoke the words, I felt a pang for his absence. To travel overseas and back would take a year or more, as he would need to make his way north to York, on the shore of Hudson's Bay, and take the ship from there to Europe.

He took my face into his hands. "I will return as quickly as I can, ma chérie."

I leaned up to kiss him, hearing a grunt of disapproval from Henry behind me. "I will wait for you," I whispered. "As long as it takes, I will wait."

THE FORT

He broke the kiss, looking around our camp frantically. "I must go. There is no time to waste. Winter is only a few months away. I must leave for France as soon as I can."

"I will ride back with you to Fort Augustus," I said, leaning down to gather our supplies. "I'm sure the Chief Factor will understand."

We packed quickly, only pausing to eat a bowl of porridge provided by one of the men. Then we mounted our horses and left Henry riding at our side. Gabriel eventually rode ahead, pushing his horse hard. I could hardly blame him, as children were not known to be treated kindly in orphanages. I thought again of my upsetting dream from the night before, my stomach clenching. I was happy to be heading back to the fort, where I could hold my child safely in my arms.

"I must say that I'm disappointed," Henry said in a low tone as we rode along behind Gabriel. "I even wrote to Margaret and called off our engagement for you. I realize you are emotional about the health of your father, but to not even speak with me before engaging in this?" He gestured at Gabriel with disdain. "And sleeping with him, out in the open like that? I thought you were a woman of good morals, Abby, and now you have sullied your reputation. And with a Frenchman, no less."

"Stop that," I snapped, feeling a newfound sense of freedom from my burden of shame. "I have not been sullied. I am a good person, Henry, no matter what I have done. Stop painting me with your ridiculous ideas of purity. Have *you* been chaste all these years? I think not."

I paused to revel at the shock on his face, then continued. "I am sorry for not speaking with you more clearly, but I was confused. I did want to marry you in the beginning, but then I realized I was falling in love with Gabriel."

He shook his head, frowning at me. "I think you are making a grave mistake. What can he offer you as a life of a trapper? Or as a farmer if you move east? My family has money, Abby. Once I am done with my service, we will be free to do whatever we want."

"I think you are better suited to someone like Margaret," I replied. "Have you not noticed I am the daughter of a blacksmith?" I held out my dirty hands for him to see. "I am not a woman of society. Being the wife of a farmer sounds lovely to me. Besides, as we have told you already, Gabriel and I love each other."

"Love?" He looked over, raising his brows. "Love is fickle. A marriage is much stronger when a woman learns to respect and obey her husband. That is the natural order of things."

I sighed, shaking my head. Perhaps Claudette was right. The English way of thinking was so rigid and stiff. "I wish you the best, Henry." With that, I urged my horse faster and caught up with Gabriel.

We made it to Gabriel's cabin just as the sun was dipping into the horizon. Henry caught up with us, politely wishing Gabriel luck in retrieving his son before departing. Then, it was just the two of us. I stood silently by the hearth as he packed everything he needed in a rucksack. He would leave at first light, making his way east and then north to sail out of Fort York, following the route of the voyageurs.

THE FORT

Finally, he was done packing, and he sank onto his bed, his head in his hands. I came over, tentatively at first, then sat beside him, putting my hand on his back.

"Can I stay with you tonight?" I asked, feeling a fiery anticipation flood my veins at my boldness. Perhaps he would refuse me, but I suspected not.

He looked up at me in surprise, his eyes rimmed red from the stress of the day. "Merci," he said, voice husky. "I would love it if you would."

I nodded, going to the basin to wash, and then quietly removed my clothing, folding it and placing it on a chair. When I was only in my shift, I crawled into the bed and watched as he stripped down to his undergarments and blew out the candle. He came in beside me, pulling a blanket over the both of us.

From his bed, I could see out the window, and the view was spectacular. The moon was out, casting its glossy light over the surface of the river. "It's beautiful," I murmured as he came close, resting his chin on my shoulder.

"You're beautiful," he said in my ear, sending a shiver through me. "I hate to leave you, Abigail. I feel like I am being punished for taking you from Henry."

"Don't think that way. I was never Henry's to have, and you wanted to collect Alexandre anyway. I am sorry for the loss of his mother, though."

"I will be nothing but a stranger to him. What if he hates me?"

"You're his father," I said reassuringly, although my stomach flipped at the thought of Ben's father taking him away. "Even if he does not remember you, he will get to know you again. It will just take time."

He sighed heavily and ran his hands from my shoulders down the length of my body. "Maybe we should wait until I return," he murmured, though he caressed my breasts through my shift as he spoke. "I don't want you to have to wonder about my intentions."

I let my hands roam his bare chest, smiling at the deep sound of appreciation he made in his throat. "I won't wonder," I said, smiling at him. "And I want to know your body now. But it would be best if I didn't end up with child. Can you be careful?"

In the distance, an alpha wolf howled, calling his pack. Gabriel lifted my nightdress over my head, then shucked off his own remaining clothing, a grin on his face. He settled himself on top, his full weight pressed against me. I wrapped my legs around his waist, my hands coming around the back of his neck.

"I love you, my Abigail," he whispered as his mouth began to move down my body. "Hier, aujourd'hui, et demain."

We woke before dawn, finding each other under the blanket once more. He made love to me slowly, running his hands over all of me as if trying to memorize my entire body. I did the same to him, swallowing back the swell of emotion that was creeping up my throat. How was it fair that I should finally find someone who loved me despite everything, only to have him ripped from my arms?

"Don't rush if it's not safe," I pleaded as he finally left the bed to get dressed. "Wait for the big ship from York. Don't try to hire a smaller one to take you across the ocean. They're not reliable." Smaller ships came

THE FORT

into the port in Montréal a few times a year but were notorious for never returning to shore.

He rubbed a hand over his face. "Please don't worry about me. I will make my way back to you, I promise." He leaned down and kissed me, nudging the blanket from where I held it at my shoulder, revealing my breasts to the chilly morning air. "You will be on my mind every second of the day."

I brought him down onto the bed again, the tears I had held back starting to fall. "I already miss you, and you have not yet left. How will I manage so many months away from you?"

His face creased in a frown before he cracked a smile. "Stay here," he said, gesturing to the small cabin. "As often as you'd like. Then I can think about you sleeping in my bed."

I laughed through my tears, letting him go so he could continue dressing. "Maybe I will. I'm sure Ben would enjoy that too."

I got up out of bed and started to dress myself, feeling his eyes on me. When I finished, I redid my braid, remembering the first time we had touched in my father's workshop. It had only been a few months ago, but in ways, it felt like a lifetime, as everything had changed.

Finally, we were ready. We made our way down to the riverbank, taking two of the canoes that were stored for common usage at the fort. He would paddle downriver, taking the route to the north, while I would go across, back to Fort Augustus.

He clung to me as we stood on the riverbank, our canoes bobbing in the water. "Au revoir, he whispered. "See you again, my love."

I kissed him fervently, not wanting the moment to end. "Come home to me, Gabriel."

He kissed me once more on the forehead, the whiskers from his beard tickling my skin. Then he turned and pushed my canoe into the water, lifting me up into the boat. I picked up a paddle and heard the *swish* of the water as I pushed off, sending me alone on my way to the fort.

Chapter Sixteen

I stood outside the fort gates, watching as Gabriel disappeared into a tiny speck on the horizon. With a heavy heart, I went inside and trudged to the cookhouse, where I found Ben finishing up his breakfast with Claudette and my father. I pulled up a chair and sat beside my father, taking his hand.

"Mary," he said, calling me by my mother's name. "Where have you been?"

"It's me, Abigail," I replied, "and I'm home now, Father."

"Welcome back, dear. How was the trip?" Claudette asked, motioning to one of the other women to bring me a plate of food.

I gave her a weak smile, blinking back the tears. "I'm afraid we didn't make it to the settlement. Gabriel was called away. His former wife in France has died, and his son has been placed in an orphanage. He's already left for York to catch the ship overseas."

"Oh my." She clasped a hand to her bosom in shock. "C'est terrible!"

I nodded sadly. "Yes. It will be a long time until we are able to see each other again."

She reached over and squeezed my hand just as my breakfast plate arrived. "You are young, Abigail. You will have many years together." She stood, taking Ben by the hand. "It's time for this young man to do his chores. Perhaps you can help me in the garden this morning? We can speak more then."

"Thank you, Claudette. For everything."

I ate my breakfast, watching my father out of the corner of my eye. He stared off into the distance, seemingly unaware that I was even there. I wished I could talk with him, to unload the burden of my heart.

"I had a horrible dream," I said in a quiet tone, knowing that he wasn't really hearing me. "George came and took Ben. But then I woke, and Gabriel was there, and we spoke about everything. He knows, Father. He knows all about George and how I'm not a widow. But he still loves me and accepts me as I am."

He continued looking away, and so I kept on talking. "He's going to be gone for so long, Father. I'm afraid that our time together was so short, and once he returns, his feelings may have changed. Henry says that love is fickle, and I just hope he's not right."

My father turned to me then, some clarity in his eyes. "But I love you, Mary. And that's not fickle."

I smiled and reached over to take his hand. "Yes, you loved Mother very much. We all did. And I love Ben and you. And our friends. Perhaps you're right, Father."

We left the table, my heart feeling a bit lighter, and I escorted him back to his room to rest, stopping by the blacksmith shop to greet Edmund. I would help Claudette this morning and then come back to the shop in the afternoon.

THE FORT

I found Claudette in a corner of the garden, pulling the carrots that were ready. We would spend the last weeks of summer harvesting the vegetables and preparing them to be put away in the root cellar for winter. Then, we could only hope that it was enough to feed us all for the long, cold winter ahead. Once the snow fell, the drifts measuring up to six feet or more would trap us in, making even the firewood scarce. Only the most hardened of men would venture out to check their trapline or hunt game to eat. By the time the spring thaw started, we would all be thinner and somewhat malnourished.

I joined her, bringing another basket. "Was my father like that the entire time?" I asked, getting down on my knees. "He seems worse."

"Oui. He seems to be far away most of the time now. He slept much of the day when you were away."

I nodded, biting my lip hard enough to leave a mark. I did not want to spend the entire day crying, but with Gabriel leaving and my father's rapid decline, misery had taken hold.

"What came to pass between you and Gabriel? I noticed a growing affection between the two of you these past weeks." Claudette sat back on her haunches, wiping sweat from her brow.

"He said he loves me. We plan to marry when he returns and move to Montréal. He wants to buy a farm and fill our home with babies." I smiled, my hand falling to my stomach. "Those thoughts will comfort me on the many days until his return."

"Oh, that is lovely. I can't tell you how happy I am for the both of you."

"There's more, Claudette." I hesitated, but only slightly. Now that I had been relieved of my secret, the heaviness of it seemed unbearable. "I told him the truth about Ben's father, and I'd like to tell you, too."

She looked over at me, raising her brows in surprise. "All right, my dear."

I revealed my tale in careful detail, filling her in on the way the earl had reeled me in with his charm. His constant attention when I spoke, how he appeared suddenly in the rooms I was cleaning, and eventually, the small touches and kisses peppered with assurances that what we were doing was out of love. As I spoke, I realized for the first time that Gabriel was right—I'd been a young girl who was taken advantage of by a man in power. In fact, I now wondered what might have happened if I had, in fact, said no. Would he have walked away? Fired me? Or taken what he wanted by force?

"It was then that my father decided we would come to the New World and make a fresh start. We left everything—my brothers, his blacksmith shop, and my mother's resting place. You see, he gave up everything for me."

"Yes, my father was much like that as well. May his soul rest in peace." She crossed herself in the Catholic way, leaving behind smudges of soil on her dress. "But I see that in you too, Abigail. You are a kindhearted soul. As for your story, do not dwell on the past, my dear. We all make sinful mistakes, but the good Father forgives all."

I leaned over, surprising us both by wrapping my arms around her in an embrace. If I had to be separated from Gabriel, I was happy that I had such a good friend to see me through.

THE FORT

A few days later, I took one of the canoes and paddled across the river, meaning to visit Elizabeth and some of the other women. It had been nearly a month since I left, and while I was hoping to avoid Henry and the Chief Factor, I was eager to see how my friends were faring.

I was only a few steps inside the gate when I ran into Henry, leading a man around the fort yard. The man was clearly out of place from the regular fort visitors, dressed in fine leather shoes, a man's dress coat, and a sharp top hat. An investor.

"Abby." Henry's mouth was set in a thin line as he greeted me. "Please greet Mr. Allen from the Old Country. He's a shareholder in the Hudson's Bay Company." He turned to the man. "Miss Williams hails from England, as well."

The man peered at me overtop his spectacles. "You look very familiar, dear. What did you say your given name was?"

My blood turned suddenly cold. "Abigail, but I'm sure we have never met. I'm a blacksmith's daughter." I looked away from his piercing gaze, frowning. I had never met this man before—or had I?

As he stared at me thoughtfully, recognition clicked in my mind. In the earl's library, as I was being publicly dismissed, there was a man by the window. The family lawyer.

I turned, not wanting the men to see the fluster that had risen on my cheeks. "If you'll excuse me, I'm just on my way to see Elizabeth and the other women," I said, trying desperately to leave.

"Wait." A hand reached out for my arm, fingers digging in unexpectedly hard. The dream flashed before my eyes, remembering George's firm grasp. My back was suddenly slick with sweat, and a tremor swept through my limbs.

"Kind sir," I said, bowing my head so as not to meet his eyes. "I'm going to visit a friend."

"I remember," he hissed, and my heart began to pound so forcefully I thought it would rip free of my chest. *No. This isn't happening.* I looked at Henry, pleading with my eyes. But no, Henry's affection for me was gone, and he stared at the place where the lawyer was still grasping my arm.

"You're the *trollop* that warmed the bed of the earl while under his employ," he said, loud enough that a few of the men close by paused in their work. He let go of my arm, and I rubbed the spot, frantically trying to plan my escape. "You certainly were neither the first nor the last. But for some reason, you caused the most kerfuffle. Elenore stayed locked away in her room for months after that."

"*What?*" Henry's hand reached out for my other arm, sending goosebumps racing up my limbs. "I thought you were a widow, Abby! You lied? And what of Ben? Is he a bastard child?"

I jerked free of Henry's grasp, hot tears blurring my vision. I began to breathe heavily, panting as my throat closed and my chest burned. I wanted to flee, but my legs were locked in place, keeping me as an audience to the disaster unfolding in front of me.

"There's a child?" Mr. Allen's face was in front of mine, and his breath, the rank odour of day-old whiskey, made my stomach churn. "The earl remains childless. He will be very interested to know this indeed."

I let out a squeak as Henry nodded. "Yes. A boy, around six years of age."

"My, my." The lawyer stroked his mustache. "I should be very interested in seeing him. Is he around?"

THE FORT

"At the North West Company fort. You know, this makes sense to me now. Abby was my betrothed a mere month ago, and just days ago, I found her in the arms of another man. She is clearly a woman of loose morals."

"Indeed." Mr. Allen pushed his spectacles up his nose. "Women like that are best to be avoided. Though it appears there are few women of virtue in this godforsaken place." His hand swept around the fort. "Take me to the child. I want to see if he is a likeness of the earl."

Ben! His name screamed through my mind, unfreezing my body. I turned and bolted out the fort gates. I sprinted down the path to the river, finding my canoe by the shore where I had left it. I nearly tipped it over in my scramble to get inside, and the underside of my skirt was soaked through by the time I was onboard.

With each stroke of the paddle, my panic grew. I did not dare look behind me to see if they had followed. As it was, my paddling was uneven and haphazard, and it took me much longer to reach the other side of the river than normal. Finally, the bottom of the boat scraped against the shore, and I jumped out, not bothering to pull the boat fully out of the water.

I climbed the hill to Fort Augustus, the water in my boots squishing with every step. Once inside the gate, I looked back and saw that, sure enough, Henry and Mr. Allen were getting into a canoe on the other side.

"Dammit, Abby," I whispered, tears falling at my stupidity. I should have floated the spare boats down the river to at least delay their arrival, but in my worry, I had not thought clearly.

I ran into the open yard of the fort, looking around for Ben. Where was he? The fort was so small normally, but it gaped open like a void as I frantically searched. I spotted Claudette coming out of the kitchen with jars of preserves to take to the cellar. I raced over to her, nearly bursting into tears.

"They're after Ben," I babbled, barely able to get the words out. "I need to find him." I blurted out the rest of the story as quickly as I could, and her face turned pale.

"There he is, just yonder!" She pointed to a group of children clustered around the side of the bunkhouse. I ran over, Claudette close behind.

"Ben!" I hissed, grabbing him by the elbow. I didn't want to frighten him or the other children, but time was of the essence. "Come with me!"

"This way," Claudette said, lifting her skirts to run. "Dépêche-toi! Hurry!"

We ran to the fur warehouse, and Claudette produced a key from her apron. The warehouse was nearly empty, save for a small stack of furs, as they had all been transported to Fort William and Montréal during the spring and summer months. There was, however, a pile of blankets on the ground in one corner, and I dragged Ben over to them.

"Ben, I'm sorry, but you must hide here. Do not come out unless it's me or Claudette, you hear?"

He nodded, his eyes full of fear. I gave him a kiss on the forehead, then lifted the blankets. He scurried underneath, and I arranged the blankets so his shape would not be visible.

"Abigail," Claudette hissed from the door. "You must go outside to the blacksmith shop, ready to distract them, and I will make sure no one finds Ben."

I ran across the warehouse, hating that the heels of my boots echoed across the wooden floor. I was not sure it was of any use, as Henry knew

THE FORT

that Ben was here. My only hope was to somehow distract them from seeing—or taking—Ben. He *was* a likeness of George, and Mr. Allen would not hesitate to claim ownership on the earl's behalf. With no husband to protect me, I was no safer than the beaver in the trapper's snare.

I had made it to just outside of the blacksmith shop when Henry and the lawyer strode through the gates. Every inch of my body was clenched tight, and my fear had started to turn into fury. How dare Henry betray me like this?

The men came over, an arrogant smirk on Henry's face. He pulled George's pocket watch out, dangling it for me to see. The idea that he had kept it on his person made it seem like he had been waiting to smoke me out, like a predator lurking in wait for its prey. Now, there would be no doubt in either man's mind about the truth of my story.

"Where's the boy?" he barked, puffing his chest in importance. "Mr. Allen would like to see your son."

"You're mistaken," I said breathlessly, still clinging onto a shred of my wits. "I was raped on the passage over from England."

Henry raised his eyebrows as if counting the number of men that had tainted me. "A lie, I'm sure. Search the place," he commanded at a few of his fellow officers who had followed them in. "If you don't find him, take her father. I'm sure she'll be more agreeable then."

I stared after him as they walked off, my whole body shaking. A cool hand came to my arm, and I snapped my head to see Edmund, his nostrils flaring in rage.

"You will not let him touch your father," he said in a low, threatening voice. He handed me the heavy iron tongs from the shop. "Do what you have to, Abby."

The tongs were reassuring in my hand, and with Edmund's words in my head and fear of losing my son or my father pumping through my veins, I ran after the men. Their backs were to me, and when I reached them, I took the tongs in both hands, set my jaw, and swung, aiming for Henry's knee.

He screamed when I made contact, a loud *crack* indicating that I had struck the bone. He fell to the ground, and I stepped over him, the tongs still firmly in my grasp.

"You selfish pig!" I yelled, spit flying from my mouth. "I *hate* you." I whirled, wielding the tongs at the other men. Mr. Allen took a few steps back, hiding behind one of the officers.

"What in heaven's sake is going on?" Chief Factor Rowand loomed over us, taking in the HBC officers, Henry, and my grasp on the tongs. "What's the matter, Abigail?"

"They're after her son and threatened her father." Edmund came up behind me, wiping his hands on his leather work apron. "I suspect this one is sore because she broke off their engagement." He nodded at Henry, who was writhing in pain on the ground.

The Chief Factor looked at me, his face a mask of confusion. I shook my head, not able to explain. He reached out for the tongs, pulling me away from the men. "Go and sit with your father," he said in a kind tone. "You are an employee of the North West Company, and I will not allow them back inside this fort." He turned to the men. "Leave. Now."

I turned and fled the scene, running past the crowd that had gathered, past Claudette, past the warehouse where my son lay hidden in fear. I ran to the edge of the garden and vomited into a bush. It was a nightmare—my worst nightmare—coming true.

Chapter Seventeen

I sat in the warehouse with Ben until after dark, replaying the scene of the afternoon over and over in my mind. How could I keep Ben safe? Claudette brought us dinner, encouraging me to come and sleep in the bunkhouse, but I refused. My guts were a twisted mess, and I would only keep the others awake. I asked her to look in on my father, and she smiled sadly and nodded.

I fell into an uneasy sleep in the late hours of the night, wrapped in one of the fort blankets on the warehouse floor. I woke again to Ben snuggling up against me, his clammy fingers grasping mine. He had become uncovered in his sleep and was cold.

The sharp smell of smoke caught my attention as I stood up to collect another blanket for Ben. I sniffed the air again. A foreboding shudder crept its way up my spine, as it seemed unlikely anyone would be using the outdoor hearth at this time of night.

I eased open the warehouse door, still wary from the events of the day, peeking my head out. The scent of fire was strong, and although I saw nothing at first, I spotted sparks coming from the direction of the

169

blacksmith shop. As I crept out further, I saw that smoke billowed in thick black plumes, making the night sky above an inky white.

I ran back inside and snatched Ben, holding his sleepy body tight in my arms. Then I ran to the bunkhouse, my heart pumping. "Fire! Fire in the blacksmith shop!"

A commotion exploded around me as men, women, and children jumped from their beds, on high alert. I pushed through the crowded rooms, my arms aching from the weight of Ben. Folks scrambled to and fro, collecting their children and prized collections. The air was smoky, and by the time I found my father I was breathing heavily.

"Abigail? What's going on?"

"Come, Father, let's go." I wanted to throw my arms around him in relief that he was lucid. A strange consolation that he remembered me on what was undoubtedly the worst day of my life. I tugged on his arm. "We must make haste down to the river. There's a fire in the blacksmith shop."

"A fire? Did Edmund not bank the forge before he left?"

"Come, Father, hurry." I helped him to his feet. We exited the bunkhouse, following the throng of people down to the river. Already, able-bodied men and women had formed a line from the river up into the fort yard, passing along buckets of water. I hesitated, wanting to help but not wanting to leave my father or Ben alone in the frenzy. I directed them both to a nearby log, with strict instructions to stay put, then headed back to assist.

A movement caught my eye across the river, illuminated by the bright moon above. There, watching us from the other side, were the murky shadows of a few men. I recognized the tall, broad stance of a man, though he was leaning heavily on a cane. *Henry.* Had they snuck into the fort and set fire to the blacksmith shop while we slept? It was unlikely that Edmund had forgotten to bank the forge since he did so every day.

"Is everyone accounted for?" the Chief Factor shouted, coming down to the bank. He came over to me and followed my gaze across the river, scowling as he saw Henry and the other men watching us. "There's going to be hell to pay for this, mark my words."

I swallowed hard, looking back up at the fort where the smoke plumed in the night air. Men came out of the fort yard with their faces streaked with black soot while more ran in to replace them. This was all because of me, because of my past. There would be hell to pay, and not just for Henry it seemed. Everything I had dreamt of—rest for my father in his final days, a marriage to Gabriel, a father for my son, more children—disintegrated into ash, wafting up into the smoky sky.

"It was because of me," I managed, my voice catching.

Squeezing my arm in a reassuring way, the Chief Factor glanced up at the fire. The flames had diminished, leaving a thick black cloud behind. "It looks like God was with us, and there is no wind tonight. Let's speak about this further in the morning." He left, going back up the slope to venture into the yard.

My hands shook as I buried my face in them. I was not this strong. I did not possess this much courage. Had I committed such a grave sin that my life would never be peaceful?

I sat with my father and Ben until the morning light began to colour the sky in streaks of yellow, orange, and red. The fire had been put out, with only the blacksmith shop and part of the palisade needing repair. Ben had fallen back asleep, his head in my lap, and I stroked his hair, bringing me quiet calm. We must leave this place—that much was clear. I would never want the other patrons of the fort to be put at risk again. But where or how, I had no notion. Would I ever see Gabriel again? What would happen when he returned and I was not here?

"Father," I said, praying that he was still lucid and able to converse, "I'm afraid our time here is at an end." I took a shaky breath. "I must take Ben. Those men are after him."

He sighed heavily. "I know, darling. I heard when you spoke with the Chief Factor. But I must stay behind. I cannot be a burden for you in your travels."

I wanted to protest. I wanted to scream and cry and bang my fists on the ground like a small child unable to get their own way. But what he said was the truth. I could not care for him while we travelled. "I will return in the spring," I promised, reaching out to hold his hand. "We will see each other once more. I'm so sorry, Father. I must protect Ben."

There was a shuffling in the grass behind us, and I turned to see the Chief Factor. His face bore the labour of the night, and his exhausted expression reflected turmoil and strife. He was a kind man and did not want to displace me.

"Come, Abigail." He spoke softly like I was a child about to receive a reprimand from a caring parent. "We must speak in my office."

I woke Ben, and the three of us followed him back into the fort. The pungent smell of burning was overpowering, and I looked reluctantly at the remains of the blacksmith shop. A group of men continued to watch

THE FORT

the fire site to ensure that all embers had been put out. Their faces were smudged, eyes red from the sting of the smoke.

When we were seated in the office, Ben on my lap, the Chief Factor poured us tea and offered a biscuit. I took them gratefully, hoping to quell the ache in my chest.

"I'm afraid this is a direct attack on me." My voice came out high and pitchy, and my stomach lurched at what I needed to say next. "They're after my son. His father is a childless nobleman whom I bedded some years ago. The man who was with Henry—Officer Davies—yesterday afternoon is their family lawyer, and he was very interested in Ben."

Ben pulled away from my chest, his blond hair askew. "No, Mama. I want to stay with you."

"No one is taking you from me, Ben. Not ever," I assured him, pulling him tight. He buried his face against me with the unconditional love of a young child. I was perfect in his eyes, and he trusted I would keep him safe.

The Chief Factor cleared his throat. "I hate to suggest this so late in the season, but maybe it's best if you leave for a while, Abigail. At least until this lawyer returns to England. I'm afraid you've made yourself an enemy of Officer Davies. And while we cannot say for certain that this was the doing of the officer ..." he paused, taking a sip of tea and looking at me with regret, "it's my job to care about the safety and well-being of all persons in the fort. Therefore, I must ask you to leave."

"I understand," I said, biting my lip to keep from crying. I cast a glance at my father, who was staring out the window. Somehow, some way, I would find my way to a nearby settlement or neighbouring fort. By the spring or summer, Henry would have left, being dispatched to his new posting, and Gabriel might return by the fall. I felt a small flicker of hope that not all was lost.

"I've arranged for you to travel with McTavish and his brigade, who leave tomorrow morning for Fort William. They wish to winter there and have agreed to take you and the boy. Your father will remain here with us."

"Fort William?" My heart sank. Fort William was across the country, on the bank of Lake Superior. It would be nearly impossible for me to make my way back in the spring alone. "Is it not possible to lodge somewhere closer? I don't know how I will make it back here by myself."

He took a long look at Ben before he replied. "If what you say is true, that they are after your son, it is probably best that you don't remain close. Or return, for that matter. This lawyer won't be able to find you easily if you winter farther away, then disappear in the spring."

I leaned back in the chair, not able to hide my emotions any longer. "Disappear?" I repeated, my voice shaking with my unshed tears. That meant I would be saying goodbye to my father forever. And what of Gabriel? Could I dare hope that he would come to find me?

Mr. Rowand cleared his throat uncomfortably. "One of the men will take you to a waiting point in the forest in an hour. I will meet with the Chief Factor of Fort Edmonton later this morning, and I think it's best if you are not here. I can tell a tale of how you fled." He held out a rucksack. "I've taken the liberty of getting one of the men to prepare a few supplies for you. Some warm clothing, new walking moccasins for you and your boy, pemmican, and a small purse of coins."

I swallowed back my grief and tried to take a steadying breath. My father snaked his hand over my lap and squeezed my fingers, his grip still

THE FORT

strong despite his ailing mind. "Thank you, sir. I hope to repay your kindness one day."

He stood, coming over and putting a heavy hand on my shoulder. "When you are able, pay the kind deed on to someone else," he said. "Now, go and say your farewells and gather any personal items of sentiment. Not too much, though, as you'll need to keep up to the pace of McTavish and his men."

I nodded, taking my father's hand as we exited the office. I wanted to go to my bed in the bunkhouse, crawl under the covers, and cry myself to sleep. Yet, I was to leave everything and everyone behind in a mere hour.

My father made his way over to his bed as soon as we entered the bunkhouse. I let him, knowing he was exhausted. It would be easier for all of us this way—when he woke, we would be gone. I helped him pull up the covers and tucked him in. My tears mixed with the saltiness of his skin as I kissed his forehead in a farewell, my heart breaking. First Mabel and Gabriel, and now my father. I wasn't sure I would ever feel whole again.

On my side of the bunkhouse, I opened the rucksack and packed extra clothes for myself and Ben. I put in our mittens and knit hats and rolled a blanket to tie below the pack. Then, I retrieved the rifle that Gabriel had given me from under the bed. I hoped I wouldn't need it, but it seemed foolish not to take it. I longed for my farrier's knife and one of my lucky horseshoes, but all our tools—any physical reminder of my father's trade—were still smouldering from the remains of the fire.

In what seemed less than an hour later, a man knocked at the door. "Ma'am? I'm to take you over to a safe shelter, where you'll wait for McTavish in the mornin'."

I nodded and took a deep breath, taking Ben's hand firmly in mine. He was frightened, not fully understanding why we had to leave. I had to stay courageous for his sake as we were led into the unknown. I dried my eyes, locking my fear away.

"Goodbye, Father," I whispered as we left the bunkhouse. I felt a small comfort in knowing that Chief Factor Rowand was a good man. He would not treat my father unkindly, and when the time came, he would lay him to rest with respect.

Claudette came running over to us as we walked through the yard, her face crumpled. "Oh sweet, Abigail, I have heard everything. C'est vraiment tragique." She thrust a small bundle at me. "Food for tonight and une figurine of Saint Christopher, for the long journey. I will pray every morning and every night for your health and safety."

I threw myself into her embrace, trying to draw strength from her for the days ahead. "In the spring, I will make my way to Montréal. It will be too far for me to return here."

"Oui." She nodded in agreement. "I shall tell Gabriel everything and that he must find you there."

"I'm afraid he may not think I'm worth the trouble," I replied, my voice cracking, not wanting to think about Gabriel too much. If I did, I would not be able to face the journey ahead.

"Ah, non! He will find you, somehow. Your love will bring you together."

I hugged her once more, blinking away hot tears. I was leaving without saying goodbye to Elizabeth and my other friends, sneaking away like a thief in the night. A swift current of anger flashed through me. Henry was like a petulant child, punishing me for choosing Gabriel over him.

THE FORT

We walked for an hour behind the man, not talking as we crunched our way through the forest. Finally, we arrived at a rustic shelter of a few logs fashioned into a rough lean-to. It would house Ben and me for the night and provide some protection from the chill, but not much. The man stayed long enough to help me light a fire for warmth, and then he disappeared back into the woods, leaving us alone.

"Mama? Is it just us now?" Ben looked around the forest, where unknown dangers lurked.

I pulled him close into my arms. "Don't fret. Everything will be all right." I squeezed my eyes shut, wishing I could believe my own words. "It's always been just us, my sweet boy."

Chapter Eighteen

McTavish was a giant of a man who towered as tall as the lean-to where Ben and I had spent the night. He scowled at me, his face a weathered brown, as craggy as a jagged mountainside.

"Up," he barked as I blinked in the early morning sunshine. I had thought I wouldn't be able to fall asleep alone in the shadows of the forest, but the events of the last week had caught up with me, and I had slept soundly.

I sat up, and his frown deepened further. He threw me a pair of men's trousers. "Change outta yer dress. You'll need to wear britches to keep up with the men." His Scottish brogue was thick, and I strained to understand him. For some reason, his accent reminded me of Gabriel, and a swell of emotion lodged in my throat.

"Be quick about it. I dinna have time to wait for a tardy Englishwoman. I'm no' too pleased I got saddled with the job of takin' ya on, so ya best cause me no trouble, ya hear?"

I nodded, waiting for him to leave and give me privacy, but he merely turned his back. I widened my eyes in surprise but climbed out of the

178

THE FORT

lean-to, not hesitating to obey his word. The last thing Ben and I needed was to be left behind in the forest by an impatient Scot.

I got dressed quickly, then took out the walking moccasins provided by the Chief Factor. The bottoms were made of a thick moose hide, and I felt another surge of gratefulness for the man, who, despite knowing me only a short time, had ensured I would be taken care of. I pulled off my boots and slipped on the thicker-soled moccasins.

A sharp *tsk* came from McTavish. "Nay, lass. Not like that." He walked over and reached down to grab my bare foot in his hand. I yelped as he pulled it up for inspection. "Yer foot is as soft as a bairn's arse. You'll be rubbed raw before midday."

Before I could protest, he took my discarded skirt and proceeded to shred it into strips, using a knife from his belt. I watched, my mouth hanging open. Had the Chief Factor left me in the hands of a madman?

Finished with the decimation of one of my few precious items of clothing, he came over, sat across from me and pulled my foot into his lap. When he pushed up my trouser leg to expose my bare calf, I tensed, trying to pull away. This man was very forward, touching my bare skin.

"The journey to Fort William will take us a month or so," he explained, not looking up as he wound the strips of fabric tightly around my foot and up to my ankle. "A hundred miles a day, by boat and on foot, ya hear? My men will no' wait on ya, no matter how bonnie ya are."

Satisfied with the binding, he did the other foot. Then he gestured at Ben. "Do the same for yer boy. Though I suspect you'll need to carry 'im through the roughest parts."

I scurried over to Ben, my heart racing. A hundred miles a day? Surely, I could not be expected to walk that far. I was stronger than most women

179

due to helping my father blacksmith, but what McTavish described was unthinkable.

I finished binding Ben's feet in the same fashion, then rolled up our blanket and slung the rifle over my shoulder. The tall Scotsman raised his bushy eyebrows at me but said nothing, leading us on a brisk march through the woods.

The rest of the voyageurs were near the river's edge, loading two long birchbark canoes full of furs and other supplies. I heard some of the men speaking in French while others spoke in the same rough brogue as McTavish. They all fell silent as I approached, and I reached out for Ben's hands, feeling my cheeks colour at their stares.

One of the men muttered something in French, earning a wave of chuckles from the others. I lifted my chin in defiance, knowing that the comment was nothing complimentary. I was a woman, and an English one, in their midst. Both the French and the Scots thought of me as their enemy because of my accent alone.

I waited for McTavish to introduce me, but he instead pointed to the middle of one boat. "You'll sit in the middle. They'll be no squirmin' about or stoppin', so I suggest ya piss before we leave."

He barked orders at a few of the men, and I took Ben over behind a bush to relieve ourselves. "Mama," he whispered as I squatted down, "I'm scared of that man."

"I know," I whispered back, "but we mustn't complain. Once we reach the fort, we never have to see him again."

"I want to see Gabriel," he whimpered, his lower lip trembling. "Why can't we travel with him?"

"Gabriel went to get his son from France," I explained with a twinge in my chest, "but he'll come to find us in Montréal. And when he does,

THE FORT

we're going to live on a farm. With a garden and crops and all sorts of animals."

His face became less fearful, and a smile pulled at the corner of his mouth. "What sort of animals?"

I stood, pulling up my trousers and belted them tight, as they were much too large at the waist. "Cows, chickens, maybe some pigs. And Gabriel's son, Alexandre, can be your new brother if you'd like."

He nodded enthusiastically, hair bouncing on his forehead. "Yes, I'd like that. How old is he?"

I smiled, my heart lifting an inch, and ruffled his hair. "He's just a few years older than you. But for now, we must not give up. The next four or five weeks will be difficult, and it might be some time before Gabriel can come to us. We will keep that dream tucked away in our hearts."

"All right, Mama. But what about Papa? We've left him behind."

"Yes." We walked out from behind the bushes towards the bank, where the men were making final preparations. I swallowed back the deep regret I had about leaving my father alone. It made my heart ache just to think of it. "Papa is too ill to make the long journey, Ben. But Claudette and Mr. Rowand will take care of him."

The man closest to me motioned for Ben and me to board the canoe. As we took our places, I turned and took one fleeting look downriver. Fort Edmonton was barely visible in the distance, covered by a thick morning fog. The men settled in around us, lifting their paddles up in unison. McTavish, who was the guide and bowman, sat in the front. On his command, the voyageurs dipped their paddles into the water, and with a swiftness that startled me, we were on our way.

The men paddled until midmorning, pausing only once to rest their arms and smoke from their pipes. The smell of the sweet tobacco tugged at my heartstrings, making me wonder if I would ever smell it again on the man I had grown to love. I closed my eyes for a second, thinking of his blue eyes when he smiled and how safe I had felt in his arms, ever so briefly.

When we finally stopped, I lumbered out of the canoe, taking Ben by the hand, my supplies on my back. I was not but a few steps onto the shore when a large hand came down heavily on my shoulder.

"Up ya go, lad," McTavish said, lifting Ben up to cling to my front. Then, using leather straps that had secured the load into the canoe, he fastened Ben to me. On top of the rucksack, he added another smaller bundle. "Yer food ration. I suggest you keep it on yer person or one of the men is liable to swipe it from ya." He paused, looking up the steep hill that we were about to climb. "Once ya reach the top, yer job will be to check the boats fer leaks. I'll show ya how, just this once. The men will be taking a few trips to carry the load, so try to stay to the side while they pass, ya hear?"

I nodded, then set on my way, not wanting to appear slow off the mark. It took a few steps to gain my balance, as I had a heavy load on both my back and front. Soon, men began to pass me, their backs laden with two or more bundles, with straps secured to their foreheads to help support the load. The canoes came past too, propped up on the heads of a few men. Their pace was fast, and I quickened mine, knowing that despite their multiple trips, they might very well beat me.

THE FORT

Twenty minutes later, I was thoroughly spent, panting loudly as I took step after burning step up the steep incline. Sweat dripped off my forehead, and Ben's head jostled uncomfortably against my shoulder. I felt weak and shaky; the food Claudette had given us was a distant memory in my stomach. The muscles in my legs screamed in agony, but I did not stop. This was only the first portage, and I would be a laughingstock if I could not make it. Instead, I gritted my teeth and focused my mind on my mission: saving Ben from the hands of Henry and that awful lawyer.

Nearly forty minutes later, I reached the top, my legs shaking something fierce as I made the final few steps toward McTavish. His arms were crossed over his chest, and I eyed the thick, ropy muscles of his forearms. His hands were so large and strong they looked like they could take a human life in seconds—and for a moment, I wondered if they had. I knew nothing of these men, and I had to trust them with my safety.

He unstrapped Ben from me and thrust a tin cup into my hand, jerking his head towards the river. I went to the bank as fast as my wobbling legs could take me, knelt, and drank three cups of the cool, flowing water. I dipped it in for a fourth, but I heard McTavish *tsk* from behind me.

"We'll portage again in an hour," he informed me, leaning down to take the cup from my hands. "You'll be emptyin' yer guts on the path if ya have more."

McTavish didn't give me time to wonder if I could possibly keep up for the entirety of the day before he dragged me over to the birchbark canoes, which were now flipped over with the bottoms faced skyward. He ran his hands over the seams, showing me where the puckered areas needed attention.

"You'll use this," he said, handing me a thick, sticky wad. "Gum of the spruce tree. Just a little will do the trick." He smeared a small amount over the area. "I expect ya to do a proper job each time we stop." With that, he was gone, headed back down the path for another load of supplies to carry to the top.

"Ben, go to the pack and get us some of the pemmican," I said as I carefully inspected the boats, applying the gum where needed. He brought over the sack, and I broke off a small piece for each of us. I grimaced as I put it in my mouth, as I didn't care for the taste. Still, the meat, fat, and berries were nourishing, and the men did not seem to be stopping to eat. I suspected that by the time we reached Fort William, I would be nearing skin and bones.

Soon, the men were done, and we were on our way on the water once more. I realized that the men were seated in the canoes according to their rank—the most important sat in the front and back to steer, while the ones in the middle did most of the grunt work. The boy that sat in front of me was no older than Edmund, though he smelled rank, like he had not washed in some time. They sang on this part of the trip, alternating between songs of the Scots and tunes in French. The repetitive stroke of the paddle served as tempo, keeping the men in time with the cadence of their voices.

By late afternoon, I was bone-weary. My legs had grown exceedingly tired with each portage and then stiffened while I sat crunched up in the canoe. My feet were indeed rubbed raw, as McTavish had predicted, and I winced with every painful step. The men had stopped only once to eat, a pot of porridge that we all shared, though I saw them chewing pemmican while they worked. The weight of my ration pack seemed too light for the days ahead, and I scoured the path for berries or mushrooms

THE FORT

that I might use to supplement this strict diet. Finally, just as the sun was sinking into the horizon, McTavish announced that we were stopping for the day. I nearly cried out in relief but managed to keep a stoic face in front of the men as I set up a sleeping area for Ben and myself. How would I continue tomorrow and the days after?

McTavish came over just as I was about to crawl under the blanket, where Ben was already asleep. Though he had not done much walking, the day had been trying for him as well.

"Let me see yer feet," he demanded roughly, a lit pipe clenched between his teeth. I sighed but did as he said, sitting and pulling off the moccasins and bindings. There was blood staining the places where blisters had formed and burst.

"Tomorro' we'll be climbing rocky terrain," he said, peering down at the bottom of my exposed feet. "Go and soak them feet in the river now for as long as ya can manage. Then come back to me and I'll bind 'em again before ya sleep. Or you'll find 'em so swole in the mornin' that ya can't get yer moccasins back on."

I nodded, wanting nothing more than to sleep, but heeded his word and limped down to the bank. I pushed the fabric of my pants above my knees, not caring in the least that my bare legs were exposed in the company of many men. Modesty seemed trivial now, and I couldn't care less what anyone thought. Then I plunged my feet and legs into the cold water, whimpering at the sharp sting. After a few minutes, though, I realized that McTavish was right in his methods, as the cold water soothed the open wounds and relieved my aching muscles.

The smell of frying fish reached my nose, and my stomach growled noisily. I glanced over my shoulder at the men, sharing food and drink together after the long day. None would be offered to me, nor would I be invited to join their circle. I was an outsider, no more than extra weight they were required to row.

The sting that had left my feet settled in the back of my throat as I tried to keep my tears at bay. I felt sorrier for myself more than ever. Everything had been stripped away from me, and I was nothing but a troublesome burden to those around me. Perhaps in the spring, instead of waiting in Montréal for Gabriel, I would board a ship to England. At least there, I would blend in with my own kind.

A large body settled next to me, jolting me out of my reverie. McTavish held out a dinner plate and gestured for my feet and legs, holding a calico cloth. Once he had dried them off, he bound them tighter than he had done in the morning. I watched him with an exhausted stare, wanting to be stubborn about accepting the food, but I was too hungry to protest. Despite his size, his fingers were nimble and swift, and he finished the job quickly, slipping my moccasins back on.

"Thank you," I said, though not even a small part of me felt grateful in that moment.

He grunted in response. "Go and get yer rest, lass. We leave before sunrise."

Chapter Nineteen

I tensed as heavy footsteps approached the wooded area where Ben and I lay. Despite being physically exhausted, I had not slept well. My entire body was stiff and sore, and I had spent the night with half an eye open. Being in the company of strange men made me anxious, on top of everything else.

"It's time, lass." I sat up before McTavish had even turned his back, shaking Ben awake. I wanted to have time to make a meal before we left, as the day before had been a struggle with so little food. The rations that McTavish had given me were a collection of oats, wild rice, cornmeal, dried beans and peas, and a few strips of salt pork. I would need to borrow a pot and hope that a fire had already been lit.

I packed up our items, Ben rubbing his eyes sleepily. It was still dark, though a smudge of orange peeked out at the far edge of the river, promising that morning was not far away. I brought our supplies out to the main camp, noting with dismay that the men were already loading the canoes.

"Will we not eat?" I asked the one closest to me, my stomach rumbling noisily at the mere mention of food.

"Non. A storm is coming in, so we need to get a head start." He pointed to my place in the canoe. "Allons-y. Get in, and make sure to sit still. It would be a catastrophe to capsize."

I sighed to myself but did as he said, lifting Ben into the boat before getting in myself. Being out in the middle of a storm sounded dreadful, and I could only hope that we would be able to stop for shelter when it did.

McTavish waded into the water, sending waves that rocked the boat. He tossed me a pair of woollen toques. "For the rain. We'll go as far as we can before we stop. Bundle up."

I pulled on a toque and gave Ben his, pulling out a strip of salt pork from the rucksack for us both. He grabbed it from my outstretched hand and then settled back on my lap, leaning against my chest.

"I like the canoes," he murmured contentedly. "Maybe when I get bigger, I can join the voyageurs."

"Aye." One of the nearby men leaned over and gave him a playful cuff on the chin. "You're a braw lad who'll do just fine."

Ben snuggled tight against me, shy at the attention. I smiled at him as we pulled out from shore and were on our way. McTavish led them at a backbreaking pace, and I marvelled at the strength of these men. I was spent just from walking, but they had rowed for hours on end and portaged much heavier loads.

Soon, we were a good distance down the river, and the sun rose, warming my face. It was a lovely morning, and the weather seemed far from stormy, but by the set of McTavish's jaw, I knew better than to judge his decision. I chewed a second pork strip thoughtfully, watching

THE FORT

the large Scotsman as he rowed. Powerful muscles flexed through his shoulders and back, the profile of his face tight and determined. I found myself wondering about him and the other men. Did they have wives and children waiting for them somewhere? Or were they men who were content to be one with the wilderness, living outdoors? Once again, I felt the heavy uncertainty of whether I would ever see Gabriel again, my own man of the woods. With each stroke in the water, I felt farther and farther away.

An hour later, the men stopped to light their pipes for a break. The one that had spoken with Ben earlier removed his shirt, dipping it in the water to wipe the sweat from his face and chest. He caught my eye as he put it back on, giving me a cheeky grin. I averted my eyes, my cheeks warm, but it was too late. He had seen me looking and had certainly gotten the wrong impression. He leaned over to talk with me but was interrupted by the watchful eye of our captain.

"McInnis, there'll be none of that. Keep yer lecherous grin to yerself, ya hear? I'll no' have any lewd behaviour with the missus here. She's all alone." McTavish's tone was sharp and intimidating, and I found my face burning as all the men turned to look.

"I'm fine," I said, pulling Ben a little tighter as a shield against my discomfort. Then, for good measure, I added, "My betrothed will meet me in Montréal when he is able. I'm only alone for now."

"Aye," one of the men near the front said loudly, "But is it the English officer or the Frenchman Bouchard? No one at Fort Augustus knew where your loyalties lay."

"Pro'ly both," another chirped, raising a chuckle from the others, the smoke of their pipes thick among them.

189

CHRISTY K. LEE

"Not both," I snapped, my ire raised. I was tired of being painted as wanton when I was, in fact, a good woman and mother. "And I don't see it as any of your business."

"Tell us your story then, lass. We've got nothin' better to do, and you'll find us a fair listenin' ear." McInnis, the one that had removed his shirt, spoke, having the decency to look sheepish at how I was being badgered.

"I think not," I replied coldly, still burning from their previous remarks. I would not share my heartbreak with these men while we sat on the open water. Keeping my pain close was the only way I could keep going. If I let it go, I would be weak, vulnerable, and as McTavish had pointed out, alone.

He shrugged and turned his back to me. The other men did the same, ignoring me for the remainder of their break. I stared out at the water, grateful for the reprieve from their inquiry, though I noticed McTavish glance at me a few times from the corner of my eye.

We rowed for another hour, and sure enough, by the time we stopped for the portage, it had started to rain. I glanced up at the path where the canoes had already disappeared on the shoulders of a few men. It was narrow and winding, taking us up a steep rock face. Once McTavish had helped me strap Ben on, I followed the last of the men up the rocky path.

As I climbed, I felt every jagged rock edge through the soles of my moccasins. The wind picked up, whipping my hair loose from its braid. I struggled to see, worried I would lose my footing. Men passed me, and although I longed to ask for a steadying hand, I refused to utter a plea. Some twenty minutes of climbing later, I reached the top, exhausted, a solid lump forming in my gut to see that the path was even more treacherous ahead. A steep wall of rock loomed on one side of the narrow path, with a sharp drop down the cliffside on the other.

THE FORT

"Mama," Ben whimpered against my chest as the wind howled around us like a wild animal, pelting rain against my face. I hesitated, wondering if I should wait for the men to return for their next load, but there was no one in sight. I took a deep breath and started out on the path alone, pressing my body as closely to the rock wall as possible with Ben strapped to my front, not daring to look down into the cavern below.

My legs shook, though this time in fear, as I carefully picked my way along the path. I could scarcely see, feeling my way along the ledge with my hands. My hair flew into my eyes, blinding me, but I did not dare to stop and retie it, as my balance was already precarious. Our clothes flapped violently around us, and the weight of the pack on my back became unbearable, threatening to send us over the edge.

"Mama!" Ben screamed as a twig flew at us, slapping him across the face. He started to cry, a frenetic wail that sent my panic into full flight.

"Hush, Ben!" I yelled over the shriek of the wind, my hands becoming clammy as I clung desperately to the rock face. Where was everyone else? Had they reached the safety of the other side and forgotten about us? I started to cry, my chest tight, and I struggled to breathe, plastered against the side of the cliff. My thoughts turned to my father, how he had given me everything, only for me to leave him and end up dead at the bottom of a cavern a few days later. I wanted to beg, to bargain, but I was almost certain God had no room in his heart for me. It was just me alone, clinging onto a precipice in the middle of a windstorm. So, I gathered my courage and took another step forward.

"Lass!" It was McTavish standing in front of me, his red tunic flapping up around his waist, his own hair askew in what was now a torrential downpour. "Give me yer hand!"

I reached out a shaky hand and he clamped it in his own, holding me steady. Then he led me, step by slow step, along the narrow ledge. Ben continued to cry, but McTavish paid him no mind, only providing me with a reassuring squeeze of the hand every so often.

After what seemed an eternity, we stepped down off the ledge and after a few more minutes, arrived at the camp, where the men had set up a shelter using a length of tarpaulin and the canoes propped up with pieces of wood. Before McTavish could lead me to it, I threw my arms around his thick waist, hugging him tight, Ben squished between us.

"Thank you," I sobbed against him, my legs barely able to keep me upright. He startled, seemingly unsure of what to do with the embrace. Finally, he patted me on the back with a gentle hand.

"There, there, lass. Ya gave us all a fright when we realized the two of ya were stuck on the ledge. It was McInnis who noticed, truth be told."

I nodded my thanks to McInnis who helped me unstrap Ben and then gave us a dry blanket and led us over to the fire. We huddled under it, sitting as close to the blazing fire as we could. A few minutes later, one of the Frenchmen handed us steaming bowls of rice and peas.

"Oh," I said, taken aback by the sudden thoughtfulness from the men. "I have my own rations I can make."

He waved me off. "Don't worry, chérie. We'll eat from yours another day."

I nodded, but his term of endearment made my heart flutter. I missed Gabriel desperately but had found newfound courage, somehow. I had brushed past death, and yet, with the help of steady hand, would see another day. I did not want to squander another moment afraid.

THE FORT

After I finished the bowl of food, McTavish handed me a mug. "Hot whiskey for yer nerves," he said, coming to sit beside me and Ben. I took a sip, coughing a bit as the spirits bit the back of my throat.

"I'm Abby," I said to him, realizing that I had never given him my name. "Do you have a name, or is it just McTavish?"

He grinned, showing a row of teeth stained brown from his pipe. "Aye. 'Tis Duncan McTavish. Should I call you Abby, then, lass? I prefer McTavish though, if it's all the same to ya."

I smiled up at him. "Yes, please. And this is Ben."

Ben stuck his hand out to the large man. "Pleased to meet you, Mister."

McTavish barked out a laugh as he took Ben's little hand in his massive one. Then, more seriously, he turned to me. "Can I give ya a piece of advice, Abby? Talk to the men. Tell them yer story. Even if it's just a part of it. We're all tired of hearin' the same tales from each other's company. Ya might find it nice to have a few men watchin' out for ya once we reach Fort William. Even if yer man is on his way to meet ya."

I considered his advice. When I had told my story to Gabriel and Claudette, they had still accepted me without condition. Others like Henry, however, had called me names and questioned my reputation as a good and honest person. I couldn't decide if I was better to hide my past, letting the secret dictate my actions, or to live freely and risk the judgement of those around me.

"All right," I said finally, taking a swig of the whiskey. "I'll tell them. But I'm warning you, you may not like me once you know the truth about me."

Without waiting for his response, I took Ben by the hand and joined the others, who were sitting close to the canoes. It was time for my son to know the truth about his father, too.

"I'm ready to tell you my story," I said to the group. "If you still want to know."

Some of the men nodded, saying yes. A bottle was passed around the circle as I found a place to sit. Then, I cleared my throat and began. I started at the beginning, telling them of how I had taken the job at the earl's estate, a good line of work for a woman of my status. Of falling in love with George. How he had left me brokenhearted and with child. That my father, my hero, had given up his life in England to ensure that his daughter would not live in shame. I told them of our time in York and how we had taken the position at Fort Edmonton despite my father's failing memory. I told them of Henry and then Gabriel. Of Gabriel's departure and how, now that I had fled, I was unsure if he would find it worthy to search for me. Finally, I told them of how the earl's family lawyer had recognized me and of Henry's betrayal.

I was met with silence as I finished, with only the sound of the wind battering the tarp behind us. I squeezed Ben's hand in comfort, wondering what he was thinking. Then, one of the men cleared his throat.

"So that dirty bastard Davies was the one that lit fire to the fort?"

I nodded, draining the rest of the whiskey from my cup. It had warmed my insides and numbed my worry like McTavish promised. "I don't know for certain, but I think it was Henry, yes."

"I know Gabriel," one of the Frenchmen piped up. "He's a good man. He'll leave no stone unturned looking for you."

THE FORT

Another man rose to his feet, offering Ben his hand. "Come, lad. I'll show you how to be a voyageur." Leaning in closer to me, he said in a low voice, "I know what it is to have no Pa. You're doin' a good job, lass."

I swallowed hard, willing myself not to cry in front of these roughened men. Their kindness was unexpected, and for the first time in days, I felt a small dash of hope for the future.

The rain had eased, and now only a light mist touched my face as I excused myself from the crowd of men, suddenly desperate for a breath of fresh air. I rounded the corner, planning to find a private place to relieve myself, when I ran into McTavish, crouched close to the ground, his head buried in his hands.

"McTavish," I ventured when the large form didn't move. "Are you alright?"

"Aye," he mumbled from behind his hands, though I could hear emotion coursing through his voice. I stared, frozen to the spot. Was this giant Scotsman crying?

I crouched down next to him, taking his hand and offering the same support he had given me earlier on the blustery path. He eased his head up, brushing his face with the back of his sleeve. He stared off into the distance, his gaze far away. I thought he might want a moment alone, but I stayed anyway, realizing what I hadn't seen before. Around his hurt he had built the highest palisade to protect himself. It was in his rough manner and stern face. It was in the determined set of his jaw, in the tense way he held his shoulders with his thick arms crossed over his burly chest. But past the fort walls was the center of him, and it was vulnerable.

"It was just yer story, lass. It reminded me of someone, is all."

I squeezed his hand. "It's all right, McTavish. I understand."

He gave a soft chuckle. "You must think me a besotted fool."

I grinned over at him. "Not in the least." I put my hand out to feel for the rain. "It's clearing up. Shouldn't we be on our way?"

He nodded, standing to his full height. I took his offered hand, and we both brushed ourselves off, ready for the next leg of the journey.

Chapter Twenty

The next days passed in the same fashion—waking before dawn, long days in the canoes and on the trail, then stumbling into camp in the evening, exhausted. Only now, there was a comradery between me and the voyageurs. Ben took turns sitting with each man as he rowed, and he became the apple of every man's eye, charming them all with his eagerness and persistent questions. Even McTavish gave him a turn at the head of the boat, giving Ben his wide-brimmed leather hat for the duration of the ride.

The ground had now become cool under my feet, a sign of the changing season, and we slept as close to the fire as possible at night. I had given up all pretense at modesty and sleeping alone but instead lay bundled up amongst the men, grateful for the shelter of their bodies against the cold.

On the eighth day of our journey, I was surprised when a small fort came into sight as we rounded a river bend. My heart gave a sudden lurch as the thick wooden spikes of the palisade reminded me of my father, left behind at Fort Augustus. Even though my mind knew I had said a final farewell, my heart clung to the wish that I might see him once more.

"Fancy a hot meal, a wash, and a fur blanket tonight, lad?" McInnis asked Ben, nodding in the direction of the fort. Ben looked up at me expectantly, hopeful that this might be our final destination. Although he had fun on the water, the days were long, and I'm sure he longed for the company of other children. But I knew this could not be Fort William, for I had heard of its sprawling gates on the mouth of the glimmering Lake Superior, and I knew we still had quite the distance to travel.

We entered the gates of the fort together, the men flanking me. Mc-Tavish had been right—it was nice to have a group of familiar faces on my side. A woman travelling alone in the barren lands of the New World could never relax her guard among strangers.

I made my way to the bunkhouse with Ben, my rifle slung for show over my shoulder. There was no spare bed to be found, and a woman pointed to the floor in front of the hearth. I placed our meagre belongings there, not missing her expression as I walked by. There was no doubt about it—I smelled as rank as my voyageur companions.

"Is there a tub for bathing?" I asked one of the younger women nearby. She backed up, shaking her head. A few others looked away, hiding their faces from me. I looked around the room with the sudden realization that these women were frightened of me. They must have lewd thoughts about me, coming into the fort with more than a dozen burly men, still dressed in men's clothing with dirt and twigs stuck in my hair. To them, I was a disreputable woman.

I squared my jaw, annoyed at their assumption. I was the men's travelling companion, nothing more.

THE FORT

"A tub, please," I said, hands on my hips. "My son and I need to bathe. Or perhaps I will just go and ask the Chief Factor for help."

"Mais oui, juste un moment," one said, scurrying away to fetch the tub. I released my stance, too exhausted to keep up the stern demeanour. After I bathed, it would be tempting to fall asleep midday despite their stares.

"Thank you," I managed when she brought me the copper tub. She smiled at me shyly, helping me bring in buckets of water. It would take an hour or more for the water to heat by the hearth, so I set off in search of some food, dragging Ben along.

Meat roasted on a spit just outside the kitchen, and the aroma made the ache in my stomach swell. I stooped through the low door of the meal hall, squinting as my eyes adjusted to the dim light inside. Much smaller than the one at Fort Edmonton, this place smelled dank and musty. My gaze fell on a swarthy man seated alone near the entrance. He stopped with his fork mid-air, staring at me, eyes dark black. He sneered, his tongue flicking out to wet his lips. I caught my breath, jerking my gaze away and moving hurriedly past him to where McTavish waved at me from a table farther back in the room.

"Thank you," I said, grateful for the protection I felt in the company of my voyageurs. I cast a worried look toward the man near the door, but his head was bent over his meal. Plates of partridge, turnip, and beets came sliding down the table, and I forgot my worry, intent on filling my stomach. I filled a plate for Ben, smiling as he dug in with enthusiasm.

I was nearly done with my plate, wondering if there was any hope of a sweet pudding, when the Chief Factor of the fort stopped by our table. He scanned the row for McTavish, then came closer, his face set in a dour expression.

199

CHRISTY K. LEE

"I'm rather afraid there's been some bad news, McTavish. Fort William's been struck with a serious case of the pox. They've closed their gates to visitors for the winter to try and slow the spread."

A hush fell over the table. I stopped chewing, and my heart seemed to skip a beat. Where would we go if not Fort William? The Chief Factor and McTavish moved to a dark corner of the room, discussing the news by the light of a single candle. I sat back in my chair, a lump in my throat.

"We can't stay here!" one of the men at my table hissed to another. "Have you seen their cellar? We'll starve before the winter's over."

"The only forts between 'ere and Fort William belong to the English," another said with a sneer. "I'd rather brave the wilderness than spend my winter with those pompous buggers." The other men murmured in agreement, a few casting sheepish looks in my direction. I shrugged back, feeling secure in my standing with them despite the difference in our nationalities.

I felt McTavish behind me as he came back to the table, looming over the talk of the men. "They've invited us to stay here, lads." He glanced over at me and Ben. "Perhaps it's best we do."

"Nay! We'll be spendin' the entire winter out huntin', freezin' our arses off. They barely 'ave enough food to feed themselves."

"We should push for Montréal. That makes the most sense."

The men rumbled their agreement with the last statement, and my heart leapt. A direct trip to Montréal would save me the hassle of finding my way there in the spring. "Yes, that sounds like a wonderful idea," I exclaimed from my seat. "That's my vote, as well."

The men turned to look at me, and my stomach clenched tight at their piteous expressions, hope drifting away like smoke from a pipe. Then,

THE FORT

their eyes darted to one another, conveying a silent message across the table.

"I think you'd be best to stay here lass," McTavish said, putting a hand on my shoulder. "We're mere weeks away from the first freeze-up. It might be hard on the lad."

"No." I shook my head vigorously, a flush of heat coursing through my veins. "Please don't leave me. I need to get to Montréal." The thought of trying to make my way there on my own in the spring was more overwhelming than I could bear.

"We'll need to move fast," McInnis explained to me kindly, reaching out to pat my hand. "We might go days without sleep."

"I'll keep up." I found McTavish's face and implored him with pleading in my eyes. "If you leave me here, I'll ..." I swallowed hard, remembering the mistrust of the women and the leer of the man at the kitchen door. If stayed here, I might never be able to find my way to Gabriel. "Please. I can pay." I had the small purse of coins that the Chief Factor had given me, although I had planned to save it for when we arrived in Montréal.

McTavish cleared his throat uncomfortably. "There'll be no need for that, lass. But you'd best make yer way to the tradin' post for some warmer things for you and the boy."

I nodded, glancing around the table. A few of the men had turned away, not meeting my eye. They were clearly not in agreement. It was true; travelling with me was likely to slow them down, and we were liable to be stranded if the waterways froze.

I left the meal hall with an unease in my shoulders, dragging a reluctant Ben away from the voyageurs for his bath. I scrubbed him thoroughly, taking some of my frustration out on the menial task of cleaning the dirt out from underneath his fingernails. When he was dried off and dressed in clean clothing, I released him into the yard in search of other children.

I washed myself quickly, worried about the situation at hand. If McTavish changed his mind about having me come along, I would have no other choice but to winter here. But could I really keep up with the men and push onward into winter conditions?

I desperately wanted to wash our clothing but sensed that the men would want to leave soon and did not want to be wearing damp clothing that would hinder my pace. I scrunched up my nose as I once again donned the filthy trousers, cotton shirt, and woollen vest. I dug out the purse of coins from the bottom of my rucksack for the trading post. Then, considering them once more, I put them away and instead took the rifle from near the hearth, where I had placed it upon my earlier arrival. It was best not to flout my coin publicly, and besides, it made me happy to think that something Gabriel had gifted me might bring me back to him.

I hesitated outside of the trading post, glancing in past the long hide that hung in place of a door. Women rarely went inside, leaving the trading to the Natives, the trappers, and the clerk. Taking a deep breath for courage, I pushed aside the hide and went in.

My nose tickled as the odour of musty furs, woollen blankets, and tobacco washed over me. A pair of Indigenous men were in the corner, and I looked away as they turned to take me in, a nervous sweat beading on my forehead. I cleared my throat, heading to the counter in search of the clerk.

THE FORT

"Hello, miss," a gravelly voice said from beside me, catching me by surprise. When I realized that it was the same swarthy man from the meal hall, I stiffened, my grasp on the rifle tightening.

"Where is the clerk?" I managed, my voice echoing too loudly over the trading post. "I need to make a trade."

"At your service, miss." He chuckled, and the sound sent a lick of fear down my spine. "How can I help?"

"This is my husband's rifle," I said, putting the gun on the counter. I wished that I had been smart enough to fashion myself a ring in the blacksmith shop when I'd had the chance. "I need to trade it for winter supplies for myself and my son."

The man raised his eyebrows at me. "I didn't see you with any husband in the meal hall, only a crowd of unsightly voyageurs. Unless you're married to one of them?"

I swallowed thickly as he leaned closer, the smell of his pipe on his breath. "Yes. McTavish is my husband."

"Duncan McTavish?" I jumped as another smaller man appeared beside me. "I've never seen McTavish carryin' on with *any* woman, let alone get married to one." He eyed me up and down, taking in my dirty trousers. "Though I suppose you're fair enough."

"Indeed," the clerk said, a tongue flicking out to wet his lower lip. "But I think you're lying. Why would McTavish send his wife into the trading post alone?"

As if summoned from the statue of Saint Christopher that Claudette had gifted me, the flap of the doorway moved aside, and a pair of large boots entered the shop. *McTavish.* The air in my chest left me in a rush, and I gave him a weak smile.

"There you are," I said cheerfully, coming over to take his arm into mine. He raised one bushy brow at me but then glanced at the counter, saying nothing.

"We hear congratulations are in order, McTavish. Who would've imagined an ol' codger like you would finally settle down?" McTavish's arm grew still under my hand as he understood the ruse. My heart thumped painfully in my chest as I waited beside him, unsure how he would react to the lie.

"Did you manage to find everything you needed ... uh ... dear?" He smiled down at me, an amused expression on his craggy face. "I've just been arrangin' extra food rations in the storehouse, but get yerself some pemmican, too." He looked at the clerk, laying his hand on mine, nodding at the rifle on the counter.

The clerk once again let out a grimy chuckle. "O' course. Right away, *Mr. and Mrs. McTavish.*" I suspected he saw through my lie, and I bit back a sharp retort. Provoking this man would be no less dangerous than prodding a bear out of its winter sleep.

McTavish stayed with me until I had chosen a fur robe for myself and Ben, and other winter supplies he pointed out. Then, he helped me with the parcels outside. Once we were clear of the trading post, he turned to me. "Dinna do that again, lass. I dinna like my name used when I'm not in hearin' distance of it."

"I understand," I said, hoisting my bundle higher into my arms. "It won't happen again, I promise. It's just that clerk is ..." I trailed off, looking back towards the trading post. "Please don't leave me here, McTavish," I begged, meeting his eyes. "I know I'm a burden to you, but I'll pitch in my fair bit. I can make all the camp meals if you like."

THE FORT

He sighed heavily. "I'll no' leave ya here, don't worry yerself. But I'll no' let my men freeze to death either."

"I won't lag behind, I promise." I threw my arms around his neck, giving him an affectionate kiss on the cheek. Then, I gathered my wintering supplies and ran off to the bunkhouse to pack. We were going to Montréal.

Chapter Twenty-One

T he days blurred into weeks as we made our way across the country. My skin grew weathered and chapped, my muscles hardy and strong. I scarcely thought anymore upon my misfortune but instead began to make plans for what I might do once we reached Montréal. My safest bet would be to find work as a maid or perhaps a barmaid for the winter, and then in the spring, I would ask around for work as a farrier in a blacksmith shop. I kept the vision of the day that Gabriel and I might be reunited tucked safely away to protect my tender heart.

As promised, I took over the making of the meals. I cooked on a rotation of our supplies, adding any mushrooms, berries, or nuts I managed to gather during the day. Weekly, McTavish took inventory of all the food rations, sitting under the protection of a nearby tree, calculating. Tonight, however, he had stayed there longer than usual, the candle casting eerie flecks of light over his frowning face.

I glanced over at his hulking frame from where I was trying to sleep. I was exhausted—we all were—but my mind was wide awake, refusing me rest. Leaving the warmth of the fire, I grabbed my blanket and stepped

THE FORT

into the crisp night air, slipping my back down the same tree trunk where he sat, the bark coming off in a scratch behind me.

"I can't sleep," I offered as the candle in front of him flickered in the night breeze. I pulled my blanket around me to keep out the chill, wondering for the hundredth time if we would indeed make it to Montréal before the waters froze for the winter. He said nothing but reached into the dark shadows, handing me an opened bottle of wine. I took a healthy swallow, handing it back to him.

"Will we be all right?" I asked, motioning to the strip of bark he had been writing on. "Will there be enough to last us through?"

"Aye," he said, voice raspy, "We'll be fine, lass. We'll fish when we can and might 'ave a stroke o' luck and come across a larger animal."

I cleared my throat, grateful when he handed the bottle back. I sat quietly, looking out into the clear night, wondering what was bothering him. "Are you all right?" I asked, taking an additional drink before I returned the wine.

He blew out a heavy breath. "Go get yer rest, lass. Dinna fash yerself over me." He threw the now-empty bottle aside and let out a quiet belch. "Nothing ya can help me with anyway."

"I can listen," I said, remembering the day I had found him in tears. It helped ease my own suffering to help carry the burdens of others. "Sometimes it helps to talk about it."

He lurched up suddenly from the ground, grabbing onto the trunk for support. As he moved jerkily past me, I realized that this bottle had not been his first. A crash sounded from the bush behind me, and he let loose a stream of curse words, punctuating the still night air.

"McTavish," I hissed, jumping up and scrambling after him. Away from the light of the fire, only a meagre moon lit my path with its pale hue. I tripped as well, sprawling headfirst into the prickly bramble.

A large pair of hands found me, helping me out of the thicket. I glared up at him as he swayed before me. "Don't you dare wander off," I scolded him. "You're drunk and liable to end up drowning yourself in the river."

He gave a bitter-sounding laugh, the smell of the wine on his breath sweeping over me, acrid and sour. "There are things ya don't understand in this wee world, lass. I'm better off drowned than continuing on as I am."

"Perhaps," I said, dragging him back over to our spot under the tree. "But I've told you everything about me, even the unsavoury parts."

He grunted in response, then rummaged around in the bush, producing another bottle from the shadows. I raised my brows at him, but he ignored me, easing the cork free with his stained teeth.

"Drink," he said, thrusting the bottle at me. "Ya willna like me once ya know the truth."

I took a drink, holding back my smile. I had said much the same to him, worried about the shame of my past. "I'm sure I'll like you just fine."

He sighed heavily, running his hand down his face. "Yer story reminded me of someone I love, someone who's far away. I just don't know if I'll ever see 'im again."

"Is she still in Scotland?" I asked, rubbing my arms against the chill.

McTavish blew out an impatient breath. "*Him*, lass. No' her."

A thick silence fell between us as I processed his words. "You love *him*?" I asked gently, realizing that he would have never revealed this truth to me if he weren't so far in his cups.

THE FORT

"Aye." He lowered his voice, though we were far enough away from the others that no one would hear. "Ya must think of me as a sordid devil."

I took a deep breath, then drank from the bottle, considering. This was not the first I had heard of men having relations with other men, and I was no stranger to the self-loathing that came along with the burden of keeping such a secret.

"No," I said firmly, reaching out and giving his arm a squeeze. "I think nothing of the sort."

He turned to me, his bushy eyebrows raised. They cast a shadow over his face, making him look formidable in the candlelight. "Well, ya should. 'Tis nothing more than a sinful affliction."

I shook my head, though I took another drink, trying to find the right words. "We can't help the way we are, McTavish. Or who we love. I've loved men who cared nothing for my well-being but it did not change my heart in the moment." I thought of Henry with his high moral attitude. "And you are a *good* man. I've known plenty who disguise themselves behind a pious mask only to reveal their true devious character in private. The measure of who you are is so much more."

McTavish grunted beside me, his breath coming out in a frigid white cloud. He said nothing though, so I prodded a bit more. "Why don't you tell me about him? Is he in Scotland?"

"Nay. He's in the American Territory. An officer. He goes by Charles. And I 'ave no way of knowin' if he's dead or alive or even if we might see each other again. Every now and again, I hear word of him, but I fear that after so long, he might not return the affection or 'ave found someone else."

I shivered, pulling my blanket closer. I knew that feeling well. "We must persevere," I said, my voice a bit raspy with emotion. Instead of feeling disgust, as McTavish had expected, knowing this piece of him made me admire him more. "We must not lose hope."

He swallowed hard beside me. "But for how long, lass? I'm feelin' a wee bit out of hope."

I smiled, tears welling in my eyes. "I'll hope for the both of us, Mc-Tavish." I sighed, looking up at the star-filled sky above us. "I have enough to share." For now, at least.

The next morning dawned far too early, and I felt the sluggish after-effects of too much wine. I peered over at McTavish, who, despite his indulgence, seemed fine, directing the men as usual. I caught his eye over the bustle and nodded in an unspoken agreement—I would keep his secret for always.

I swallowed back a bout of nausea as I stirred a large pot of porridge resting on some large stones set in the fire. Ben ran to and fro, getting in the way of the voyageurs until one of the men gently scolded him.

"Ben!" I called, irritated. I stood up to beckon him over, gasping as a sudden wave of dizziness washed over me.

"Lass!" It was McInnis, a steady hand under my elbow. "Watch yerself near the fire." He peered at my face. "Are ya ill?"

"I'm fine," I assured him, clearing my throat as my stomach continued to churn. I didn't dare admit that I had been drinking the rations of wine

THE FORT

with McTavish late at night. Above all, it would seem improper to be spending time alone with a man at night.

Within the hour, we were on our way, pushing the canoe out past the frozen edges of the river. Morning frost clung to the long grasses along the shore, a stark reminder that we were racing against the impending winter. The men talked among themselves in hushed tones as they paddled. "At this rate, we'll be lucky to cross Lake Superior before the freeze-up."

"Aye. 'Tis a fool's errand. We've been out near on a month already, with another to go. We'll be tradin' in the canoes for a pair o' dog sleds, if we're lucky. Or else, we'll be arrivin' to Montréal on foot."

"Did you hear that, Mama?" Ben whispered loudly from my lap. "Dog sleds!"

I smiled, leaning down to give him a kiss, but my mind started to reel at the men's words. Had we been out almost a month? In the sudden departure of Gabriel, coupled with the appearance of the lawyer and the fire at Fort Augustus, I had completely lost track of time. A startling realization shot through my gut: I had not had my monthly courses for quite some time.

The conversation swirled around me as I thought back. Yes, the last time had been just before we'd moved from Fort Edmonton to Fort Augustus, and after that, I had bedded Gabriel. I blew out a long breath as I considered that I might, in fact, be with child. He had taken some precautions like I had asked, but I was not blind to the ways of conception, as evidenced by the six-year-old in my lap.

Ben shifted to look up at me, and I turned my face away, blinking back tears. How could this have happened to me once again? It was true that Ben was a blessing, and Gabriel had professed his love and commitment, but my future was nothing but uncertain. How could I possibly survive the wait for him in Montréal with a child on the way? It was one thing to disguise myself as a widow with an older child but quite another to be pregnant after spending two months travelling alone with a band of men.

For once I was grateful when we disembarked, looking forward to the walk to have time alone to think. Ben trotted alongside me, collecting rocks and twigs until his pockets were nearly bursting.

"Mama?" he asked after we had gone some distance, and the men were far out of sight, "What will happen to us if Gabriel does not come? What if he cannot find us?"

My heart seized at his question, my hope from the evening before having evaporated with the realization of the morning. What would I do if he did not come? How long would I wait before doing the only thing I could to survive? I would have to find another man to marry and support us. The only other option—sailing home to England and begging one of my brothers to house us—filled me with gut-wrenching shame.

"He'll come to us," I said, almost sternly, more for myself than to answer Ben's question. "I know he will. He loves us." I was desperate to believe my own words.

A strange mewling interrupted me, and I turned to see a pair of deer eyes staring at me from the side of the path. Its brown gaze met mine, and I realized that its antlers were stuck in the branches of a nearby tree. In normal circumstances, I would free the creature, setting it free. But not now, with our supplies dwindling and winter nipping at our heels. I winced, knowing what I must do.

"Ben!" I hissed as quietly as I could. "Run and catch up with the men. Tell them there's meat and to bring a gun."

THE FORT

Ben took off down the path, and I turned back to the animal, reaching out to pet its nose. It reared, more afraid of me than I was of it. It could be a danger to me if it escaped its tangle, but I felt no alarm. Instead, devastating remorse flooded me for the need to kill it, though I knew it would relieve McTavish of the worry that our food rations would not be enough.

The deer let loose another cry, this one louder, as if it had realized its fate. A cry escaped my own lips, and I felt my face to find it wet with tears, an overflow of everything I had been keeping inside. Mabel, Gabriel, my father, and now, an unborn child in my womb. I sank to my knees in front of the creature and wept. My sobbing grew loud and untamed as I let it all go—the love, bright and beautiful, and the loss, dark and lonely.

A piercing shot echoed through the woods, and the animal fell with a *thud*, the ground shaking under my knees. I looked up to see McTavish coming towards me, a smoking rifle in his hand. He made a *tsk*, frowning, then lifted me up, trapping me against his chest with his impossibly large arms.

"There, there, lass," he crooned as a fresh wave of tears burst out of me, making his shirt damp. "'Tis not as bad as all that."

"But it is," I said, my voice shaking violently as I struggled to control my grief. "I think I'm carrying a child. Gabriel's child."

He made a deep noise in the back of his throat, then pulled me away to look at him. "I did wonder if something was amiss," he said, surprising me. "Not that I know much about lasses, but I 'ad six sisters."

"But ... what if he doesn't come? We're still unwed. What if—"

"He'll come," he said gruffly, cutting me off. "I'll 'ave enough hope for the both of us. And until then," he continued, reaching down to the deer

213

and smearing some of the blood between his fingers, "you're stuck with me. I promise I'll not leave yer side."

We wrestled the dead animal out from the brush together then I watched with awe as McTavish lifted the entire beast onto his shoulders, grasping the two legs in each hand. "Come now, lass. We'll be eating meat tonight."

The men cheered as we came into view, rushing over to take the animal off McTavish's broad shoulders. A few of them took me into an embrace, saying I was their lucky charm. I smiled along with them, wiping away the last of my tears. I wasn't alone. These men had become like brothers. A family bound not by blood but by something more important. Trust.

Chapter Twenty-Two

We passed Fort William without a word, though I gazed up at the massive gates, thinking of how far we'd come. There was no consideration of going inside, not with pox rampant among the patrons. My father and I had been inoculated before leaving England, but I doubted that the men of the canoe brigade, who were small-town farm boys for the most part, would have received such treatment.

McTavish stared out over the expanse of Lake Superior, over three-hundred and fifty miles across. It would take us a good portion of a week to make our way to the other side, barring any weather that might set us off our course.

"She's naught but a beast," he murmured as I came up next to him. "Storms that can pick in a minute or fog as thick as yer hand. And that's in the summer." He pulled his wool toque down over his ears, grey hair sticking out, and crossed his arms over a plaid-covered chest. "How are ya feelin', lass?" he asked in a quieter tone so that the nearby men didn't overhear.

I cleared my throat, his question making the ever-present nausea swirl in my stomach. "I'll be fine. I'm just looking forward to arriving in Montréal." Truthfully, I was exhausted in a way that sleep couldn't cure. I felt weary down to my very bones, deep into my soul. I knew that McTavish had slowed our pace over the last few days, likely on my accord. The men had noticed and there was tension among them, as there was now no doubt—we would not reach Montréal before the onset of ice and snow.

We managed the first day across the great lake without any debacle, pulling the boats out of the water just after sunset. The daylight hours had become shorter, and most evenings, McTavish pulled us in from the water late in the day, Ben and I chattering with cold while the men made haste to set up camp.

A few of the voyageurs warmed themselves by the fire while the others busied themselves setting up our sleeping area.

"I reckon he's gone daft," one said as I prepared the evening stew nearby. Though the meat from the deer was long gone, I had been able to save a good collection of bones, gristle, and fat to make broth for meals. I longed for the days when Claudette had served me spiced meat pies and piping hot tea while we sat and chatted in the sun.

"Aye. Somethin' got into 'him, to be sure."

"Who's gone daft?" I asked, stirring the pot, my stomach growling. The last few mornings, I had not managed to eat breakfast, my appetite taken over by a vicious queasiness, and by evening, I was nearly fainting with hunger.

"McTavish. The wine's gone amiss, but he doesn't seem to care who stole it. And now, he's slowed down the whole brigade, like we 'ave time to spare. Maybe his ol' age is showin'."

THE FORT

"I think he's hidin' somethin'. He always has."

"It's on account of me," I blurted out, not wanting the men to talk amongst themselves about any secret McTavish might be hiding. To know that he loved another man would ruin his reputation for good. "I'm carrying Gabriel's child. I just found out."

The hiss and crack of the fire joined the rush of the wind through the trees as the men stared over at me. I saw the thoughts written clearly on their faces—that, for the second time, I would birth a child alone without being wed.

I thrust my chin up, daring any one of them to make mention of my morals. "I'm sorry that we've been forced to slow our pace. I have not been well these past days, but I'm sure it will pass soon."

The men nodded, shoving hands deep into their pockets with hunched shoulders as they walked away to help the others set up camp. I knew that news of my condition would be known by all before the end of the meal, but somehow, I didn't mind. It was likely that I would be showing far before we arrived in Montréal anyhow, and I doubted anyone would scorn me with McTavish nearby.

An odd quiet blanketed the camp as I dished up and delivered dinner to the men. Each one took his bowl, not quite meeting my eyes. Even Ben seemed to notice something amiss and ate without his usual chatter. Then, as had become the usual, the men carried their empty bowls to a bucket, which I had filled with water, warmed over the fire. There, I would clean up and set some wild rice to soak for the next day.

I had just dipped my hands into the water to start washing the dishes when one of the Frenchmen came over to me. "I heard of your condition," he said, blushing slightly. "I will go personally to York in the

217

summer to collect Gabriel and bring him to you in Montréal. That way, he won't waste time heading west to find you."

"Oh, my. Thank you ever so much," I replied, wiping my hands on my apron, giving him my full attention. "That's so very kind of you."

He patted me awkwardly on the back as McInnis came over. "Abby, I just wanted you to know you're not to worry," he stammered, his face also flushed red. "If it so happens that your man cannot make his way to you, I'd be happy to marry you."

My mouth dropped open in surprise, as McInnis was no more than twenty, but I recovered quickly as he stood before me, serious in his proposal. "Thank you, McInnis. I shall keep that in mind."

By the time I crawled under the blanket with Ben that night, I had received several marriage proposals, an offer of employment working on a farm, and more promises to ensure Gabriel made his way to me. McTavish grinned at me from across the camp, his smile saying everything.

Just after noon on the second day, the wind picked up, a soft rustling at first. McTavish kept his eye trained on the clouds forming above and motioned that we would head into shore.

"Nay!" a man from the second boat shouted over. "It's nothing but a breeze! If we stop now, we'll waste the rest of the day!"

Another voyageur shouted in agreement, and McTavish nodded reluctantly, though his mouth grew tight and thin, his opinion evident. The consensus outweighed his authority—we were losing the daily race

THE FORT

against the impending freeze-up. That morning had seemed a bit warmer but no less forgiving as I watched with trepidation as the waves of Lake Superior grew choppy, the spray splashing over the sides.

After another hour, we were entirely soaked through. It started to rain; sharp icy droplets that drove into us sideways from the wind. Ben pressed against my chest, and I silently prayed that McTavish would indeed make the decision to pull us ashore. Finally, the call came a mere motion of his hand, slicing through the darkened sky.

They had just maneuvered the boat towards the direction of the shore when a pool of frigid water collected at my feet. I looked down to see a gaping hole in the seam, the canoe rapidly filling up with lake water.

"There's a leak!" I shouted, barely audible through the wind and the rain. "The boat's ripped!" Half a dozen heads whipped around to look at me, then down at my feet, where the water was already halfway up my calves. Panic surged through me at the fear that flashed on their faces. McTavish fumbled around with something at his feet, then tossed me a pair of tin cups.

"Scoop, lass! You and the lad!"

I nodded, grabbing the cup and began collecting water from the bottom, throwing it back into the lake. Around me, the men were paddling furiously, counting aloud together to keep their rapid strokes in time.

"Look, Mama! I stopped the water." I looked up to see Ben standing in front of me, covering the rip with the length of his foot. He looked up at me, grinning his toothless smile. Then, in a horrifying instant, the tear ripped further, a loud sound that turned my heart to ice. Both Ben and McInnis, who had been paddling beside him, plunged into the black depths of Lake Superior.

"Ben!" I shrieked, trying in vain to reach after him. A wave hit the side of the boat, and the entire canoe capsized, throwing me into the water below. The water hit my face and chest, a vice around my lungs, paralyzing my limbs. I tried to scramble towards the surface, only to be brought down by another wave. Fright overtook my senses as I lost my sense of direction, my legs and arms pulled every which way. I pried my eyes open, trying to see anything in the murky abyss. I could see nothing, only inky black shadows.

Forcing my arms and legs into movement, I swam towards one, knowing that I would not be able to stay under much longer. *Ben! Where was he?*

My hand grasped onto something solid, and I was being dragged through the water, filling my ears with a rushing gurgle. My head broke the surface, and I gasped, my chest seizing as I tried to breathe. There was a thump on my back, and I coughed and spluttered, finding myself face to face with McTavish, his hair plastered to the side of his face, lips blue.

"Ben!" I managed in a raspy sob, and he left me on the surface, swimming again down into the depths of the lake. My chest ached as I tried to gasp in more air in the frigid cold. I was tossed around in the waves for a moment until the second boat paddled up next to me. Two pairs of hands reached over, hauling me roughly into the boat.

"No," I cried out once I had righted myself. The boat was packed tight with others who had also gone overboard, shaking forcefully with the cold. "Ben is still down there. I must look for him."

"Non," one of the Frenchmen exclaimed as I tried to throw myself overboard. He tucked me against him, banding me with thick arms around my waist. "You must let McTavish look. You're liable to drown."

THE FORT

A giant splash broke the surface of the water a short distance away, and the men in the front hauled over McTavish with Ben in his arms, the weight making the boat rock violently in the waves. I tried to stand, to make my way to him, but the same Frenchman clamped a hand on my shoulder, keeping me down.

"Vite, vite!" The men at the front of the boat crowded around Ben, stripping him of his clothing. They wrapped him in a blanket, rubbing his body to create warmth. McTavish turned and vomited over the side of the boat, the lake water he had swallowed making its way back up.

"Ya arrogant fool!" McTavish roared when he had finished, his teeth clacking together from the cold. He pointed at the voyageur who had suggested we not turn in an hour before. "We very nearly drowned!" Then men started to argue, their gestures making the boat rock, lake water coming over the sides. One of the Scotsmen passed Ben into my arms, and I gathered him close, peering down at him, his face so tiny and frail in the hood of the blanket. He was breathing, but it was coming in short pants, and his skin was mottled and blue.

"Please," I begged, raising my voice over the men who were still arguing with each other, "We must get him ashore."

The weather remained turbulent, and it took the better part of twenty minutes to paddle to shore, where the damaged boat lay, its gaping wound facing skyward. A few of the men lay on the shores of the bank, exhausted with the effort of swimming the damaged canoe to shore.

"We lost much of the cargo, I'm afraid," one man reported to McTavish, yelling above the fury of the wind. The rain whipped against our faces, and it took all my will to stand upright. He looked us all over, then frowned. "Do ya not have McInnis with ya?"

I froze mid-step, Ben lying heavy in my arms. "McInnis," I whispered. I turned to McTavish, a scream building in my throat. We looked out at the water, which still raged, dark blue and black. "He went down with Ben."

McTavish's went white. "No, lass. Say it isn't true." He turned and headed back towards the lake but was held back by a couple of men. To search for him now would be a loss in the vast, choppy waters.

McInnis was gone.

A cry left my lips as I sank to the ground, crumpled together with Ben, his limbs flying loose from the blanket. There was murmuring above me for a moment, and then I was lifted into warm arms. My head had suddenly gone murky, and I collapsed against the man carrying me.

"You've got to get out of these wet clothes, ya hear?" the voice said, a soft burr in my ear. "Then wrap yerself in a blanket."

I was plopped down in front of a sputtering fire, Ben lying nearby. Jolting out of my reverie, I crawled over to my son and pulled him into my lap, rocking back and forth slowly. Behind me, the men shouted at one another as the tragedy sunk in.

"You've killed him!" I recognized McTavish, though his voice was hoarse. There was a scuffle, and I turned to see fists flying; at least five men were involved in the fight.

"Stop!" I yelled over the shouting. My chest heaved, heavy and painful. The anguish was too much, weighing me down like my sodden clothes. "That's enough! He's gone. Killing each other won't bring him back."

McTavish looked at me, his lip bleeding, and cursed loudly. Then, nostrils flaring, he whirled and stomped off into the forest. The rest of the men dispersed in different directions, each one going out alone to grieve. With the camp now empty, I removed my wet clothes down to

THE FORT

my shift, then lay down, pulling Ben against me and wrapping another blanket over us both. My own sorrow overwhelmed me, and I fell into a dark, dreamless sleep.

Chapter Twenty-Three

When I woke in the morning, the camp had dispersed. Only McTavish remained, crouched on his haunches, stirring a pot over the fire. Ben sat on a nearby log, and though he looked more pale than normal, relief washed over me to see him awake and alert. McTavish, on the other hand, looked like death awakened. His complexion was dull, with purplish-blue blotches in his cheeks. The dark shadows under his red-rimmed eyes told me that his night had been long, filled with turmoil and grief.

I sat up, careful not to expose my undergarments under the blanket, though I knew he wasn't of harm to me. The rain had slowed to a drizzle, dripping through the leaves. "Where is everyone?"

He stared at me for a moment, as if only realizing I was there. "They've gone, lass. A few decided to take their chances at Fort William, and the others ..." His voice trailed off, and he looked away, deep in the forest.

"What happened to the others?" I demanded, trying to stand. I took a few steps and sank back down weakly onto the log with Ben. The events

THE FORT

of the day before had taken a toll on me, and I was completely spent. Yet my heart pounded as I tried to understand what McTavish was saying.

"We fought. They ... they left."

"They left?!"

"Aye. Took the canoes with them." McTavish ran a hand down his face, looking as weary and disheartened as I felt. "I may 'ave told them to bugger off."

I took a deep breath, trying to calm my racing pulse. The other men were gone? And they had taken the boats. What would we do? We were on the shores of the massive lake, and winter was fast approaching.

"McTavish—"

"It's up to you, lass. I reckon I'll be either deliverin' ya to Fort William or to Montréal. Yer choice."

I stared at him. "How in heavens are we going to get to Montréal? The canoes are gone."

He shrugged, his giant shoulder seemingly smaller than normal. "We start by walkin'. Yer things are there." He nodded towards my rucksack, which lay wet and dishevelled. "Eat. We'll stay 'ere for the day to rest, then head one way or another." With that, he heaved himself up and abruptly disappeared into the bush.

Ben and I ate, and then I arranged our clothes properly around the fire so they might have some semblance of drying over the course of the day. I did the same with our belongings from the rucksack, torn over the turbulent events of the past day. From what I could tell, Ben seemed to be none the wiser about the drowning, so I stayed quiet, not wishing to see my son wrestling with the same anguish that McTavish and I had been forced to bear. It seemed that only a moment ago, the men of the canoe brigade had offered me their hands in marriage, and now they were ...

gone. And McInnis ... I shook my head in a firm resolve. I couldn't even begin to dwell on what had happened to him if I was to stay strong for the days ahead. We were still in the wilderness, far from civilization. To fall apart now, to give in to the wounds of my heart, would mean certain death. No, I must let the cuts form a scar to stay strong. I found myself understanding why McTavish had learned to protect his heart, to erect a fort around himself. Against nature, man was nothing if his mind was not formidable.

What should we do? The thought of backtracking and spending the winter at Fort William, despite the outbreak, was tempting. My hand fell to my belly, where my unborn child grew. *Gabriel's child.* Gabriel. If we were to stay at Fort William, I would have to find my own way to Montréal in the spring or hope that I could send word to Claudette, who would deliver the news to Gabriel. I counted the months and realized the chances of travelling in the spring were slim as I would already be heavily pregnant. And it would be much the same with a newborn, as no brigade would want a mother with a child and a baby in tow. No, it would be better to take the chance now and with McTavish as my guide.

A few hours later, Ben had fallen asleep again, and I sat by the fire, staring mindlessly. McTavish came crashing through the forest, a pair of rabbits in hand. He gave me a curt nod, then took out his knife to skin and prepare them to eat. I managed a weak smile, my stomach growling at the thought of a proper meal.

"Montréal," I said, without preamble. "If you think we can arrive safely, then I'd like to make our way there."

He looked over at me, his eyebrows raising in surprise, but then a thin smile crossed his features. "Aye. I reckoned that would be yer choice. You're not afraid of much, are ya?"

THE FORT

I gave a wry laugh. "I'm afraid of plenty. Of everything, really. I have one shred of hope left, McTavish. I can't let go of Gabriel."

"And ya shouldn't." He cleared his throat gruffly, and I knew he was thinking of his own love, Charles, wondering where he was and if he was safe. "I can't let go either, lass."

"Do you think they think of us as often as we do them?" I asked, grateful to share a part of my loneliness. My father entered my thoughts too and I let out a heavy sigh. McTavish merely shook his head at me, not knowing the answer either.

We ate together in silence, setting aside a portion for Ben when he woke. I cleaned up, taking stock of our now meagre supplies. "I have some coins," I said, bringing the purse to McTavish. "We may need them in the days ahead. I think it's best if you hold on to them for now."

He nodded, taking the purse from my hands and tucking it into his sporran-type pouch around his waist. "It's best if we act like we're married. If we encounter other folks, I'll sleep next to ya for safety. I reckon ya understand that I will no' be a danger to ya."

"That's fine, thank you." I came over and sat next to him. "And thank you for staying and not leaving me alone." I took a deep breath, finding that my mind was indeed hardy and strong. "I'm so sorry about McInnis."

He looked away, but not before I saw the torment that flashed across his face. "McInnis was a good lad. 'Tis not the first occurrence of death on the water, lass, nor will it be the last. It's just part of the life of a voyageur."

Ben coughed in his sleep, a deep, barking sound that made us both turn and frown. "Our first stop will be to an Indian camp," McTavish said, carefully wiping his blood-stained knife and sheathing back into his belt. "We'll trade for some snowshoes and a remedy for yer lad."

"What will we trade?" I asked, gesturing to my threadbare belongings laid out to dry. "Should we use the coin?"

He shook his head, giving me a grin. "I figure it's time to put those blacksmithin' skills of yours to good use." Turning to leave, he nodded at Ben. "Get yerself some more rest. I'll be out huntin' for the rest of the day."

I laid down after he left, but I could not fall asleep. I let everything wash over me, trying to calm my inner storm. How had it been only months ago that I had been kissing Gabriel outside the palisade at Fort Augustus? Now I lay here in the wilderness with my fate at the hands of a large Scotsman, heading into the harsh winter conditions on foot, my six-year-old son in tow. I hoped Claudette was continuing her daily prayers for us. We would need it.

Two days of trekking later, we stood at the edge of an Ojibwa Native settlement. While McTavish went in alone to speak with the Elders, I waited on the outskirts with Ben, wiping my hands nervously down my trousers. We planned to stay the night, or maybe two, so that we could barter for supplies and regain our strength. I had noticed that even McTavish travelled with a weary step, the loss of his crew having drained him.

THE FORT

"They've no need of a blacksmith," he said as he came striding back in our direction. "But they've agreed to let us stay. Perhaps I can hunt for a few days and trade that way."

I swallowed hard, peering past him at the moose hide tents, standing tall and proud. I had never stayed at an Indigenous camp and was feeling rather unsettled about it. I longed desperately for the company of Gabriel, a flood of emotion that had come on suddenly in the past few days, weakening my resolve to be strong. I had begun to think about him all the time, unable to push it away any longer. At night, I would imagine myself in his arms, his beard scratching my bare skin. The heartache of being a world away, wondering if I might ever see him again, was becoming almost more than I could bear.

"Abby." McTavish took my chin in his large hand, directing my eyes to his. "You must put it aside, lass." He lowered his voice so Ben would not overhear. "If we're to survive out here, ya cannot let yer heart do the talkin'."

I squared my shoulders and closed my eyes, my mind's eye settling on an image of my father. He would not want me to be weak. I could do this for him. I opened my eyes and reached out, taking Ben's hand. "All right, let's go."

McTavish reached down and lifted Ben into his arms. "Call me Pa, ya hear, lad?" A hand reached down to my waist, drawing me closer to him. Our married ruse.

As we walked through the camp, I put on my warmest smile, reminding myself that I was as different to them as they were to me. McTavish's fingers squeezed my waist encouragingly, and I looked past their darker skin and clothing adorned with feathers and beads to see that their camp was not unlike the fort—children ran around us, playing games with sticks and balls, and women carried babies on cradleboards while completing daily chores. Only a few older men lingered within, telling me that the younger men were away, likely hunting and gathering food before the snow and ice arrived.

We made our way to one of the tents, McTavish pushing aside the flap of the hide. I followed him inside, surprised at the immediate warmth. A small circular hearth sat in the middle, the smoke twisting its way upward through a hole at the top. Furs and blankets were heaped in one corner to be used for sleeping and, to my delight, a bucket of water for washing in another.

"You can stay in the tipi if you'd like, lass. Wash and rest. I'll see about gettin' us some food and an ailment tea for yer boy."

I nodded my thanks, watching as his broad back disappeared through the slit. As far as make-believe husbands went, I could do worse than McTavish. In fact, I had come to consider him something of a companion, a friend. It was an unlikely pairing, as men and women did not often have common associations outside of marriage, but life had thrown us together, and we fit.

I brought the bucket over near the fire to warm. It wasn't enough to bathe entirely, but I was eager to wash the grime from my face and hands. I had just finished washing Ben when the flap opened, letting a gust of cool air into the cozy space. It was a beautiful young woman, her long black hair swishing elegantly over her shoulders. I smiled, though I patted my own hair, suddenly self-conscious about the state of my physical appearance.

"Hello," she said, coming over and sitting down next to me. "Your husband said you might want some help. My name is Nishime." She pulled out a hairbrush from a leather bag slung over her chest.

THE FORT

"Oh my. Thank you," I said, grateful for her unexpected offer. "I'm Abby."

Nishime knelt behind me and started to untangle my braid, which I was certain was full of dirt, leaves, twigs, and perhaps a few insects. Her hands were gentle and soothing, and I felt myself relax for what seemed like the first time since we'd left Fort Augustus. The brush moved through my hair painfully at first, but then the strokes became even and smooth, and she expertly braided it into a tight plait.

McTavish burst into the tent, carrying a pot of stew and a birchbark bowl of tea for Ben's cough. Nishime blushed, a deep, dusky rose, then left the tent without a word, darting a quick glance at my Scottish companion. I bit back a laugh, wondering if she found him handsome or was impressed by his behemoth size.

"A stroke o' luck, lass," he whispered excitedly, making my eyes pop open in anticipation. "As it happens, the Chief needs a message delivered to a man in Montréal. He's agreed to supply us with what we need in exchange. We can leave first thing in the mornin'."

I clapped my hands together, pleased with the outcome. As inviting as the warm tipi was, time was against us. "That's wonderful, McTavish. How soon until the snowfall, do you think?"

"A week, maybe two," he said, dishing up three bowls of stew. "If you're feeling rested, we'll push hard the next few days."

I nodded, taking a bite of the savoury stew. I hoped that, for once, the winds had turned in our favour, and it was a true stroke of luck indeed.

Later that evening, I slipped out from the warmth of the tipi into the brisk night. Both McTavish and Ben had fallen asleep, and although I didn't feel brave enough to roam the Ojibwa camp on my own, a breath of fresh air from the musky buffalo tent was much needed.

A figure came up to me in the darkness, and I recognized Nishime. She wore a sleek fur robe to keep out the night chill, her hair now pulled back in a thick braid like my own.

"Hello," she said, her voice lilting like a rippling wave in the water. "I've brought you a gift." She retrieved a bundle from inside her cloak and handed it to me. "There's pemmican and some berry tea to keep away the winter illness."

Her hand found mine in the darkness and clenched tightly. I tensed, not sure if she meant harm, as her grasp was almost painful. "Please, miss," she whispered in my ear, her words now clipped and tight, "you must take me with you."

"Take you?" I hissed back at her, unease rising in my chest. "Take you where?"

"Shhh, please be quiet." She put her hand across my mouth, dragging me by the hand around the tent. I allowed her to lead me away from the camp into a forest grove, my heart beating loudly through my chest.

"I can help," she said, her eyes black and wide under the moonlight as she implored me. "I am used to the ways of this land, and I can hunt. Please."

I shook my head, trying to understand her urgency. "Why do you want to come, Nishime?"

"I am betrothed to marry a man whom I despise," she said, wringing her hands together, "and I feel like I would rather die. I will take my

THE FORT

chances on my own in Montréal. I've heard there are Indian women like me working on the docks, cleaning fish."

I blew out a hot breath, my heart tugging in sympathy. My father had always allowed me some freedom of choice in my marital status. Most women married as their fathers dictated. I could only imagine the life-long sentence of being married to the wrong kind of man, like Mabel's husband.

"I shall have to ask McTa—er, my husband," I said, reaching out and squeezing her hand. "But I cannot promise anything. He is a man of his own mind." Truthfully, I would not mind a female companion, but I doubted McTavish would agree, as it was another mouth to feed, regardless of her hunting and foraging ability.

Nishime bowed her head in thanks. "I will wait for your word in the morning."

She led me to the camp, then disappeared as silently as she had come, back into the inky darkness. I stood there for a moment longer, hugging myself against Nishime's confession. Our plights were not all that different, I realized, despite the differences in our appearance, clothing, and day-to-day life. Nishime, Mabel, Elizabeth, Claudette, and I—we were all striving to make our mark, like the imprint a blacksmith left on their life's work. While our imprints were diverse, our need to carve our own path—and to belong—was the same.

Chapter Twenty-Four

McTavish shook his head, the line between his eyebrows thickening. "Nay, lass. 'Tis a very bad idea. Have ya not thought it through at all? We're liable to start a war by taking one of their women."

I nodded, looking down into my hands folded in my lap. I knew taking Nishime along with us would be a bad idea. But I had wanted to ask, as a woman who wanted to help another woman, something McTavish could never understand. "You're probably right," I said, looking across the tent at him, where we still sat tucked in our sleeping blankets. It was as if we both understood that this might be the last moment we would feel truly warm for many days ahead. "It's just ... I don't think she would be a burden on our travels. She seems strong and knows much of the land."

He sighed heavily, laying back down on his bedroll. Ben had awoken during our conversation and was now gazing over at the older man. "I understand yer sympathy, lass, but I'm afraid the answer is still no."

I lay back myself, staring up at the hole at the top of the tipi, where the wooden beams crossed together in a star. The smoke from the morning

THE FORT

fire swirled up lazily, escaping into the heavens above. "I wish we could stay here for the winter," I murmured softly. "It's comfortable."

McTavish chuckled. "Aye. Though many bairns 'ave been conceived in these tents, between the white fur traders and the Indian women." He grinned over at me. "Pro'ly on that very bedroll you're lyin' on."

I sat up straight, throwing the bedclothes off. "That's quite enough, McTavish," I said sternly as he howled with laughter at my reaction. I stood and padded barefoot over to the flap of the tent, peering outside. Dawn had broken, and the ground was a glittering, frosty white.

"We'd best be on our way," I said, gathering my clothes from where I had piled them on a rug. "The sun is already up."

McTavish barked out another laugh. "I reckon I've turned ya into a voyageur, lass. Up at the break o' dawn, raring to go."

I laughed, then solemnly agreed. No doubt if I met Gabriel on the forest path, he wouldn't recognize me. An hour later, we were dressed, packed, and fed. The Chief met us at the outskirts of the camp, our snowshoes and winter supplies in hand, along with a message that McTavish would deliver once we'd reached Montréal. I scanned the group of men for Nishime, but the girl was nowhere to be seen. Glancing up at McTavish's now stern demeanour, I didn't dare ask to speak with her but instead set a brisk pace as we left the Ojibwa camp, once again on our way.

We pushed ourselves hard, travelling over the rough terrain from dawn until dusk over the next week. McTavish seemed pleased with our progress, and even the weather seemed to hold in our favour. Then, late one afternoon, when we stopped for a quick bite to eat, the first flakes appeared. Throughout the rest of the day, we watched with dismay as the snow grew thick underfoot, adding a crunch to the sound of our footsteps through the forest.

"No matter," McTavish said encouragingly as we set up camp for the evening a few hours later. "I daresay travel with the snowshoes is easier." His frown said otherwise, though, as he gazed up at the steady snowfall falling from the night sky.

"What about a dogsled?" Ben asked, his energy thankfully returned to normal after our visit to the Native camp. "Might we travel on one?"

"Perhaps," McTavish answered, though his eyes were now trained on the darkened forest beyond the clearing we had chosen for the night. He held a hand up to silence us, slowly reaching for his hunting rifle. "There's something there," he whispered.

I nodded, putting my finger to my lips to encourage Ben to be quiet. We were in desperate need of a proper meal, something other than pemmican and rice. McTavish crept into the trees, nimble and light despite his size.

"Bloody hell!" he shouted from the woods, making me jump. He stepped back into the grove, a pair of partridges in his hand. "Unbelievable," he muttered, shoving them at me.

"What's the matter?" I asked, turning over the birds in my hands. They seemed in fine form and would make a delicious dinner. "Where did they come from?"

THE FORT

"We're being followed," he said, eyes narrowed, trying to discern a form in the shadowy cover of trees. "These are a gift."

"A gift?" I asked, and then realization dawned on me. *Nishime.*

"Aye." He sighed heavily, muttering something in Gaelic and raised his eyes towards the heavens. "Two women and a boy, with 'undreds of miles to go. I hope you're the praying type, lass, 'cause me and the good Lord don't see eye to eye, and we've got one hell of a journey to make."

I pursed my lips, wanting to take offence to his statement, but instead threw my arms around his thick neck. "Thank you," I whispered, tears coming to my eyes. McTavish was all thorns and prickles to the world around him, but I knew that his inside was molten gold. He was a kindred spirit through and through.

He grumbled but then took the partridges from me, thrusting his head towards the trees. "You'd best go and find her, then."

I took the lantern from where McTavish had fashioned a makeshift tent and carefully made my way into the snow-covered forest. I had only made my way a few steps in when I felt a cool hand touch my arm. I brought the girl into my embrace, feeling the thump of her heartbeat through her chest.

"You shouldn't have followed us," I scolded, knowing very well that McTavish would be within his rights to send her back. "It was dangerous."

"What of your husband?" she asked, peering past me to where McTavish was showing Ben how to prepare the partridges for roasting. "Will he allow me to travel with you?"

I pulled at her hand, coaxing her out of the forest. McTavish glanced up at us as we emerged, wearing neither a smile nor a frown. "He'll be all right," I said in a low tone, "but you must know, he's not actually my husband. It's a farce for my protection."

Nishime nodded, but her gaze fell to Ben. I knew she wondered about my circumstances, but I did not want to elaborate, not just yet. My belly was already beginning to swell under my loose trousers, much sooner than I had with Ben. It was likely by the time we reached Montréal, I would have to explain myself to more than Nishime.

The partridge was indeed delicious. After we finished, Nishime smiled at me then made her way back into the forest. I looked over at McTavish, surprised that she did not want to sleep closer to the fire, but he shrugged, busying himself with his own bedroll. I took one more glance into the trees, then did the same, preparing for the evening ahead.

Later that night, I woke, finding that she had, in fact, crept to the edge of the clearing, sitting with her legs tucked close to her body, trying to stay warm. I sat up, beckoning with my hand for her to come closer. The fire was banked, but the embers still provided some warmth against the frigid night air.

She nodded and came beside me, and I opened my arm, inviting her to share my blanket. Nishime hesitated a moment but ducked in beside me, pulling the wool over both of our shoulders.

"Thank you," she said in a whisper as not to wake Ben, who lay beside us. "Perhaps it seems foolish, running away from my people."

I shook my head, thinking of Henry. To be forced to marry a man who did not have any consideration for his wife seemed terrifying, but I knew well that having any choice in the matter was not a luxury afforded to all.

"I understand," I consoled her, wondering if she was having second thoughts. "Thankfully, my father allows me some liberties."

THE FORT

Nishime swallowed back what seemed like tears. "Mine as well," she said hoarsely, "But he took ill and died a few months ago. Since then, my uncle has been making the decisions about my future."

I took her hand and squeezed it. I shared with her about my father's ailment and the constant worry that sat lurking deep within me. "He did everything for me," I said, trying not to let tears fall lest they freeze on my cheeks. "He taught me his blacksmithing trade so I could survive alone, if need be."

She smiled back at me. "I think the Creator has brought us together," she said. "For my father also taught me to hunt and live off the land, as our ancestors intended. I have no need for a husband."

I thought of Gabriel, so far away. "Perhaps one day, Nishime, we will find happiness when we least expect it." I smiled, though it did not reach my eyes. Ben stirred beside us, so we tried again to sleep, huddled side by side, protecting each other from more than the cold.

As I had thought, Nishime was not a hindrance to our travel but an asset instead. Her footsteps were swift and sure, and she helped carry Ben through the difficult parts that he could not manage alone. Sometimes, she would disappear for hours at a time, rejoining us later in the day. Those times, she would often return with game in hand—squirrels that had not yet hidden away for the winter, rabbits, and even a red-tailed fox. Although McTavish did not engage in much conversation with her, I could tell he was impressed with the constant source of food.

"It's damn chilly," McTavish commented one morning while he helped Ben fasten on his snowshoes. The rounded foot support, fashioned with a wood frame and leather straps, helped disperse our weight across the snow so we did not sink into the deeper parts. "Best bundle up today."

Nishime came tramping back into camp, covered in fresh snow from her early morning scout. "There's a trapper's cottage an hour from here," she reported, helping herself to pemmican and the cup of berry tea I had prepared earlier. It was now cold, but she didn't seem to mind, drinking it down in one gulp. She turned to speak with McTavish directly. "There's a dog team outside. If we hurry, perhaps you can talk to him."

I widened my eyes in hopeful delight. If the trapper was heading east, and we were able to catch a ride, we might make it to Montréal before the worst of the winter set in. Otherwise, we might be forced to stop and seek shelter, doing our best to survive in the bitter cold.

Our trek to the trapper's cottage was slowed by a sharp wind that bit into my cheeks, the snow swirling thick around us. Each step seemed slower than the last, and I pulled my fur robe over the lower part of my face, doing the same for Ben. The temperature had seemed to drop drastically overnight, my lungs burning with each breath.

Eventually, the trapper's hut came into view. It was a rough lean-to, crudely constructed of fallen lumber and not large enough to house more than one person. Nishime, Ben and I waited a few paces behind while McTavish rapped sharply at the door of the hut. For a moment, it seemed that no one would answer, but then the door flew open, revealing a lone man. He was a greasy character, tall and thin, his beard and mustache stained a deep yellow. He stared at McTavish without speaking then his gaze flitted to us, bushy eyebrows raised.

THE FORT

"We require a lift east, as far as Montréal," McTavish said, though I heard the wariness in his voice. Even by sled, the journey would take the better part of two weeks. He glanced over his shoulder at us, waiting in the snow. "My wife is with child."

I stared straight ahead as Nishime shifted beside me, hearing McTavish's words. She had seen me sharing a tipi with him and was no doubt coming to a scandalous conclusion about our pretend marriage. I brushed the shame aside, no longer allowing it to define me. Regardless of whether I ever found Gabriel, I would no longer wallow in self-loathing. My children were a blessing, not a burden, as my father had said to me long ago.

The trapper raked his gaze over me, then shifted his beady eyes to Nishime. I shivered, swallowing down a strong sense of revulsion. "I cannot carry the lot of you," he rasped, his tone entirely unfriendly. He sized up McTavish with his large girth and height. "Just the women and child."

My heart caught in my throat as McTavish looked back at me, a forlorn expression on his craggy face. He was going to agree and be left to navigate the wilderness alone. "No," I said firmly, walking over and placing my hand gently on his broad back. "I won't leave you behind."

McTavish took me by the elbow and propelled me away from the door. The greasy trapper shrugged, going back into the cabin, shutting the door against the cold. "Listen to me, lass," McTavish said, keeping his voice quiet. "This might be yer only chance. Dinna worry yerself o'r me."

I shook my head, even though I knew that I would eventually agree. "I don't like that man, McTavish."

"Aye," he agreed, casting a look at the hut, where the deer hide flap moved back over the window, the trapper watching us. He directed his attention to Nishime, standing with Ben. "You keep an eye on Abby, ya hear? No more adventures into the woods alone."

Nishime nodded furiously, her face grim. "Yes, sir."

McTavish blocked the trapper's view of us, sliding a small hunting knife out for me, then rummaging around in his rucksack for the purse of coins. "Take these. I'll come to find ya once I reach Montréal."

My throat was thick with emotion, and I blinked hard, not wanting the tears to freeze my eyelashes. "How will you find us?"

"I'll find ya, lass," he said gruffly, reaching down to pat Ben fondly on the head. "Just like yer Frenchman will." He turned and marched back up to the cabin, rapping on the door once again. When the unsavoury trapper answered, McTavish held out one of the coins in his palm. "For yer trouble. I'll expect you'll deliver them to the city itself."

The man grabbed the coin from his palm, pocketing the treasure. "We'll go as far as the dogs take us," he said simply. "I'm leaving shortly."

We arranged ourselves on the narrow sled, me sitting on a pile of furs with Ben on my lap. Nishime had no choice but to sit at my feet, and I encouraged her to lean back, head resting against my legs. McTavish helped harness the dogs into their leads, a collection of a dozen mangy-looking animals. Finally, the trapper took his place at the front of the sled.

With a lurching jolt, we were off, bumpy at first, as the dogs found their footing with the additional weight. Soon though, we were sliding through the snow, the wind whipping my hair. I craned my body, watching as McTavish melted into the horizon. My heart, which was now nothing more than shards, broke once more as my giant Scotsman disappeared into nothing.

Chapter Twenty-Five

Nishime held back my hair from my face as I emptied my churning stomach onto the snowbank. My nausea had become exacerbated by the rapid ride on the dog sled, especially as the trapper, who had still not provided us with his name, seemed fond of driving the dogs hard. We whipped through the patches of ice at a neck-breaking speed, jolting to and fro on our precarious perch. Even Ben seemed a bit green.

"It must be a healthy babe," Nishime said in a low tone as she passed me a cup of water to rinse my mouth. "She's reminding you of her presence every day."

I gave a half-hearted chuckle. "Yes, well, I'm much more ill than I was with Ben." I shook my head as she held out a chunk of pemmican. "Best not chance it until my stomach has settled a bit."

Nishime nodded, tucking the precious staple back away in her beaded pouch. She glanced around the clearing where we had stopped for the night, then over to the man, who was tending to the dogs. "I'll go out again tonight after he sleeps. There may be some animal carcasses left behind after the cold snap." She rubbed her hands together, her breath coming out in a white stream. It had indeed been frigid.

Ben, Nishime, and I slept as close to each other as possible, with our fur robes laid between us and the frozen ground. I was fraught with worry for McTavish, though Nishime reassured me that he was hardened against the weather and had likely stayed in the trapper's cabin.

"Perhaps we should have done the same," I muttered to myself, casting a wary eye on our escort. Sleeping together not only provided warmth, but safety too. The man had not given me a second glance, but I had noticed his lecherous stare resting on Nishime more than once.

I crawled into our makeshift bed exhausted, my arms wrapped tight around Ben, but I lay awake for some time before I fell into an uneasy slumber with Gabriel in my dreams.

The sun shone warm on my face, the perfect spring morning. I tended to the garden, coaxing the seedlings, a babe gurgling on a blanket nearby. My heart felt whole and, except for a small tinge of worry, I felt happy.

I was accosted from behind, lusty kisses trailing down my neck, his hands roaming indecent places, considering we were outdoors in full view of anyone who happened to pass by.

"Stop that, Gabriel," I said, laughing as he gave a desperate groan. "You'll have me pregnant again in no time. Little Edmund needs his time with his mother's milk to grow."

"What's a man to do when his wife is bent over in the garden? It was such a delightful view."

I turned to him, kissing him fully on the mouth. "Don't be greedy, my husband. You had me just this morning." I stroked his beard, which was neatly trimmed these days, along with his hair. He was nearly fully grey now, with deep lines etched around his eyes.

THE FORT

"Ma chérie, I am just making up for the time we spent apart. It was the longest year of my life."

"Year and a half," I corrected him, tracing his features with my fingers, leaving remnants of soil behind. "But now you've been home for three, with two more babes. My body needs a rest." He gave me a loving smile in response, which set my heart ablaze. Truthfully, I would never say no. I wanted all the children he would give me, and although I would never admit as much, I couldn't get enough of him either.

"All right," he said, taking my hand and pulling me to my feet. He leaned down to pick up the baby, then looked at me, his smile replaced with a solemness in his deep blue eyes. "It's time."

I let him lead me away from the garden, but my gaze rested on the hills that lay in the distance beyond our farm. Three years. The worry that had been just an ember the moment before grew tenfold, like when my father pumped the bellow in the blacksmith's forge. Three years with no word or sign. Ben and Alexandre rode into the city weekly, checking the docks and the local public house for any whisper of him, but there was none.

"Frozen to death, more than likely," Claudette had said to Gabriel one morning in the kitchen when she thought I was still asleep. "Or eaten by some animal, organs and all."

Gabriel and I rounded the corner of the barn, where the others were waiting. Claudette and Nishime stood together, Nishime's rounded belly between them. It was her first, and she was nervous as her time grew near. They looked up as I approached, coming over to gather me into their embrace. Their husbands were already out by the cherry tree, shovels in hand, tasked with laying my father in his final resting place.

"He lived a good life," Claudette murmured as she drew me into her ample bosom. "And he loved the company of the children."

245

I smiled at my children, who were gathered around Gabriel, clamouring for his attention. Ben and Alexandre stood near the barn door, empty sacks at their feet. They would head out after the funeral to check their traps. Gabriel had taught them well, and the meat and furs provided us with a good trade value in the Montréal markets. We wanted for nothing, falling asleep at night with our bellies full and our family safe and warm.

I had taught the older boys as well. I ran a small local horseshoeing forge, and Ben had taken over for me during my last pregnancy. He gave me a wide grin, reaching behind the barn door to produce a pile of small lucky charm horseshoes.

"I fashioned imprints for all of us," he said, coming over to show me his own, marked with his initials. He was taller than me now, growing into a man. "I'd like to lay them to rest with Papa."

"Oh, Ben, that's such a lovely idea," I said, tears coming to my eyes at his thoughtfulness. I had already grieved the loss of my father in Gabriel's arms, my husband comforting me in his soothing French whispers. I sorted through Ben's collection of charms, my heart stopping cold at the last one. D.M. Duncan McTavish.

"He would be here if he could, Mama. One day, he will, I just know it."

I reached out to squeeze his hand. My son was always a beacon of hope. "Ben—"

"No, Mama, he's not gone." He thumped his chest, which had started to fill out, muscular and strong. "I can still feel him, here."

I woke with a start, my heart racing as a heavy weight settled on top of me. I blinked in the darkness, a foul-smelling breath filling my nostrils. I managed a gasp before a rough hand clapped over my mouth and nose.

Another hand roamed my body, intrusive and rough. "Where is it?" the man's voice growled in my ear, his weight pressing hard against my swollen belly. I squirmed, suddenly aware that Ben was not beside me. I struggled frantically, vomit rising in my throat.

There was a sharp pain in my side as the man began to pummel me with his fist. I screamed behind the hand over my mouth, tears streaming down my face. He had no intention of raping me, that much was clear, but what he was after, I could not guess.

"I saw the Scotsman give you a purse. It's not in your sack." He gave me another punch to the stomach, the pain so fierce I struggled to breathe. The coins were hidden with Nishime, but he wasn't going to give me the chance to explain.

He stopped hitting me, his free hand instead coming to the front of my throat. His fingers quickly found their place around my windpipe, and my blood ran cold to realize that he likely had killed before. My life was disposable to him, a mere inconvenience in search of the coins. As his fingers tightened, I tried to again scream for Ben.

There was a scuffle in the pitch black above me, and an additional weight came down on top of me. The man's fingers were tight, and my consciousness became dull, my thoughts fading back to my dream. McTavish was gone, dead in the cold, barren wilderness. I was soon to follow at the hands of an unnamed man. Gabriel would never find me, as my remains would be picked clean by spring.

I was dimly aware of a gurgling, a sound like a babbling brook in spring. The man's fingers loosened, and the weight was lifted off me. I gasped in a breath, my head and heart on fire.

"Abby!" It was Nishime, shaking me. "Are you all right? Did he hurt you?"

I shook my head weakly, unable to speak, but the throbbing ache in my womb filled me with a cold dread. "Ben," I managed, struggling to sit up. "Where's Ben?" The man lay crumpled to the side of me, dead. I wasn't sure how, but Nishime had saved my life.

Nishime widened her eyes and frantically looked around the clearing. There were clouds overhead, and it was difficult to see. I started to sob, a rough sound in my throat, my bile rising. I raised my hands to my face, then stopped short. My hands were wet and sticky, covered in the man's blood.

"Ben!" I yelled hoarsely into the dark night, as loud as my bruised windpipe would allow. Nishime was fumbling by dog sled, looking for the lantern. The dogs, awakened by the ruckus, were barking and whimpering. I pushed myself to my feet, gasping as a sharp pain shot through my side. *No. My baby. Gabriel's baby.*

There was a bob of light as Nishime lit the lantern. "You stay here," she said, coming over to me, her voice panicked. "He can't be far."

"No." I shook my head stubbornly, knowing that no amount of rest could stop what had already started. Tears streamed down my face, but I shook my head again. "I'm coming with you."

Nishime took my bloody hand in hers, and we scoured the clearing for any sign of my son. Panic rose hot in my throat with each corner searched, and my frantic sobs echoed behind us. The dogs, aroused by the scent of their master's blood, yelped in a high-pitched frenzy, jerking on their leads.

"Ben!" I screamed over the noise. Nishime dropped my hand, ducked into the forest, and dragged out a deer from her late-night hunting. She retrieved a large knife from her belt, slicing the animal open. She cut out the organs with a deft hand, then tossed them to the dogs, who instantly forgot their worries, fighting over the fresh meat.

THE FORT

"Mama!" The cry came from the far outskirts of the clearing, and I ran to Ben, ignoring the hot splash of fluid that ran down my legs, soaking my trousers. I sank to my knees, checking him over with my hands, leaving behind streaks of blood.

"I'm fine, Mama." He sobbed, clearly shaken. "I left to relieve myself in the forest, but when I came back, that man was on top of you."

I gathered him in my arms, crooning over him like he was a baby. He pressed himself against me, probably trying to remove what he had seen from his mind. Nishime came over to us and wrapped her arms around me from behind.

I turned to face her, suddenly remembering how Gabriel had also embraced me in my dream. How happy we had been, together as a family—but that's all it had been. A dream, nothing more. In the present, my stomach was starting to cramp, my womb vacating the only reminder I had of him.

"I'm losing the baby," I whispered, my throat raw from where he had tried to squeeze the life from me. "I need your help, Nishime."

Nishime's face fell, reflecting the grief on my own. We sat together for a moment on the frozen ground, and then she took Ben from my arms. "Come," she said, leading me towards the fire. "Let's get you cleaned up."

Chapter Twenty-Six

I looked the other way as Nishime shrouded the remains of my delivery with a blanket, her body shielding Ben from the view. Dawn was breaking; morning light reflected silver off the snow, making the world much too bright for my liking. I let my head slump down to my chest, my head foggy from the tea Nishime had prepared.

"To help with the pain," she'd said, coaxing the hot liquid down my throat. I was grateful for her beaded pouch, which seemed to hold an assortment of herbs and remedies. It had not only numbed the pain but also my grief.

She handed me a plate of deer meat, fragrant and hot. I pushed her hand away, repulsed by the idea of food. She shoved it back at me. "You need to eat. We need to be on our way again."

I shook my head. "I'm going back to McTavish," I slurred, tossing my head in the general direction of where we'd come. My dream still lingered, and I worried for him. "You go on without me."

THE FORT

Nishime squatted down, her long braid trailing down her back. "No, Abby. There's a storm coming." She cast a pensive look to the sky. "We need to find some sort of shelter."

I followed her gaze up over the trees, not understanding what she saw, but I didn't question her. My heart gave a sudden lurch, knowing that I would have to carry on once again through my brokenness. A keening wail left my lips, and I fell back on the furs that I had birthed on not moments before. The wail became a scream as the loss ripped through my chest, echoing through the clearing and setting the dogs into their own panicked cries.

"Mama!" It was Ben, trying to curl up against my chest. I forced myself to rise, to put away my rage, as the night had scarred my child as well. A mother's care knew no bounds, even when she needed care herself.

"It's all right, Ben," I soothed, choking back my agony. I picked up the plate I had discarded beside me. "Let's eat. And then we shall be on our way." I glanced up to Nishime, who gave me a half smile, tears rimming her eyes.

We packed quickly, astutely avoiding the man, who still lay crumpled in the snow, a dark patch of crimson beneath him. We would neither take the time to bury him nor would I leave my baby to rest in this clearing. It was Ben who lifted the tiny bundle into the sled, tucking it safely away. He had grown so much, aged well beyond his years.

"Do you know which direction to Montréal?" I asked as Nishime took the lead in the front of the sled.

"East," she replied, her brown eyes trained on the path ahead. "The Creator will lead us."

I pulled Ben snugly against me, closing my eyes as we left. There was so much pain, but I had no more tears. It seemed my heart had become

251

separate from my body, unable to contain any more hurt. I had been foolish to allow myself to be separated from McTavish. Two women alone with a child in the wilderness were mere prey to both men and beast.

Shaking my head vigorously, I discarded the dream of the night before, of the farm and a family with Gabriel, onto the icy path below us. Hope and dreams made me weak, nothing but a fool. I squared my shoulders against the biting wind and constructed my own high walls around my crumpled heart. I built my palisade thick and strong, a fortress that no one could enter.

The wind bit into my flesh, chunks of snow and ice pelting my face. My gloved fingers were numb with cold, grasping the reins that controlled the dogs. It had been some time since they had been fed, and I could feel their exhaustion through the lead. My arms ached with the effort, my side still throbbing from the trapper's assault. I bled heavily, and although Nishime had helped me fashion a rag from a rabbit pelt, it was soaked through. I knew we must stop soon for a rest, but the storm threatened the horizon, and we still had found no shelter.

"Over there!" Nishime shouted, her voice barely audible over the wind howling past my ears. I didn't bother to respond, as my lungs were already burning from the cold. I was weary to the bone, and any distraction might result in my dropping the lead and losing control of the sled. I scanned the horizon and saw a dot in the distance. I prayed that it was

THE FORT

shelter, as to be out during the worst of the storm would prove fatal for us all.

It was indeed a small cabin, and the three of us nearly fell on the doorstep in our haste to knock on the door. Ben's teeth were chattering uncontrollably, and I pulled him close, though I could not offer him any additional warmth.

The door opened, bringing with it a gust of warm air, a hearth roaring within. An older man stood in the door frame, and behind him, a plump woman. They scanned our faces, frowning.

"Please," I managed, wondering if my lips were blue, as I had lost feeling in them. "Please give us shelter for the night."

The man started to speak in French, and I desperately tried to remember any of the words I had learned from Gabriel. Those days spent in his arms seemed a world away, like a distant dream that had all been a figment of my imagination.

Beside me, Nishime conversed with the man in broken French, and I once again found myself grateful for her presence. I hoped that she would stay with us once we reached Montréal, but I did not want to impose on her kindness. Without her, I would likely still be in the dreaded clearing of that morning, overwhelmed with anguish.

"D'accord," the man said, though he gave Nishime a long look. "Seulement parce que c'est Noël."

Nishime cleared her throat beside me. "It's Christmas," she translated, squeezing my arm. "And they will give us shelter from the storm."

We stripped off our outer furs, handing them to the man, who took them to the stable to dry. The woman gasped as I stepped out of mine. I looked down and saw that I had bled through the entire length of my trousers, a grisly reminder of the tragedy of the night. I turned my head away, as I did not have the heart to try and explain.

The woman shooed her husband away, taking me into her arms. I stiffened, trying to push her affection away, but she held tight. I gave in, melting against her, a sob escaping my lips.

Nishime explained the situation to the couple, explaining in English to me that she left out the part about the trapper's fate. I nodded, understanding that we should not speak of him, for she had, in fact, killed him. Any officer of the law would not side with an Indigenous person, even if it were in defence.

The woman's face pulled into a deep crease, and for the first time, I noticed the absence of children in the cabin. It seemed that maybe she understood my loss, woman to woman. She set about the cabin in a flurry, hauling out a large copper basin. I tried to wave her off, but she insisted, getting her husband to haul buckets of snow to heat by the fire. Then, sending him and Ben out to tend to the dogs in the stable, she helped me undress. There was another gasp as she saw the side of my stomach where the man had beaten me. It was blue and purple, and I moaned in pain when she lightly touched it.

"Qu'est-ce qui t'est arrivée, ma chérie?" she murmured, as I turned my head away once again. I lowered myself into the warm water, willing myself not to cry. Yet, as the kind woman began to help me wash, my walls broke, and tears poured down my face.

"Gabriel." I sobbed into my shaking hands as the warm water washed away the blood and grime. "I'm so sorry, my love. I'm so sorry our child is gone."

THE FORT

Nishime came to my side, taking one of my hands in hers. "Perhaps we should ask her to bury your baby," she suggested gently. "They seem like kind folk."

I nodded through my distress, and Nishime asked the woman, who crossed herself in the Catholic way, then ran out the door to fetch her husband again. I widened my eyes. Surely, she would not make him dig into the frozen ground during a storm.

Nishime gave a low chuckle as she washed my hair. "It seems that she gives the directions, and he follows her command."

I laughed with her, some of my brokenness washed away with the bath. "She reminds me of Claudette, a French woman at Fort Augustus." I paused, remembering when she had stubbornly left Gabriel with her religious figurines as he recovered from the cougar attack. "Actually, Nishime, Claudette gave me something when I left the Fort. Will you fetch my rucksack? I'd like to bury it with her."

"Of course." She stood, starting to walk away. Then she came back, reaching into her beaded pouch and held out a birchbark match. "Will you allow me to place this with her? My people believe her spirit will use it to light the way on her journey to the other world."

I smiled at her, touched beyond measure. "Yes, thank you. Thank you for everything, Nishime. You saved my life."

She blushed and turned away. "I only wish I had saved hers, too."

Although I did not know if my child had been a daughter or a son, I named the baby Mary, after my mother, and we laid her to rest under an apple tree. Joséphine, as she introduced herself, and her husband, Jean, assured me that it would blossom to a lovely pink in the spring and that they would pray for our safe journey to Montréal. Joséphine had found a hand-knit blanket in a chest of drawers and her husband had fashioned a rough wooden box in the stable. Inside, I placed the statue of Saint Christopher that Claudette had bestowed upon me inside the box, with the match from Nishime. I longed for one of my lucky horseshoes but instead settled on a lock of my hair, as well as one from Ben.

When it was finished, we barricaded ourselves indoors against the storm. Joséphine put us to work in the kitchen, retrieving extra food from the cellar to feed us a Christmas feast. After we stuffed ourselves, Ben sat with Jean, playing chess, while Nishime helped clean up the kitchen, insisting I rest. I tried to relax, but I found myself missing my father terribly. Was he still alive? Or had he, too, passed, buried in the frozen ground? And what of Gabriel on this Christmas day? Was he safe, celebrating the holiday with his son? A painful lump grew in my throat at the thought of him, an entire world away.

"Don't worry, Mama," Ben whispered as we settled down later that night in front of the hearth. "Mr. Jean says we're only a few weeks away from Montréal. Gabriel will find us, and we can have the farm with the animals, like you said."

"That's right, my sweet boy," I said without much conviction in my voice. I kissed him on the forehead, exhausted. It had been the longest day I had ever known.

I closed my eyes, ready for sleep to take me away, but Ben nudged me awake again. "He's coming for us, don't worry, Mama." He thumped his chest, lean and scrawny from our long journey. "I can still feel him, here."

Chapter Twenty-Seven

WINTER 1807, MONTRÉAL

Montréal was a bustling hub of activity, even in the bitter cold. I rubbed my gloved hands together, trying to keep them warm as I made my way back outdoors from the steaming laundry room. The three of us had arrived four weeks prior, a sight for sore eyes after pushing hard through the shortened winter days. Nishime had quickly found a buyer for the sled and dogs, though I'd shuddered at the thought of someone recognizing that they had belonged to the greasy man—now likely nothing more than bones, picked clean by some hungry predator. Since then, we had found a mishmash of jobs to get us by, starting with gutting and cleaning fish first thing in the morning. Then, Nishime went to one of the fur warehouses, where she had procured work finishing the furs. Some were stripped of their hair to make use of the hides, while others were cured for the long journey overseas.

I had gotten a job in the afternoons working for the local laundress. While I didn't get paid in coins, it allowed us room and board above the shop, the three of us sharing a single space. All in all, it was hard work, but we were surviving.

The late afternoon was brisk, and the sun had already started to make its way onto the horizon, shining into my eyes as I made my way to the city center. I allowed Ben to roam freely in the afternoons after he had finished his job of hauling and stacking firewood for the laundress. He had been desperate to play with some of the local children, and I didn't need him underfoot while lifting the heavy, wet clothes from the basin to the washboards and then up to dry. Around the dinner hour, I ducked out to find him, as he was always too caught up with his play to notice the setting sun.

I rounded the corner of the church courtyard, where Ben was most often found, playing a game with sticks and a puck on the icy surface with the other boys. Scanning the crowded area, I found his ruddy cheeks and toque quickly and motioned with my hand for him to come. He groaned and pouted at the other boys, wishing he could stay out longer. I gave a short laugh at his dramatics, but then my attention was pulled to the far side of the courtyard, where a skirmish had broken out.

As the crowd cleared, I gasped as my gaze fell to a large, foreboding man at the edge of the drunken brawl. My heart leapt at the sight of him—he was a good head taller than all the others, with a firm set to his jaw and a scowl set on his features. My giant Scotsman.

I started over to him, cupping my hands around my mouth and shouting his name across the yard in the most unladylike way. His head jerked up, meeting my eyes for a split second. His eyes widened, then, without any further hesitation, McTavish turned the other way and ran to the nearest alleyway.

THE FORT

I stopped short, shaking my head in confusion. "That's strange," I said to Ben, who was now standing beside me. "I could have sworn that was McTavish." Not waiting for him to answer, I left him behind. I dropped into a jog, careful of the icy patches on the cobblestone beneath my feet.

"McTavish!" I called again as I reached the entrance to the alley where he had vanished. It was deserted, with only large footprints in the un-cleared snow indicating that anyone had been through it. I frowned, a dark worry edging its way into my guts. Why on earth had he run away from me?

I called his name again as I followed the footprints. Perhaps I had been mistaken? No, I recalled the moment his eyes had met mine, and something had flashed across his face. Fear? Regret? Displeasure?

"Dammit," I swore softly to myself, tears pricking the corners of my eyes. A light snow had started, the flakes melting on my cheeks, which had become flaming hot with my realization. He had run *away* from me. The worry that had sat in my stomach the moment before roared to life as something new, something fierce. A boiling rage erupted from me. How dare he run from me? To think he had discarded me like a heavy pack at the end of the voyageur's long day. And yet he had done exactly that, tossing me aside like chaff in the wind.

I picked up an empty pail that sat waiting on the street for the milk-man's delivery. I swung the pail hard at the side of the building next to me, the strike sending pain reverberating back into my muscles. I swung again and again, letting out a high-pitched scream that echoed through the alleyway.

"I never liked you anyway, you god-awful Scot!" I yelled, discarding the now-ruined bucket on the ground. Tears streamed down my face, and a growl rose in my throat. "You're a coward and a horrible excuse for a man!" My stomach churned, and I turned and ran back the way I had come, lest he see me be sick from wherever he was hiding. I would not waste one more thought on Duncan McTavish.

"What happened?" Ben asked anxiously as I stormed out of the alleyway. More than a few people looked my way, likely alerted by me shrieking like a feral cat. I straightened my back, tight and stiff from the day's work, and wiped my face clean.

"Nothing happened. He just doesn't care to see us, is all, Ben. He was commissioned to take us on the journey, and now that's over."

"But—" Ben frowned as he trotted alongside me, my pace fueled by my fury. I knew what he was thinking, remembering all the moments we'd shared with the crew along the way. I stopped, taking his hand in mine. He was only a boy of seven but had already lived through so much.

"You must understand that in this life, some people will disappoint you. I thought McTavish was our friend too, but it seems that he wants to go his own way now."

Ben nodded, though I noticed that he swallowed hard. "Just like my father, right, Mama?"

I winced, regretting that my son knew the bitter tonic of rejection at such an early age. "Your father didn't leave you. He doesn't know about you. That's why we had to flee the fort and leave Papa behind. I couldn't risk that lawyer taking you away from me."

We started to walk again, the snow crunching under our feet. Ben was quiet, mulling over the situation. My anger started to dissolve, and in its place was a piercing hurt. I replayed my last moments with McTavish, when his brow had been furrowed in concern at having to separate. My own creased into a frown at the memory. I desperately wanted to believe it wasn't true, but I was wise enough to believe my own words: McTavish had abandoned us.

The next morning, I feigned illness due to my monthly, which had Nishime fussing over me with tea and biscuits. I had not felt like myself since the miscarriage, and although I tried to keep the symptoms private, Nishime seemed to have an all-knowing understanding.

"It takes the body time to heal from tragedy," she said, handing me a cup of black tea. "It's normal that you feel unwell."

I shrugged her off, as I knew the source of my grief on this particular morning had more to do with McTavish. As for the baby, I had tried to push the memory into the far corner of my mind, locked tight.

"I think I'll rest this morning if that's all right with you," I said, leaning back against the pillows she had propped up on my bedroll. We had slowly begun to accumulate more belongings, and our room was starting to feel cozy. Nishime had woven a rug, helping to keep out the winter chill. There was a small window on the far wall, and Ben was seated on a wooden stool, staring out of it. He had been quiet the entire evening before, and I regretted my overt emotional reaction of yesterday. I should have just kept quiet or pretended that I had been mistaken about McTavish's identity.

"That's fine," Nishime agreed, walking over to join Ben. She followed his gaze out the window. "That poor woman is back out there. It's the third time this week."

I sat up in my bed, nodding. "The one with the two little boys? Yes, I saw them yesterday, asking for food." They had been huddled together, panhandling on the street. It was a dangerous position for a woman alone to be in, liable to be robbed, beaten, or worse.

Nishime nudged Ben, indicating it was time to leave for the morning work on the docks. She met my eye before gathering up the remainder of our breakfast to give to the woman and her sons. I smiled to myself as they left, the door banging behind them. Nishime was a kind-hearted soul, and I was forever grateful for her companionship. I had told her everything about Henry and Gabriel, and she, too, kept up hope that Gabriel would return to us someday.

After a few moments, I dragged myself from the warmth of my bedroll and put on my clothes. I took a few deep breaths to calm myself, then made my way outside. The ache in my heart wouldn't cease, and I was determined to make McTavish *say* the words to me. I wanted him to look me in the eye and explain himself like a grown man.

I trudged down the same route I had taken the day before, an anxious fluttering in my stomach. I peered into the doorways along the way, not sure where or even if McTavish might be staying in the area. When I reached the end of the alleyway, I let out a disgruntled sigh. There was no inn or public house where one might lodge. It was no use. Montréal was well-established, with many nooks and crannies where any man not wanting to be found could hide.

My footsteps were heavy on the way back to the laundry shop, but I pushed the thought of McTavish away. I instead focused on planning our future once the winter was finally over. I had already inquired at a few of the local blacksmith shops, and one smith had reluctantly agreed

THE FORT

to take me on as farrier come the spring. It would be better money than cleaning fish, and perhaps I could still manage the laundry.

I nearly stumbled across the woman and her boys, who were still sitting outside the laundress, the food that Nishime had delivered already devoured. I gave another hearty sigh, then crouched down to their level.

"You shouldn't be here," I said to the mother, not able to look into the faces of the hungry little boys. "It's not safe."

"My husband died two months ago. I'ave no way of puttin' food on the table." Her eyes were filled with melancholy and despair, and she pulled her youngest child tight against her.

I sat down next to her, ignoring the way the snow seeped into my dress. "I lost my baby around the same time," I said softly, not sure why I was sharing my pain with a stranger. "And in the fall, I had to leave my father behind at Fort Edmonton. He's ill, and I will likely never see him again." One of the boys started to whimper, but I continued, raising my voice. "I was betrothed to a vile Englishman who betrayed me in the worst possible way. And," I ranted, my tribulations flooding the dam I had built around them, "just yesterday, I ... I lost a friend."

The woman stared at me with her eyes wide, but I just shook my head, refusing her pity. "You have plenty of ways to put food on the table. I have a son to take care of, too. You must find work. You must survive."

I stood, extending my hand to her. She hesitated but then took it, gathering her children and her belongings. I left her on the curbside while I went to speak with the laundry lady.

"Don't need her," she barked, pushing me aside with a heavy basket laden with bedsheets from the local brothel. "I've got enough help at the moment."

263

I frowned, then gave her my sweetest smile. "She needs help. Her children are going hungry."

The owner shrugged. "Then give 'er your job. It's a hard time for everyone, lass."

I left the shop, feeling disheartened once again. "She doesn't need anyone," I said gently to the woman. "But I will take you to the docks tomorrow. There's plenty of work there if you don't mind the smell of fish."

I walked with the woman to her home, surprised when she stopped in front of a vacant blacksmith shop. I peered inside, the darkened windows filling me with nostalgia. I missed the weight of the tongs in my hand.

I missed my father.

The boys trudged through the shop to a set of stairs that led to a dwelling above. "Do you live here?" I asked though it was apparent they did. My mind whirled with potential.

"My husband was a smith," she explained, making to follow the children upstairs. "I suppose I could put the shop up for sale, but where would we live?"

My chest filled with excitement, and I barely contained a squeal. Surely, with the leftover coins from the Chief Factor, along with what we had earned from the sled and dogs, would be enough. I put a hand on her shoulder, a wide grin on my face. "I've got just the solution."

Chapter Twenty-Eight

The sharp twang of the hammer on the anvil echoed in my ears and my muscles were heavy with fatigue as I closed shop for the evening. It was already mid-summer, and the Montréal air was thick and humid. My clothes clung to my body, perpetually damp with sweat. I was already looking forward to my weekly wash in the neighbouring spring the day after tomorrow.

I wearily climbed the stairs to our lodgings, my feet heavy with more than exhaustion. The week before had marked one year since I had fled Fort Augustus since I had seen my father. I had thought about him often since I had opened *Abby's Horse and Saddlery* in early spring. At first, I worried that people would not trust my work, as I was a woman, but I had found that folks were eager to have their tack repaired without having to wait in line at the other blacksmith's. My skill rivalled any man's, and my reputation kept me busy from dawn 'til dusk.

Ben and Nishime were not yet home, so I took the opportunity to lay on my bed for a quiet moment before starting the preparations for our evening meal. Although exhausted, I was content in a way I had never felt before. I was taking care of myself, my small business was thriving, Ben was attending the local school, and although I missed Gabriel, I no longer worried about what would happen if he did not find his way to me. I would be all right.

I heard Nishime and Ben chattering excitedly through the open window, and I smiled, wondering what they had procured from the weekly market. Not fish, given the way Ben grinned as they opened the door. Fish was plentiful and inexpensive, but my son found it unappetizing.

"Beef today, Mama," he exclaimed excitedly, and I raised my eyebrows at Nishime. She was excellent at bargaining at the market, often bringing some of her beaded work, weaving, or a cured hide to trade, but the cut of meat Ben held was large and costly.

"It was a gift," she explained, blushing from head to toe. "From Daniel."

"Another one?" I teased, giving her a knowing grin. Daniel was a Métis man who Nishime had met at the fur warehouse. He was smitten with her, and although she didn't say much, I thought Nishime felt the same way about him.

Nishime took the meat and started to cut it into smaller pieces while I prepared the vegetables and barley for a stew. She was quiet, glancing over at me occasionally.

"We saw McTavish today at the market," she said softly, not quite meeting my eye. "Just from behind. It's strange that's he's still here in the city."

I gave the pot a stir as she came over and added the hunks of meat. "I'm sure I couldn't guess why," I replied, a cold edge to my voice. It was the second sighting of the man since he had run from me on that cold winter day. I, too, wondered why he had not rejoined the voyageurs, but I refused to let my mind dwell on him.

"Thank you for sharing your gift. And please thank Daniel, too," I said, standing to move away from her and change the subject.

"Yes. About that, Abby." She stood, grasping my hand, looking at me directly. "He's asked me to marry him. He wants to travel east to the Métis settlement to live among his people. Some of mine, the Ojibwa, are there, too."

I let out a heavy sigh, smiling at her, though my eyes pricked with tears. I had known this day was coming, though I had selfishly hoped it wouldn't. I had tried to keep my loneliness at bay by keeping busy, but with the news of Nishime leaving, I felt the acute sting of it in my throat.

"That's wonderful," I said, hiding my face as I embraced her. "I'm truly happy for you."

"Come with us," she whispered into my ear. "I can't bear to leave you here alone."

"No." I smoothed her sleek black hair as I let her go. She was a sweet soul, sent to help me through the last leg of my journey, but now it was time for us to part ways. "I have Ben, and the blacksmith shop. We'll do just fine here, Nishime. You don't need to worry about me."

She nodded, brushing away a tear. "I know. We'll leave in two weeks. We must make haste before the winter comes." She took a deep breath before bending to stir our dinner. "I'm nervous, Abby. You must tell me everything there is to know about men."

I gave wry chuckle, remembering the feel of Gabriel's hands roaming my body. It felt like a lifetime ago, but I longed for it once more. "All right," I agreed. "We'll speak of it tonight, after Ben is asleep."

We said goodbye to Nishime a fortnight later, and although I kept a brave face, I mourned the loss of her like a sister. It made me think of Mabel, and I wondered what had happened to her, where she was settled. I turned my mind away from those goodbyes as the shop was busy and I was putting in extra hours, both to keep up with the demand and prevent my thoughts from leading me down a forlorn path.

A shadow fell over the shop, blocking my light. I turned to see who had approached, letting out a groan of dismay. It was Monsieur Laurent, Montréal's most eligible bachelor. He had bumped into me one day at an outdoor market, and since then had been as persistent as the flies around a horse's ass.

"Abigail," he dragged out the 'ee' sound, his French accent thick and dramatic. "We meet once again."

"Fancy that," I muttered, thoroughly annoyed. "Since you're in *my* shop." I would never admit to as much, but I was a bit frightened. Ever since the incident in the wilderness when I had lost the baby, I was afraid of unwanted male attention. I was very much isolated in my shop for most of the day when Ben was at school.

"I was hoping you had considered my previous offer," he said, catching a glimpse of himself in some scrap metal and admiring his reflection.

I wiped the sweat from my brow, turning to face him. I kept the tongs in my hand for protection, a pang shooting through me at the memory of my first encounter with Gabriel. I bit my lip, hard. "I have already told you that I'm betrothed, sir. To a Frenchman like yourself. I am sure he will not react kindly to hear of your insistence."

THE FORT

Monsieur Laurent grunted in a displeased manner. "He should know better than to leave a fine woman like yourself alone." He looked around the shop, glancing at the stairs that led to our dwellings above. "For you appear to be just that. Very much alone."

"She's not alone, but very much loved." A loud voice rang out over the shop, making me weak in the knees. My chest heaved as she came into full view, looking rather travel worn, but still very much the person who would comfort me despite her own weariness.

"Claudette," I breathed, not wanting to blink or move, lest she disappear. It seemed like a dream that I didn't dare believe to be true.

"Come, my dear." She held her arms open, and I ran to her, pushing past the Monsieur. I fell into her embrace, not able to control the tremor that ran through my body. Was it real? Was she really here?

"My blessed girl," she crooned, holding me tight against her. "I've prayed for you every day. The good Father was with you every step of the way."

The palisade inside of me burst, and I wept in her arms. "I'm not so sure he was, Claudette. I've lost so much."

She tightened her hold on me and sighed. "The Lord giveth, and the Lord taketh away, Abigail. We do not always know the reasons why. But He will never task you with a burden too heavy to carry alone."

I nodded against her, hearing the truth in her words. "But why does it have to be so hard? Just for once, I'd like things to be easy."

She pulled me away from her, looking into my face. Her journey had been hard too, I saw, by the lines etched into her forehead and the shadows under her eyes. "Like the blacksmith, who takes something old and forges it into something new, so works the Lord." She smiled, reaching out to smooth my hair back off my face. "Your past is in the past, Abigail, and today you start anew. Come now, we must wash up. Gabriel is waiting by the docks, with Alexandre."

I shrieked as I leapt backwards, nearly knocking over the Monsieur, who had been eavesdropping behind us. "Gabriel is *here*?!"

She laughed, and my whole body warmed at the sound. "Oui, chérie. With my husband, and some voyageurs. I wandered off, in search of food, and the Lord led me here." She crossed herself, eyes raised to the heavens.

I whirled, turning to Monsieur Laurent. "Stay here," I instructed, wagging my finger at him. "Keep an eye on the forge."

Without waiting for a response, I picked up the length of my skirts and ran towards the river. My heart thumped in my chest with both excitement and fear. So much had happened since he paddled away from me many months ago. I stopped suddenly, afraid to tell him the fate of our child. Perhaps he would be angry for putting myself at risk and travelling with only Nishime at my side. Or perhaps he would not be concerned at all, as it had not yet been born.

I shook my head, tucking my worries away, and started once again on my way. I walked more slowly now, trying to calm my racing heart. I must look a fright after working the day with the horses. And the smell—Claudette had been right—I should have washed first.

I stopped again, ready to head back to my place, when I saw him, searching the streets with a wrinkled brow. His hair was now trimmed short, but the beard remained the same, and his eyes—those eyes—blazed blue.

"Gabriel," I whispered. He held the hand of a young boy, around the same size as Ben, but pale and drawn. His son.

He turned towards me, likely feeling my eyes on him. His face crumpled for a moment, then relief washed over his features. Dropping

THE FORT

Alexandre's hand, he ran the rest of the way to me. We collided together, a fury of kisses and words, our bodies fused as one on the busy street. Finally, breathless, we pulled apart, and I noticed his son standing awkwardly beside us.

"Hello," I said, not letting go of Gabriel. "My name is Abby—Abigail," I corrected myself, smiling back up at my handsome Frenchman. It was time to use my hard-earned wisdom and let go of the past. To begin again.

"Bonjour," the boy said meekly, pulling at his father's shirt. Gabriel chuckled and leaned down to lift him into his arms.

"He doesn't know much English," Gabriel explained, giving me another kiss. "And he's a little afraid."

"Moi aussi," I said, earning a grin from them both. I had learned quite a lot more of the language during my months in Montréal, as many of my customers were French.

"Ma chérie," Gabriel put Alexandre back down and he ran to join Claudette and her husband. "I'm so sorry. I've been sick with worry since I heard the news. Please tell me your journey was without danger."

I swallowed hard, my face buried against his chest. "Claudette's prayers sent some angels to guide my way," I murmured, thinking of Nishime, and then reluctantly of McTavish. I pulled back to look at him, my heart heavy with the news I was about to share. "I became pregnant with your child, but I laid her to rest on Christmas Day."

The blue in his eyes became stormy and dark, and a cry left my lips. He shook his head with a furrowed brow, crushing me against him. We stood there, just holding each other, but I found that I had no more tears, just peace.

"Claudette told me your father also passed away on Christmas," he said, his voice husky in my ear. "It seems that he held our daughter's hand into heaven."

I let out an exhale, the weight of it suddenly leaving my chest. My father had always carried my burdens with him, even into death.

"Come, my Abigail." Gabriel's hand was firm on my waist, and I never wanted him to let go. "There is much to tell."

Chapter Twenty-Nine

G abriel lay beside me, asleep, his bare chest rising and falling under my hand. He still bore the scar from the wild cat, though it had faded to a puckered pink. I thought of my own wounds, wondering if my heart looked the same.

Sleep threatened to pull me under, but I resisted, untangling my legs from his and slipping out of the bed. I padded over to the basin, pulling a cool cup of water from the pail beside it. Then I made my way over to the open window, letting the night breeze wash over my bare form.

They were home. *We* were home.

The afternoon had been a blur. The entire group of us had walked over to pick up Ben from school. He had flown down the stairs with a cry of elation, launching himself into Gabriel's arms. He'd hid his face in a bashful manner from Alexandre, though. It would take time for the boys to adjust to our new family.

It would take me time too, I realized, coming back to the bed. I was not the same Abigail that had kissed Gabriel goodbye a year ago. I noticed a difference in him too. He was more protective, and softer, somehow. He did not leave my side for the entirety of the evening, burying his face in my neck and hair whenever we managed to find a moment alone. Finally, Claudette, who insisted on finding other accommodations for the night, dragged everyone out the door. Ben and Alexandre stayed behind, and for a while, we'd sat all four around the hearth, enjoying the feeling of togetherness.

I slid my hand back onto Gabriel's chest and he stirred, a faint smile on his lips. Our lovemaking had been frantic and hurried, neither one of us able to speak for a moment afterwards. Then we'd come together again, and he held me while I cried. First for my father, and then for myself. I cried in relief, overwhelmed with sudden exhaustion now that I was no longer alone.

"Tell me again," I said, running my hand down the length of his thigh. He groaned, gathering me in his arms, while his eyes remained closed.

"Ma belle fille," he replied, opening one sleepy eyelid. "What do you want to hear?"

"The whole story. Everything from that moment to this."

He chuckled, opening his arm to tuck me in next to him. "The trip to France was horrible. The waves were choppy, and I only thought of you, ma chérie. I was both seasick and lovesick."

I swallowed hard, remembering the nights camped out with the voyageurs, when I had yearned desperately for him. "I thought I might never see you again."

He turned to me, his eyes alert in a sudden wakefulness. "You made the right choice, Abigail. Henry would have taken Ben from you and banished you into the winter alone. Claudette told me he made life rather difficult for them at the fort after you left." His brow furrowed in anger. I reached out to smooth it flat again, and he pulled my fingers to his lips.

THE FORT

"I managed to collect Alexandre from the orphanage without trouble," he said, returning to the story. "And found a small ship destined for Montréal. I could not bear to wait the full year, so we took the risk to come. We came through Montréal a month ago, headed west."

"And you found Claudette with her husband, headed east on the voyageur's trail."

"That was a miracle, to be sure, but I was devastated to hear of what had happened. I did not know if you were dead or alive, my love. I felt ill every waking moment, and our pace was slow and cumbersome with so many."

I leaned up to kiss him, my fingers in his beard. "I'm so happy you're here," I whispered, as his grip around me tightened. "I didn't dare dream you would arrive so soon."

"We must be married at once, ma chérie. I cannot bear to be apart from you."

I shook my head. "No, I want to wait. Until we are able to buy a farm and build a home. I want to have our wedding there."

He heaved a sigh. "Mon Dieu, Abigail. I cannot wait that long to live as man and wife." He pulled back the blanket to reveal our naked bodies, pressed together. "We are already as one."

I laughed at his pained expression. "All right, you stubborn Frenchman. I shall let you have your way this once." I kissed his cheek. "But only because I love you."

He did not reply, as his lips had become occupied, moving down my neck to the top of my breasts. His embrace was comforting and safe, and I fell into slumber at last, deep in the warmth of his arms.

In the end, we did not get married until the spring, as Claudette would hear of nothing less than a farmyard celebration. I refused to sleep anywhere except beside Gabriel, and by the time the dewy morning of our wedding rolled around, I was several months along with another baby.

"Gabriel, you mustn't be here," I scolded as he came into the woodshed where Claudette was helping me get ready. "It's unlucky."

He gave a chuckle, doing nothing to avert his gaze from my wedding gown. His blue eyes twinkled in approval, and he leaned down to give me a kiss. "Luck is nothing between us, my love. Still, I've come to give you this." He opened his hand, revealing a rectangular metal block. I gasped to realize it was an imprint, like the one I had previously used to mark my lucky horseshoes with a rose.

"I know you had to leave everything behind," he said, pressing the block into my palm. "And I thought you might like a new design."

The blacksmith who had fashioned it had taken his time, creating a flawless likeness of a voyageur's canoe, complete with a paddle and waves. My journey.

"I love it, Gabriel. It couldn't be more perfect."

"There's one more thing, ma chérie. I went looking for McTavish, and I found him."

My heart gave a painful lurch at the mention of him, but I gave a brave smile to Claudette, who excused herself from the room.

Gabriel pulled a stool up to mine and took hold of my hand. "I thought perhaps I could convince him to come to our wedding. But the

THE FORT

man I found was a drunk, Abigail, nothing of the hardy voyageur you described."

"A drunk?" I frowned, remembering when he revealed his truth to me, of his love affair with another man. He had been intoxicated that night too, by the willow tree. "Did you speak with him? What did he say?"

"He did not say a thing. He only turned his back to me."

I sighed, pushing myself up from the seat, and running my hands over my swollen belly. Gabriel's fingers met mine, and we caressed our unborn child with soft, loving strokes. I didn't know if time healed all wounds completely. I looked lovingly into the eyes of the man across from me. Perhaps I would just have to learn to accept myself, jagged edges and all.

Claudette poked her head back in the door. "We are ready, mes amies." Her gaze fell to where we held my belly, and she smiled softly. "Dépêche toi. Before this sweet babe arrives."

Gabriel smiled, dropping a kiss on my forehead before he obediently followed Claudette through the door. Ben and Alexandre came in a moment later, ready to walk me down the aisle. I took one boy on either side, and together we left the woodshed, into the yard.

Our homes lay to the west, standing proud and tall in the morning sun. Ours was painted a sunny yellow, with a wide porch, where I sat on many evenings, playing cards with Gabriel and the boys. Claudette and her husband shared the other home, a dusky blue homestead where Claudette kept the children and men stuffed with delicious baked goods from her kitchen.

The community had pitched in to raise our barn, and between Claudette's family and ours, we had purchased a cow and a few chickens and pigs. I had planted my first garden, and tended to it carefully, as I tended to my soul and my child growing within. As for the blacksmith shop, I had sold it to a young smith and his family, but he allowed me to visit as often as I liked, running my hands over the forge in memory of my father.

I caught Gabriel's eye across the yard, where he stood waiting, ready to make me his wife. My stomach was not aflutter, but instead filled with a calm assurance, mixed with a heady desire for my Frenchman of the woods.

At long last, I had arrived.

Epilogue

SPRING, 1811

The rain pelted against my face as I struggled through the sodden farmyard. The milk pails were filled to the point of overflow, and the hot liquid split over the sides, drenching my aching hands. Ben's husky, Sam, trotted in circles around me, hopeful that I might have a morsel for him in my pockets. I finally reached the door of the kitchen, pushing it open with my shoulder.

"Mama!" two small voices chimed together at my arrival, though I had only left their side twenty minutes before. Louise ran forward, clinging to my skirts, while her younger sister, Madeleine, stood back, her round face still bearing the remnants of breakfast. They both had the look of their older brother, Alexandre, though Madeleine surprised me with a likeness of my father on rare occasion.

"Mes filles, let your poor mother in the door. It's raining like the devil," Claudette said from the sitting room, with her basket of darning.

I smiled gratefully at her, handing her one of the heavy buckets. "I must take the butter and cheese into town, regardless of the weather. Monsieur Dupont does not take kindly to the goods arriving late." I glanced down at my gown, which clung to my once-again rounded belly. "Though I suppose I must change." The rain had tapered off, but it was still miserable conditions to take the wagon into town.

"Or perhaps we can wait for one of the boys to take it," she suggested, glancing out the window. Ben was now twelve, and Alexandre a young man. They were practically inseparable, although in recent days Alexandre had taken an interest in a girl in town, which had left Ben feeling amiss.

I shook my head. "No, they've gone out to the far field today. They'll likely work through lunch to finish the day early with this rain. I'll be back within the hour, don't worry."

Claudette nodded reluctantly, taking the children further into the house to play with the new kitten litter that had arrived last week. I made my way into the bedroom and changed into some dry clothes. I looked longingly at the bed, as I was so very tired on this last leg of the pregnancy. Gabriel had scooped me up the evening before, tucking me into bed hours early, but I still felt the weary weight of my womb with every step.

I plodded out to the kitchen, patting the girls on the top of their heads in farewell. They barely looked my way, now enraptured with the balls of fur in front of them.

The rain had tamed down by the time I hitched the wagon and led the horses into the yard. I had loaded in everything to go the market, covered with a length of tarpaulin: milk, eggs, butter, fresh vegetables from the garden, and a few cured fox skins from the trapping Gabriel had done earlier in the month.

THE FORT

"Ma chérie, où vas-tu?" Gabriel came running across the yard from the field, clad in an oilskin jacket and a wide-brimmed hat to keep himself dry while working the farm. I waited for him, grateful for a hoist into the wagon, as my current girth made it quite cumbersome.

"Just to the market. I'll be back soon," I said, smiling as his hands made their familiar route over my body. He could never get enough of me, and I the same. Many a morning he was late to the morning chores, spending time instead buried under the bedclothes with my legs wrapped around him. That was one thing about the French: you could not hurry them through the simple pleasures of life.

He cast a worried look to the sky. "But this weather—"

"I'll be fine," I reassured him, holding my hand out for him to lift me up onto the bench. "I did once travel 'cross these lands like the voyageurs," I said, winking at him. When he gave me a grudging smile in response, I lifted the reins and set the horses in motion, leaving him behind in the yard with his hand lifted in farewell.

After twenty minutes of jostling and clenching my teeth at the poor condition of the road, the wagon bumped into a deep crevice and lurched to a halt, the sound of the wheel splintering making me groan in despair.

"Dammit," I swore, my head tilted towards the heavens in a silent bargain. It would take me another twenty minutes to walk into town, and there, I would have to try to procure a way home. And the whole journey would be for naught, as I could not carry the market goods along the way.

I climbed down from the wagon for further inspection, shaking my head in frustration. When I was finished, I turned to see a stranger, coming along the road in the misty distance. A stranger, yet, I would know his broad stance anywhere in the world. "No," I whispered as he came near. "It can't be. Not now."

McTavish lumbered closer, still unaware that it was me. "Hullo lass," he shouted through the rain. "Can I be of help to ya, miss?"

"It's me," I said, stepping into view and lowering my hood to reveal myself. "Abigail."

The figure stopped short, straightening up to his full height. I thought for a brief moment he might turn and flee, but I kept my eyes locked with his.

"McTavish," I gritted out, vaguely aware that the winds had picked up around us. "It appears that I am in need of some assistance."

His eyes fell to my swollen belly, then back up to my face. He tried to keep himself stoic and stern, but I saw a flash of something in his eyes. Something that had cracked his hard shell. Then he frowned, reining it back into himself.

"Aye," he said, his eyes becoming cold and defensive. The sky above us opened, and the rains grew tenfold in a frigid torrent. He shouted above the sudden downpour. "I'll continue this way, and let yer husband know."

I choked back a cry, as his intention to leave me alone tore open an old wound to bleed. I turned my back to him, trying to find shelter from the pelting rain against the horses. I could not let him see how much his rebuff still stung.

There was only the pitter-patter of the drops behind me, and when I finally turned, he was still there, head hung low. "Lass," he croaked, not meeting my eyes, "I reckon I owe ya' an apology."

I shook my head, refusing to let him in. This was Duncan McTavish, who had fled from me on the streets of Montréal, almost five years prior.

THE FORT

Who had refused to come to my wedding, despite his promise to keep hope for Gabriel's return. No, this man was not deserving of my time.

A large hand reached out to cover mine, and when I tried to pull away, he held on tight. "Abby, I..." he began, but then took a step back. "Never ya mind. I'll just go fetch yer man."

He tried to pull his hand away, but this time I was the one who did not let go. A small piece of my armor loosened, and a tiny shred of compassion fell over me, like the early morning light that danced through the cracks in the barn wall. This was Duncan McTavish, who had led me through the wilderness, who had shared with me his deepest secret. A man in a hardened, weathered cage who possessed a kindred heart like none I had ever known.

"McTavish," I whispered, voice barely audible over the pouring rain. I had started to shiver from the cold and tried to pull my coat closer to my body. "What happened?"

His long hair covered his eyes, water streaming in rivulets down his face. Three silent heartbeats passed, and he gave me no answer. Then I heard a loud *pop* and a sharp sting shot across my belly. My eyes widened as a rush of hot fluid ran down my legs.

"No, not now," I whimpered, dropping his hand to embrace my child within. As if in answer, another radiating swell of pain tore its way up my body. It was strong enough that I groaned, reaching out to the side of the wagon for support.

"Lass?" He peered down at me, his craggy face creased in concern. "Is there somethin' amiss?"

"Isn't it obvious?" I hissed, my empathy from the moment before gone. "Just leave, McTavish. It's what you do best."

He stumbled backwards, as if I had slapped him. Then he stood up straight, nostrils flared. "I left you alone for *yer* protection, not mine!"

I snorted at him, my temper hot. "I lost my baby at the hands of that vile trapper mere days after you left. You certainly didn't protect me then."

A silence fell between us, and I flicked my gaze up to see his face gone pale. A twinge of guilt flashed through me—I knew it wasn't fair to blame him for what had happened. I tried to apologize, but was instead consumed by another birthing wave, this one more intense than the last. Clinging to the side of the wagon, I panted as it reached its peak.

"When I arrived in Montréal, I received word that Charles had been killed in the line of duty in the Americas." His voice came through the mist, coaxing me to the other side of the contraction. "I was swept up in despair, lass, and I often thought of taking my own life, just to be with him." He shook his head sadly, and I knew that he still wrestled that demon. "When I saw ya and yer lad in the church courtyard, I ... well, I couldn't share my burden with ya, lass. I knew ya still held hope for yer happy ending. I've been moping around these parts since then, tryin' to figure myself out."

"I'm so sorry," I said, reaching out once again for his hand. "But you're wrong. Burdens are meant to be shared with the ones we love. You would never ask one voyageur to carry the whole load alone. He might be able to manage at first, but after a while, he would falter in his step."

"Aye. I suppose you're right about that," he said, grasping my small hand between his large ones. "But it's too late now."

"No. It's never too late, McTa—" I broke off as another contraction started, taking away my ability to speak. There was a familiar pressure building inside me that indicated the baby would be arriving, much

THE FORT

sooner than I wanted. I squeezed my old friend's hand, not able to keep in a groan as the pain racked my body.

"Lass," McTavish frowned at me as it ended, "we'd best be getting you home."

"No." I shook my head, casting a worried glance up at him. "There's no time. My last babe came before the midwife could arrive." I looked up to the wagon bed, half full of goods to be delivered to the market. "Do you think you could arrange the tarpaulin so I might have some privacy?"

His eyes widened, and for a moment, he stood still, processing my request. Then he jumped up onto the wagon bed, untucking the tarp. With a deft hand, he stacked the goods in the back corners, re-tucking the canvas sheet to make a tent of sorts.

He jumped back down, sweeping me up in his arms in one swift movement. Then, he climbed back into the wagon, with me clinging to his thick neck. He set me down onto the floor of the wagon with a gentleness that would seem unlikely in such a hardy man, but it did not surprise me. I knew of his caring nature, and that I had ever doubted it seemed so foolish.

Another wave started, and this one had me bearing down, gritting my teeth to keep from pushing. McTavish watched me whole time, looking a bit terrified. Then, he leaned down and wiped the tears from my cheeks. He caught my gaze with his, and with a thick swallow, he nodded.

"Aye. Tell me what I need to do, Abby. I'll not leave ya alone this time."

"I need to remove my bloomers," I panted, trying to catch my breath. "And you'll need to catch the baby as it comes."

He swallowed again, but did as I said, trying to avert his eyes as he removed my undergarments. The situation suddenly struck me, and I giggled uncontrollably, laying back to rest for a moment. He sent me a

285

bemused look, but continued with his task, securing the tarpaulin for further protection against the rains and then removing his overcoat and sweater, to wrap the baby.

"I'm happy for ya, lass," he said, sitting on his haunches, waiting to help me through the next contraction. "Ya 'ave everything ya wanted, it seems."

I nodded, thinking of our beautiful farm, my children, and my husband. It had been nothing short of perfect, and yet, from time to time, I was reminded of the things I had lost. "I missed these last years between us, McTavish. You were my friend."

"Aye. I'd like to repair that, if ya wish. If yer husband don't mind."

"Gabriel understands. He knows everything." When McTavish raised his eyebrows, I waved him off. "He's French. They're more accepting of these things."

He rumbled a laugh, but then peered at me as I let out a guttural moan. The urge to push came swift and strong with each contraction thereafter, and it was only about ten minutes later that the babe burst free of my womb, squalling in McTavish's big hands.

"'Tis a lad, Abby" he said, staring at the newborn in his arms. "A bonnie one, if I've ever seen one."

I shifted to sit beside him, smiling down at my healthy baby. Then I turned to the man beside me, whose expression was filled with the joy of a life renewed. "Let's name him Charles," I said, squeezing his arm. "After your love taken from you too soon. Charlie for short."

McTavish caught his breath. "Lass, I ... yer husband, I'm sure he—"

"He won't mind," I said, taking the baby from him. "He's a fair and reasonable husband. And besides, it suits him, don't you think?"

THE FORT

"Aye, it does." McTavish's voice was calm and steady, and I knew, without a doubt, he would dote on Charlie all his days. My son would be a beacon for a man who had lost his way in the dark forest of grief, trapped by the thorns of his secret. It was time for him to put down his heavy burden and rest.

"Come," I said to my burly Scot, my heart repaired by the antidote of forgiveness. "It's time to go home."

Acknowledgments

The Fort is a story that remains close to my heart, for while writing this novel, I was going through one of the most challenging chapters of my own life. Without realizing it, I made sure that Abby was never left alone to face the trials of her journey, because I also had hands that lifted me up when I felt as if I could not go on. So, these acknowledgements are not superficial, but rather reflect on the importance of community through thick and thin.

Tina and Alex at Rising Action, your faith in our stories is unwavering. True leaders shine by example through integrity, courage, and strength, and you are two of the best. I am so proud to call Rising Action home.

Marthese, thank you for helping my stories become stronger with your amazing edits. I love having a friendship with you, even though we have never met in real life! One day! Nat Mack, your talent amazes me, as once again I am blessed with such a striking cover. Your ability to translate ideas into art is truly incredible.

Carrie, I could not have written this book without you. Your constant guidance led me to historical research, knowledge of time and place, and the ways of the Indigenous peoples in a fragile moment of their history.

Jodie, Carleen, and Laura, your first reads and edits were so valuable and helped shape the trajectory of the story. Thank you so much for your time, effort, and advice, and keeping me on the path to completion. Jamie and Valerie, thank you for beta reading the book in its completion.

Jodie and Lisa, thank you for aiding me with so much French! Thank goodness for friends who are bilingual!

To all of my writing friends, co-authors and social media pals—you are the best! I know who to turn to when I feel down and need a writing chat. □

To my friends, old and new. Your support is never taken for granted and never unnoticed: Sarah, Erin, Maia, Joy, Danielle, Adele, Juna, Rachel, Marie, Kendall, Kim, Dawn, Brittany, Shivani, Kortney, Carmen, Jeannie, Drea, Stef,Tessa, Shannon, Kim.

To the crew at JKE, you have been like one big family, and I miss you so much! To my new community at DPCS, I look forward to more adventures with you. To all the kiddos that chat with me about writing, thank you for striving with me to create stories with words.

Jess, for your partnership, compassion, kindness, love, and always believing in me. I was alone on a cliff in a windstorm, and it was you holding out your hand.

To Mom, the writer who made me a writer! Thank you for indulging me with countless trips to the second-hand bookstores, both when I was a kid and even now. I love that we can enjoy books together. Dad, thank you for always checking my work for the mechanics of things and historical accuracy. I appreciate how you are willing to read my never-ending screenshots. Amy and Joyanna, thank you for all your support in all the small and big ways. Love you.

To my family in New Zealand and other parts of Canada, thank you for getting excited for me and sharing my books with your family and friends.

Finally, to my three daughters, Leyla, Serra and Ayla. Thank you for making every day an adventure and for filling my life with purpose. I love you each for your own unique strengths and I love watching you grow! I love you forever and always.

About the Author

Christy K. Lee is a lifetime writer and storyteller. She is obsessed with stories of women who break all the rules, and is sometimes a bit of a rule breaker herself. When she's not writing, she can be found spending time in her classroom, in the local library digging through historical archives, or having a bevvie with a friend. Her first historical fiction, *The Roads We Take*, was released in October 2024.